Spiralling

out of control

MICHELLE DENNIS EVANS

Spiralling Out of Control
© Michelle Dennis Evans 2013, 2024

Published by Armour Books
P. O. Box 492, Corinda QLD 4075

Cover Images: Nixprint | Baby B, Etsy; cove703 | Creative Fabrica
Spirals: rarinlada | Creative Fabrica
Cover and Interior Design and Typeset by Beckon Creative

ISBN (Second edition): 978-1-925380-71-2

First edition published by Lilly Pilly Press 2014, Cover Design by Melissa
Dalley and Lilly Pilly Press, Model –Kristy Hutchinson, Photography by
Bek Grace Photography, ISBN: 978-0-9923557-5-3 (paperback)

A catalogue record for this book is available from the National Library of Australia

This book is a work of fiction set in Australia and any resemblance to
persons, living or dead, or places, events or locales is purely coincidental.
The characters are productions of the author's imagination and used
fictitiously.

Note: 16+ Young Adult Reading Material. Australian spelling and
grammar conventions are used throughout this book.

For the girl who has made dumb decisions...

Today is a new day,
leave the past in the past and
take a different path.
Choose life from this day forward.

Spiralling out of control

MICHELLE DENNIS EVANS

Contents

Prologue

The plane landed.
He filed off
lacking emotion,
a common trait.

Dad missed
my solo.
He misses everything
while he's working
away.

Mum and Dad
gathered us close
for a family meeting
dropped a bombshell
that would blow…
A city
A country
A nation

Moving
out
of
town.

I blew
        my
    mind.

            Moving
                interstate.

Promotion, he said.

To me
it was demotion.
All
the
way.

Just when I'd made the lead,
just when I was at my peak,
just when I was finally somebody,
they didn't give a damn.

Pack now,
think later.

Removal truck
loaded.

Spiralling Out of Control

Car
full.

Ripped

from life
as I knew it.

Nine
hundred
kilometres
in our rattling car.

Too close.
Too long.
Enough gum trees.
Enough countryside.

Let me out.
Take me back home.
Let me go.
Before

I
spin
out
of
control.

The Move

Chapter One

Adrenaline surged through Stephanie as the auditorium fell into a suspended hush. She wanted more. More attention, more spotlight, more dancing. She took a deep breath as the faint echo of music and applause resounded through her ears, nourishing her core. Hairs pricked at the back of her neck as she waited, expecting the curtain to swish back. Easing one foot in front of the other, her built-in rhythm clock knew more time had passed than they'd rehearsed. What on earth was happening with the curtain?

Stephanie turned her head, looking for answers.

'Don't stress,' mouthed her best friend, Tabbie.

Finally, the curtain swung open and Stephanie took a bow with the other dancers. Flustered and unfocused, she stepped forward to begin her solo. Behind her, the other dancers ran off to the sides, creaking the floorboards and sending a fine mist of dust into the air. It was a glitch, just a minor glitch. Every professional dancer would have to deal with incompetency at some stage. She stood alone, centre stage, ready to blow them away with her performance—her parents, her teachers and any scout that may be in the crowd waiting to discover her.

Stephanie blinked as the bright beam flooded into her eyes. Five, six, seven, eight—the music bounced off the walls of the school as she danced her solo. She spun a pirouette and leapt across the floor, silencing the audience as she owned the stage. This was her moment. This was going to be her year. The realisation of a dream she'd held close to her heart since being accepted into Hill Top Private, nearly three years ago. She finished upstage. The house lights came on and she caught her mother's eye.

Is that a tear? Can she actually be proud of me?

The crowd cheered, rising to their feet. Stephanie turned, seeing Tabbie slip through the side curtains to present her with a colourful bouquet.

A week later, her award-winning performance may as well have been a lifetime ago. She was sure their torturous drive from Sydney to Toowoomba would inflict PTSD, post-traumatic stress disorder.

Stephanie's sister, April, spoke after everyone in the car fell silent. 'You nailed the solo last week.'

'Yeah.' Stephanie chewed a fingernail as she looked out the window. 'But as if this stupid country town will have any good dance schools.'

'It's a city, isn't it? I bet they'll have a dance class at school.' April scratched a piece of cracked upholstery.

'You're right, April. And we'll just have to wait and see what's available when we get settled in.' Her mother faced the windscreen as she spoke. 'We might have to check the fees first.'

Her mother's tone screwed with her heart. Dancing in competitions and being discovered now seemed as likely as getting hit by a meteorite.

    Spiralling Out of Control

They arrived at the hotel after ten that night. Stephanie unclipped her seatbelt anticipating her escape from the confines of the family car as she watched her father walk towards the dark reception room. He knocked, pulled out his phone, knocked again then spoke to someone on his phone. A minute later, he shoved his phone in his pocket and returned to the car.

'Blast!' He thrust open the car door and started the engine with a rev. The spinning tyres sent a shower of loose gravel against the motel wall. The clatter loud enough to wake someone from a coma.

'What? John, what's going on? Where are we going?' her mother asked.

Her father drove off, red creeping down his neck and his jaw bone protruding. 'Diane, girls, this is it,' he said as he pulled into a driveway.

'Our new home?' Diane said.

John nodded as he climbed out of the car.

'You're not even sure of what our new home looks like?' Stephanie stared at her mother.

'You know I've only seen pictures.' Diane shook her head.

'We don't pick up the key until tomorrow.' Her father drew in a deep breath. 'And there's a rodeo this weekend, so it appears the whole of Toowoomba is booked up, including our room that they gave to someone else because we didn't get here before the office closed.'

'What? That's not good enough.' Her mother's voice bounced off the car windows. 'Wasn't there something you could've done?'

'They gave our room to someone else. What did you want me to do? Go and tell them to get out?' Her father's mouth formed a thin line. 'One thing I do know … I can't spend another minute in the car today. I'll wait under the porch 'til morning. Girls, try and get some sleep.'

Stephanie yawned as her father walked away from the car. Before she could get comfortable, April spun in her seat and kicked her feet up onto Steph's lap to stretch out.

'April, stop kicking me!' Stephanie shoved her away.

'Oh, Stephanie, stop it.' Her mother levered the front passenger seat down as flat as it would go. 'Move here, to the front. April, put your pillow on the door. Here like this.' She climbed out and went to the back door to fuss over April.

'It's too cold to sleep.' Stephanie's teeth chattered in between words.

'Try wrapping this around you.' Her mother handed her a woolly pullover then stepped towards their new home. She shivered in the chilly mountain air, then walked up the three steps to sit beside her husband on the porch.

Stephanie went to open her window and realised Dad had taken the keys. She cracked open the door slightly without activating the interior light and tried to hear the conversation.

'We should have left earlier.' Diane folded her arms.

Her father stared at the ground in silence.

Stephanie closed the door to shut out the cold air and the conversation. April breathed heavily in the back, already asleep. Stephanie focused on her parents sitting on the porch with their backs to the wall and a picnic blanket wrapped around them until her eyelids fell.

The next morning, she woke, shuddered and stretched her cramped body. She straightened her neck and blinked away the early sun. As she rubbed her finger on the damp windscreen, she formed a circle in the condensation. Her parents weren't on the porch. With April snoring in the back seat, Stephanie crept out of the car and rested the door closed without letting it click. Tightening the woolly pullover, she breathed white fog in the still morning air.

No one was in the front yard. She spun around as her chest tightened. Surely Mum and Dad wouldn't have walked to the real estate office to get the key.

Chapter Two

The front door of their new home was slightly ajar.

'Hello? Mum? Dad? Are you in here?' Steph entered the house.

No one was in the lounge room or kitchen. She mounted the first step and paused. Silence. She inched her way up to the next. The house was still. *Where are they?* She bit her lip, as she climbed the rest of the stairs, then walked down a short hallway, checking the rooms on either side. Through the last doorway, her parents lay on the floor of what looked like the master bedroom.

Her father rolled over to face her. 'Steph, good morning. How did you sleep?'

'Why didn't you tell us you got in?'

'Just as it was getting light, your father decided to check under all the pavers and rocks for a spare key.' Her mother chuckled.

'They left a key?' Stephanie spat the words.

'It appears that way.' Dad yawned.

'Why didn't you check last night?'

'Is April awake?' Dad asked.

'Are you crazy? We could've been inside.' Stephanie spun the doorknob between her thumb and fingers. 'That's so typical of you!'

'Stephanie!' Her mother sat up.

'Not much we can do about it now.' Her father climbed to his feet.

April entered the room, pushing the door out of Stephanie's grasp. 'Can we go to Maccas for breakfast?'

'Good morning, love. Yes, McDonalds sounds good. I could do with a coffee.' Diane pushed herself up off the floor.

Stephanie looked from one to the other. *Is this some weird fairy tale I've woken up in?*

When they returned to the house, the removal truck doors swung in the breeze. Two burly men were ready to unload. Stephanie cheered. Finally something was happening as scheduled.

Stephanie helped unpack box after box. By the end of the day most things were rehomed and she left the confines of the house.

Her mind spun with all the changes. Tabbie wasn't a five-minute drive away. She wouldn't be walking into Hill Top Private College Monday morning and there would be no dance rehearsal this week.

Stephanie took long strides away from the house as dusk approached. Maybe a walk would clear her mind. The grey sky seemed to hover low, like it was falling on her, choking the voice inside that wanted to scream. The weight of fear forced her back home. Her heart raced and her head pounded as she darted into her room.

She found her posters, the ones she'd carefully taken off the walls of her Sydney bedroom. With no order or pattern, she slapped them on the walls, blu-tacking them haphazardly to cover the duck-pond green paint. Everything began to spin. Stephanie fell onto her bed, smothered her face with her pillow and sobbed.

'Stephanie,' April called.

'Go away,' she mumbled from under the pillow.

'Steph!' April flung the bedroom door open. 'Steph, I'm practising my routine. Come watch.'

Stephanie pulled a tissue from the box to wipe her face. Nose running, she grabbed the box and dragged her feet along the hallway and halfway down the stairs. Slumping, she hugged an arm through the vertical posts. April flipped and cartwheeled around the empty lounge room while Mum watched from the kitchen doorway. Stephanie glanced at her mother and clenched her teeth. April. *Always the favourite!*

'Gymnastics display finished.' April took a bow. 'Your turn.'

'Where's Dad?' Stephanie asked.

'Oh, he had to pop into the office for a bit to sort things out there.' Mum shook her head.

Will we really see more of him now his office is so close?

April stood at the base of the stairs. 'Come on, Steph. Dance.'

Stephanie ran back upstairs. Her stomach churned.

'Don't you want to dance?' her mother called after her.

Of course I want to dance. But you can't seem to find the money.

Stephanie closed her bedroom door and leaned against it. She cried until she'd saturated the wad of tissues in her hand. Flinging her wardrobe open, she dug out all her dancing gear and threw it into the bin. Done. Over. Gone. Season of life finished.

Her mother's words stung. 'We might have to check the fees.' *Urgh!* It seemed the star gymnast's fees came first.

She needed to hide. From the world. From her parents. From her sister. Climbing into bed, she pulled the covers over her head and drifted on the verge of sleep until she was startled awake. Light shone through her doorway. Musk, the scent of her mother. Her body stiffened. She squeezed her eyes shut. The last thing she wanted was a conversation with her mother.

'Lord, watch over her,' Diane whispered.

Stephanie held her breath until her mother padded out of the room and clicked the door closed. Then she let her tears roll again until she slept.

Stephanie pounded her fist on the vanity. *Great! Just great! Look what I've done.* She splashed cold water on her face, hoping to calm her red, puffy eyes.

'Girls, we'll be leaving in ten minutes,' her mother called from downstairs. 'Coffee's waiting on the bench, Steph.'

April leaned on the door frame.

'What do you want? Go away. Can't you see I'm getting dressed?' Stephanie wished her parents had allowed them a week to settle in instead of insisting they begin school straight away. Her mother was so keen for them to start, she'd pre-ordered their uniforms.

'It'll be okay, Steph,' April said.

'Get out!' *What would a stupid ten-year-old know?*

She closed the door in April's face, put on her new uniform and brushed her hair into a loose ponytail before heading downstairs.

In a swift move, she grabbed her coffee cup from the kitchen bench. As she turned, her school bag slipped off her shoulder, jerking her elbow. The entire cup splashed down the front of her blouse.

'Argh!' She clenched her teeth, fighting another fury of tears.

Her mother clicked her tongue. 'You have another uniform hanging in your wardrobe. Go and get changed. I'll have to clean this up before we leave.'

Stephanie ran the bathroom tap and sponged the coffee off her arms and chest, now pink from the hot drink. She pulled on the clean blouse, stomped back down the stairs and climbed into the car.

'First stop, April's school.' Her mother started the car.

St Maria's co-ed primary school covered most of a low-lying flat block. The high school had been built next door on the top of a hill. The parish church was attached, yet separated from the high school. Its steeple stood tall, keeping watch over both younger and older students.

'April, I'll come in with you and make sure you're okay,' Mum said.

'I'll be right. They know I'm coming, don't they?' April jumped out of the car, then turned back. 'Ah, actually… Yeah, could you come?'

'I'll wait here,' Stephanie said under her breath.

'Back soon.' Her mother slung the words over her shoulder.

Stephanie pulled at her fingernails. Her nerves forced shallow breaths. She could see the church from the car, shadowed in the morning sun by a large red brick building with historic arched windows. *Probably where a bunch of old nuns live.*

She glanced back towards the primary school and saw her mother. As she stared into her lap, a shiver raced through her skin. *How far would I get if I made a run for it?*

'There was such a lovely vibe in there,' her mother said.

Maybe time travel was a better escape option.

'April's new teacher, Mrs Day, was so welcoming.'

'Sure.' Stephanie sighed.

'Now for your turn.' Diane drove up the hill and around the corner. 'Are you okay?'

'What do you reckon?' Stephanie clenched her teeth.

'I reckon you'll settle in fine. It's similar to the school I went to. You'll make friends easily. You'll soon be having so much fun, you won't have time to think about Sydney.'

Stephanie glared at her mother. *You've got to be joking.*

'Right, here we are.' Her mother's voice bubbled unnaturally. 'Just enough time for me to drop the forms to administration before you need to be in class. Come on. Stop dawdling.'

Stephanie tightened her ponytail, trying to remember the way out, in case she needed to leave quickly. She followed her mother along a walkway into the administration office. Pungent cleaning agents clung to the atmosphere while the receptionist took the paperwork. She handed Stephanie her timetable and a map and gave her the directions to her homeroom.

'Thank you.' Her mother took the map.

'Mum.' Stephanie snatched it back. 'You can go. I have the details.'

'Okay then. Have a good day.'

Stephanie rolled her eyes and set off to meet her new homeroom teacher. As she walked through a cool leafy area with tables and chairs, a sense of peace came over her. *I could come here to eat lunch.*

The directions on the page led her towards another building where she counted the stairs. Ten. The bell rang and students rushed everywhere. Stephanie side-stepped to avoid colliding with anyone.

She gripped the straps of her school bag until her knuckles turned white. Curling her fingers in, she hoped to hide her trembling hands. By the time she found her homeroom, she was late.

Chapter Three

'YOU MUST BE STEPHANIE. I'm Mrs Bardon.' The teacher's chins flapped as she turned her well-rounded body to face the class. 'Students, meet, Stephanie.'

Voices mumbled, heads turned and hands smothered snickers. Stephanie looked for some support, hoping to see a friendly face, but she couldn't find anyone to connect with.

A loud wolf whistle speared her churning stomach. 'Check it out. Check out the new piece!' the shaggy-haired boy said.

Mrs Bardon cleared her throat until the sound echoed off the walls.

Stephanie swallowed as fire moved up her neck and exploded in her cheeks. She'd never been whistled at before. *Co-ed sucks.* She repositioned her feet for escape. A quick dash and she'd be gone. But her soles felt glued to the floor. She looked to the teacher, hoping for some help or, at the very least, a rebuttal.

Mrs Bardon cleared her throat for the second time and dropped a heavy textbook on her desk. 'Find a seat, Stephanie. Anywhere is fine.'

Stephanie held her head down, glancing from desk to desk to find a seat.

'Come here, sweetheart. I saved this one just for you.' Wolf Whistle Boy smacked the desk beside him as the class erupted in laughter.

She waited for Mrs Bardon to reprimand the boy. But she didn't. Did this teacher have any clue? Hoping to shrink away from any more attention, Stephanie slinked into an empty seat between two girls. She smiled towards their blank faces. Both girls focused on her with icy eyes, then shared a look and grinned. What was that supposed to mean?

'Class!' Mrs Bardon slammed a pile of textbooks down on the wooden desk. The thud silenced the class. 'Let's get back to the roll … Melinda Black …'

'Uh huh.'

'John Class …'

'Yow!' It was Wolf Whistle Boy. *Yeah, all class.*

Mrs Bardon looked up from the roll. 'John, this is your last warning. Your behaviour this morning is unacceptable and I will be reporting the whistling.'

The class giggled, bringing more heat to Stephanie's cheeks.

Mrs Bardon continued. 'Monica Hannack …'

'Yep,' said the blonde girl next to Stephanie.

Stephanie zoned out for the rest of the lesson. Her heart was still thumping in her chest when the bell rang. She let the flow of students carry her to the hallway. Like a fish in a duck pond, she searched the sea of students and approached a group of girls to ask for directions. Without speaking, they pointed to a map on the wall and walked away. *Stupid.* She shouldn't have asked in the first place. She pulled out the map she was given on arrival.

Stephanie shook her head. Surely this was a nightmare. When the final bell sounded for the day, she left the school grounds ahead of the other students to meet her mother in the car park.

'How was it?' Diane asked.

'This school sucks.'

'Stephanie, please don't use that word.' Diane manoeuvred the car away from the school.

'Well, in my vocab, I can't think of another word to express my day.' Stephanie swallowed the hard lump in her throat. Tears blurred her vision, smudging the world through the window.

April twisted around in the front seat grabbing Stephanie's attention. 'Tomorrow will be better.'

Her little sister's beaming smile didn't reduce her anger. It fuelled it. Stephanie turned back to the window and set her eyes on a dirty smear. When her mother parked in the driveway, Stephanie ran inside. She slammed her bedroom door as more tears erupted, pain gripped her heart and tore at her mind. She yearned for her life in Sydney. The promise of spending the Easter holidays with Tabbie was too far.

She tiptoed out to the hallway and grabbed the cordless phone. This time she closed the door without alerting the household and rang Tabbie. 'It's worse than you could ever imagine.'

'Why? What happened?' Tabbie asked.

'The boys whistled at me and no girls would talk to me.' Stephanie's voice wavered.

Tabbie's sigh crackled through the line. 'There's a comp coming up.'

'Let's not talk about dancing.' Stephanie held back tears through clenched teeth.

'Do you have heaps of hot boys to perve on?'

She shook her head. *Far from it.* 'I'd rather be back at Hill Top. I've never been humiliated like today.'

'Oh, Steph. You know it'll take time to settle in. Remember our first term in year seven? We had no idea.' They were both silent for a moment.

Her head throbbed as she returned the phone. How many ways can a best friend say, 'things will get better?' She found the heaviest music she owned and played it as loud as her speakers would go. She tried to dance, but her breasts pounded against her, reminding her of how Wolf Whistle Boy had stared at her chest. She went to write in her journal, but couldn't see the page through her tears. She did care about the competitions her best friend was entering, but it hurt too much to talk about it. And now she'd hurt Tabbie by cutting her off at the mention of dance. She went to the family computer and began typing an apology to Tabbie, but again more tears rolled. She deleted it and closed the screen.

Minutes later, she lay on her bed, looking at the ceiling, fists clenched. If only the music would take away the pain.

Her mother knocked on her door. 'Steph, dinner is ready.'

Stephanie didn't reply.

'Look.' Diane stepped inside her room. 'I know it wasn't the best start, but why don't you come down for dinner? Dad's home and he wants us to eat together.'

Rolling off the bed, Stephanie dragged her feet downstairs.

'Hello, Steph.' Her father spoke while focusing on the newspaper. 'Mum said you didn't have a good day.'

Stephanie wanted to rip the paper from his hands, but didn't.

They sat at the table while April dissected her fabulous day. 'Oh, there's three girls in my class who do gymnastics. They go to the best club. I just have to join it.'

Her father looked up from the paper. 'We can book you in for a trial, if you like.'

'There's a birthday this weekend. Jenna has invited me. Is it okay if I go? Well, I kind of already replied but I … well is it okay?'

John tilted his paper forward, peering over the top. 'I hope you didn't invite yourself.'

April shook her head. 'There's a play coming up and I'm trying out for a part tomorrow.'

Diane smiled. 'Do you need to learn some lines? Maybe Stephanie can help.'

Stephanie pulled a face at April and shook her head, rolling her eyes.

'Mum, can you come and help at school?' April asked.

'Yes, I should be able to fit in one or two days.'

'Dad, they're asking for fathers to help with some of the backdrops and props. Can I put you down for that?'

He folded the paper in half, putting it down. 'It depends what time and which day they need me.'

'Mum, I can't believe they gave me readers. They're so easy. I can read way better than that!'

All Stephanie heard was, 'Blah blah blah,' while April continued to prattle on. Argh!

After dinner, Stephanie resumed her position on her bed, staring at the ceiling, letting the loud music thump off the walls until her mother asked her to turn it down for the night. She held her aching head in her hands and cried herself to sleep.

Nightmares interrupted her sleep. Up-close faces raced in front of her one after the other, laughing.

Diane stopped right in front of the school gate for the third day in a row.

'Mum, could you stop a little further away from the gate?'

'Why? There's no other cars right in front,' Diane said. 'Saves you the walk.'

Believe me, Mum, you are making my life worse. Stephanie groaned as she leaned against the car door that never closed on the first shove. Before she even looked up, the banter had started.

'Wanna have lunch?' one boy asked, followed by one of his friends with, 'Oh, no she already has a lunch date ... with herself.'

'Shut up, idiots.' Stephanie urged her feet to move faster.

The boys erupted with laughter. The only difference each day was different boys delivered the lines, adding obscene remarks about her body parts. Wolf Whistle Boy was always in the centre, finishing with a whistle each day.

'Get a life,' she told them as she walked away.

Chapter Four

Aloneness
isolated
endless.
In denim jeans
I'm the same.
But new school uniform
I'm the odd one out.
Private schoolgirl
arrives
awakens
rattles
the chip
on their shoulder.

 Spiralling Out of Control

Hiding
Turning
Running
Senseless low-act teasing.
Out of touch.
Completely
off
the
   rails.
Big city girl
lost
misunderstood
in country town mentality.

STEPHANIE SOON LEARNED WHERE all the classrooms were and didn't need to ask for help. Classes were boring without friends. She thought back to her life in Sydney, and realised how much she missed the routine of dancing after school.

She pulled out her lunch box in the break. Foodwise, nothing had changed with the change of address. An apple, peanut butter and honey sandwiches, a juice popper and a couple of biscuits. Stephanie had stopped enjoying peanut butter and honey years ago, but had given up saying anything. Mum made it daily no matter what she asked for.

As she closed her locker, she bit into her apple and headed to the leafy courtyard. The table was empty today. She'd had company yesterday. She'd introduced herself and tried to make conversation, but it fell on deaf ears and loneliness sat with her again. The calming sense she'd felt on the first day was now nothing but a daily blur of misery.

Stephanie watched a group of girls practise a jazz dance routine in one of the classrooms. Maybe she had been too quick to throw out her shoes. She asked if she could join in.

'Sorry, we're full,' the leader told her. The others shook their heads and curled their lips in snarls.

Cliquey much? In Sydney, if she took one step forward, she'd always been welcomed with open arms. Here, in Toowoomba, the people she wanted to befriend may as well have spat in her face with their snide remarks and lack of acceptance.

'Mum?'

'Stephanie, can this wait? I've got a mother-daughter morning tea with April's class.' Mum jingled the keys in her hand as she opened the front door.

'I guess.' *No. It can't wait.*

'Come on, Mum. I don't want to be late,' April called from the car. Stephanie watched them drive off, then noticed her father. She wasn't about to interrupt him as he pushed the lawnmower like he was racing a hare. She closed the door to block out the roaring mower.

Jealousy churned inside as she watched her parents and sister settle in to this new town. She was short with them to avoid communication. But, the constant looks and comments from her mother made things worse. 'I'm sure you'd make friends more easily if you wiped that sullen frown off your face,' Diane said when they were alone in the laundry. 'What about those dance competitions you wanted to do this year?'

'They're all in Sydney,' Stephanie said.

'And now that we're here, we can find out what's coming up.'

Stephanie gritted her teeth. 'No. I don't want to do comps anymore.'

'Well, let's at least find some classes.'

'I thought you said they were too expensive.'

'We could have a look and see.' Her mother continued to fold the washing.

'Forget it. I don't want to dance ever again!' She ran upstairs.

Stephanie knew she was being difficult. But as soon as the words fell from her tongue, she was sure it was meant to be. Fate had thrown this horrible town at her and somehow, she had to find her place in it—without dancing.

No friends, no dancing, no passion.

An unnerving pressure held her eyes half shut. Rain fell every other day outside as her life fell into a swamp.

But there was Tabbie. She was the speck of light at the end of the tunnel, the one person who brought happiness with her. The ringing of the landline interrupted Stephanie's thoughts. She ran to answer it.

'Hiya!' Tabbie said.

'The time isn't passing fast enough.'

'Not long now. I can't wait!' Tabbie's voice was irritably happy. Stephanie could only dream of being so happy.

'Yeah, same. This town is a hole.'

'There's this—'

'The worst is in the mornings.' Stephanie cut her off and moved into her bedroom. 'When I walk through the school gates, the boys' hoohaaring and wolf-whistles grate on me.'

'Oh, Steph …' Tabbie sighed. 'Why don't you just smile and say hello? That should shut them up.'

'I'll try tomorrow.'

'The eisteddfod—'

'Tabbie, I've got to go.' The competition was the last thing Stephanie wanted to talk about.

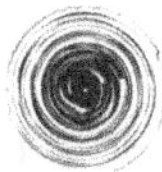

The whole of Saint Maria's High School funnelled into the steepled stone church for their Easter service. One class per row.

Stephanie sat on the pew with Monica to her left, already kneeling. Looking to her right, she discovered everyone was kneeling.

Monica pointed to the wooden platform. 'Don't you know anything? You're meant to be kneeling.'

Stephanie thought back to the times she'd gone to church services with her parents. She'd been young and rarely knelt when they did.

Small bells echoed and a pungent scent filled the church along with the tones of an organ. A student choir stood in rows to the side of the altar, attempting an operatic hymn which echoed through the walls. A procession of students carrying candles and urns walked down the aisle, in front of the priest.

'Check out Jason,' Monica said to the girl on her left. 'He's so hot.'

Stephanie assumed the taller, ridiculously good-looking boy bowing at the altar must be Jason. He turned with a half-smile and gave a two-finger salute to his friends before retreating to the front row.

When the music ended, the priest moved forward. 'In the name of the Father, Son and Holy Spirit.'

'Amen.' Stephanie remembered the response she'd said years before.

'I've asked Crystal to hook Jason and me up,' Monica whispered to her friend.

'No way. He'd never go out with you. He's never dated anyone in our year.'

'Shh.' Someone behind them silenced Monica's conversation.

As the service continued, Stephanie was slow to respond at the right places but found her autopilot when the congregation began reciting the Nicene Creed.

Her eyes were drawn to the tall, broad-shouldered boy in the front row. He'd have to be Monica's crush. He elbowed his neighbour as his shoulders bounced in silent laughter. Monica leaned to her right, pushing Stephanie aside to get a better view. Stephanie shuffled her knees to move out of the way just as Monica jabbed her elbow into Stephanie's arm.

Note to self. Avoid sitting beside this girl EVER again. She walked out of the church, rubbing her arm, thankful the school only held one service a term.

That afternoon, Stephanie dumped her school bag on her bed and called Tabbie. 'This place is such a hole.'

'Hey, the way you talk about Toowoomba, I don't know if I want to come.'

'You're coming to see me, not the town. At least you get to leave. I'm stuck here.'

'It's not forever, Steph. You're nearly fifteen. Maybe you could go to boarding school or … Hey, I've just had a great idea. What if you could come and stay here and finish school back at Hill Top?'

'Tabbie, you're a genius.' Stephanie jumped off her bed and kicked a leg high, then spun around on the spot.

'Mmm.'

'We'll have to make a plan when you come and stay. You're the bestest friend.'

Chapter Five

FOR THE FIRST TIME SINCE THEY'D MOVED, Stephanie fell into a deep peaceful sleep. Sydney dreams captured her mind. If she endured life in this inland city for the rest of the year, perhaps she could go back to her old life. Maybe things would get better. She could only hope.

'Morning.' Stephanie breezed into the kitchen.

'Good to see you up so early and cheerful.' Her mother smiled.

'Would you like a coffee, Mum?'

'That would be a lovely change, you making me a coffee.'

Stephanie reflected her mother's smile.

'Wouldn't have something to do with a certain friend coming this afternoon?' Her mother winked. 'It's nice to see you happy and not moping around.'

'Mum, you get on well with Tabbie's parents, don't you?' Stephanie hoped planting early seeds would ease her mother into the idea.

Her mother's response was an underwhelming nod.

Stephanie caught her father's attention before he left for work. 'What was boarding school like? Why didn't you send us to one?'

By the way her father laughed in response, she knew it was a financial choice. She'd have to devise a plan on how to approach the subject without having them fob her off.

Diane pulled up outside the school at the usual time. Stephanie walked through the gates to Wolf Whistle Boy and his friends saying the same things. She'd grown tired of being bothered by it, but they still irritated her. 'Morning.' Stephanie tried Tabbie's suggestion, and looked them straight in the eye with a cheesy grin. The boys turned away and laughed. It was one step up from being called names and getting ogled.

Stephanie's brain buzzed with the slowness of the school day. She jumped when the bell rang at the end of the second last period and ran through the front gates to meet Mum, thrilled to leave school early for the day and begin the Easter holidays.

'It'll take us just over an hour, hey?' Stephanie climbed into the car.

'Yes, possibly closer to two, but we have plenty of time. Tabbie sent me a text message to say her flight had been delayed forty-five minutes.'

Stephanie put her headphones on, wound the chair back and relaxed. She dozed to the sound of music until both lanes slowed because of an accident.

'Mum, do you think I could go and spend some time at Tabbie's in term two, maybe during the June-July holidays?' she asked.

Diane kept her eyes on the road. 'Why not? That should be fine.'

After another ten minutes Stephanie asked, 'At what age do you think it's okay to leave home?'

Her mother didn't answer, she just looked at Stephanie with raised eyebrows.

Stephanie tried from a different angle. 'Would you let me or April go to boarding school if we wanted to?'

Her mother rubbed her chin. 'What are you thinking, Steph? What's going on?'

'Oh, nothing.'

'Are things all right at school?'

'It's okay.' Stephanie looked away.

'You know Dad moved us up here so we could all be together. Why would we want to send you off to boarding school?'

'It's not like we see more of him.'

'Do we need to talk about this with your father?'

'Nah, it's cool.' Stephanie didn't want to get into an argument. She turned her music back on. It was time to back off and wait until she had cemented a plan with Tabbie.

'All aboard,' Mum called two hours later, as she pulled into the airport pickup zone.

'Hello!' Tabbie squealed. 'Good to see you. Where's April?'

'She's at a friend's house.' Mum helped Tabbie throw her luggage into the boot, then climbed back into the driver's seat. 'Hope you don't mind us picking you up here. Parking is just so expensive.

'No, that's okay,' Tabbie said.

The girls embraced, both with eyes welling up.

'April loves it in Toowoomba, go figure.' Stephanie swallowed, pushing her tongue to the roof of her mouth in an attempt to stop the tears. She trembled as a trickle released, rolling down her cheek, and quickly wiped it away.

Stephanie slid into the back seat, followed by Tabbie.

'Well, what have we got planned?' Tabbie asked.

'Nothing really, but I think exploring is on the agenda tomorrow.' Stephanie plastered a smile across her face.

Diane cleared her throat. 'Are you sure about that? How do you think you'll get around? Don't you think you should run that by the driver first?'

'It's okay, Mum. We can catch the bus.'

'We don't know the timetable. I haven't got anything planned tomorrow. I'll drop you off and come and pick you up.'

Stephanie looked to the car roof, then at her mother. *Stop treating me like a kid.*

The girls caught up on the in-between bits they hadn't discussed over the phone. Every time Tabbie brought up dancing or school,

     Spiralling Out of Control

Stephanie changed the subject. In a lull in conversation, Tabbie pulled her phone out to read a text message.

'Is that your new phone?' Stephanie picked at her fingernails.

'Mum's old one. When are you getting one?'

'When I can pay the bill.' Stephanie rolled her eyes.

She'd begged her parents for a mobile phone on the drive up from Sydney. Her father had told her, 'You can get one after you get a job, and we don't want you working until you turn sixteen.'

'When are you getting your internet hooked up?' Tabbie asked.

'It's up and running, but only on the computer in Dad's office.'

Tabbie squeezed in her eyes, mouth and nose to resemble something like the rear end of a cat.

'Don't ask.' Stephanie shook her head.

'Have you talked about moving back to Sydney?' Tabbie asked in a small voice.

Stephanie leaned across the back seat to whisper, 'Just a couple of hints but not really. We'll have to chat at home.' She glanced at her mother.

They drove up the Great Dividing Range as the sun fell behind the mountain and twilight clung to the air. When they picked up April, she badgered Tabbie with question after question. Stephanie ignored her, willing her mother to speed so they could get home quicker. As soon as Diane parked in the driveway, Stephanie fled from her little sister, leading Tabbie upstairs.

'No, April, you can't come in!' Stephanie closed the door.

Tabbie looked at the crooked posters. 'What happened here?'

'Suits my mood. I'm leaving them that way.'

'So has there been any change at school?' Tabbie lay on the bed.

'What do you mean?' Stephanie fluffed her pillow to lean on it.

'Have you ignored their comments and just smiled?'

'I started trying it.' Stephanie groaned. 'But no, they're still the same.'

'Give it time.' Tabbie raised her eyebrows. 'You keep shutting me down when I mention dance. Tell me, why aren't you dancing?'

'Tabbie!' Stephanie heaved a breath.

'Come on Steph—you love dancing and you're so good at it.'

'I guess I was just angry with Mum and Dad and everything. I told them I didn't want to dance. Like, ever again. Now I've said it, I guess it's true. It feels cemented.'

Tabbie looked into Stephanie's eyes. 'Just because you said it to your parents doesn't mean you can't ever dance again.'

Stephanie sighed, clamping her mouth closed. *I couldn't stand dancing with those cows from school.*

'Let me show you part of the new routine we've just started.' Tabbie jumped up, started the music on her phone and grooved out a few moves. 'Make you want to join in?'

'No.'

'Just a little?'

Stephanie's eyelids dipped, leaving her eyes half open. 'No. I've made my decision.'

'There's more to it than the fact you told your parents you didn't want to, hey?'

Tears choked her voice. She swallowed. 'The girls who dance here hate me.' *How could I have gone from amazing friends like Tabbie to this town where everyone hates me?*

'All of them? They just don't know you yet.'

'They don't want to know me, Tabbie. They hate me. They're mean. They're rude. And they're different to us.'

April knocked on the door. 'It's dinner time!'

Stephanie blew her nose and went to the bathroom to wash her face before leading Tabbie to dinner. She sat at the table to find her father's seat bare. 'Where's Dad?'

'He had to work late.' Her mother shook her head. 'He'll arrive any minute.'

'What are you doing tomorrow? Can I come?' April asked.

Stephanie glared at her. 'You have gymnastics.'

'Can I come after?'

'No.' Sharing Tabbie with her little sister was not an option.

Her father breezed in halfway through the meal. He sat at the table and read the paper while her mother reheated his dinner. Stephanie stabbed the last piece of food on her plate and shoved it into her mouth. Still chewing, she stood. 'We're going back upstairs.'

'Can I come too?' April jumped up.

'No!' Stephanie glared at her.

'Maybe you can spend some time with the girls tomorrow, after your gymnastics class.'

Tabbie and Stephanie ran up to the bedroom. 'Sometimes April is just so annoying!' Stephanie pushed her bedroom door closed behind them.

'You think? I think she's sweet.'

Stephanie screwed her nose up. Tabbie shrugged.

'I need to get back to Sydney.'

'So let's work it out. How can we get you there?'

'Mum and Dad are against boarding school. I don't think Dad has good memories of going himself.'

'What if you come and live with us?'

'Have you said anything to your parents?'

'I asked if you could come for the next holidays and maybe stay for a while next year.'

'What did they say?'

'Mum said it should be fine. Peter's moving out next year to study in Melbourne. So we'd have a spare room.'

'Really?' Stephanie hoped Tabbie hadn't noticed her voice almost squeak. She'd had a huge crush on Peter when she first met him. Remnants of her dreams of dating him flooded back with the mention of his name.

Tabbie nodded.

Stephanie pushed Peter's image to the back of her mind. 'I just have to talk Mum and Dad round.'

'Imagine that! Living together. It'd be so much fun.'

The girls giggled.

The next day Stephanie's mother dropped them in the centre of Toowoomba. 'Make sure you keep enough change to ring from the public phone if you need me before three o'clock, okay?'

Tabbie pulled her mobile out as Diane drove away. 'Has she forgotten I have this?'

'She's seriously clueless.' Stephanie shook her head.

They walked in and out of old-fashioned shops, most with faded signs and flaking paint. After shopping for a couple of hours, they watched a movie, then bought some sandwiches to eat at Queens Park, just a short walk away.

'This park is gorgeous.' Tabbie looked around with bright eyes.

'I guess it is nice. First time I've been here.' Stephanie followed Tabbie's gaze towards the trees and flowerbeds.

Tabbie spun around with her arms out.

'I don't feel like walking any more today,' Stephanie said. The weight of her slumping shoulders urged her to sit down. 'We can see more tomorrow.'

'Let's sit under that giant tree.' Tabbie skipped ahead.

They lay on the grass chatting for a couple of hours, breathing the fresh mountain air before calling Mum to pick them up. Even when a deluge of rain dampened the rest of the week, the lingering glow of happiness took Stephanie back to her old self. She actually began to look forward to school returning.

Her resolve to cope when school started back stood firm. Could she endure the pressure?

Chapter Six

Term two, day one. Stephanie pulled her uniform on and tied her hair back in a tight ponytail. No longer would she allow others to reduce her to insignificance. Her freshly inspired intentions spurred her to wait for the perfect time to talk to her parents about doing her last years of school in Sydney. But first she had to brave the creeps at the gate.

Stephanie walked with casual steps through the gates. The usual boys were doing their usual things, whistling and yelling remarks about her body. *They're just getting off on trying to embarrass me. I won't let them get to me. I'm fine.* She smiled, held her head up, and stopped in front of them. 'Hi there, how are you? Great to be back, isn't it? How were your holidays?'

The boys laughed. *I can do this.* Stephanie stood firm. She wasn't going to be shaken from her newfound self-assurance. She squared her shoulders, kept the smile on her face until the boys left, and then continued on her way. Just beyond the gate, a group of older boys lingered.

'Morning.' Stephanie kept her voice airy, her smile firmly in place. Moving her body forward helped keep her calm.

A girl's voice butted into her resolution. 'What do you think you are doing, b****? You think you have a chance with those boys?'

Recognising Monica's voice, Stephanie climbed the stairs and sucked in air, filling the deepest point in her lungs. She forced her legs to move forward, trying not to let the "b" word cut deeper than it already had.

'She's got to be dreaming!' Monica said to her posse as Stephanie passed her.

I did it! I got through without caving.

On the outside, Stephanie looked strong, perhaps even arrogant, but on the inside she wavered. On Wednesday, she smiled politely at the boys by the gate while hiding her shaking hands. Her dry throat shut off her vocal cords, shortening her greeting to, 'Hello.'

By Friday, she was ready to bury her head in a pillow again.

'Tabbie, this sucks!' Her forever best friend was always there when she needed to talk.

'Oh, Steph, what's happened?'

'Nothing. Not one change.' Stephanie clenched the cordless phone.

'Really?'

'I guess Wolf Whistle Boy and his friends weren't as bad by the end of the week. But I …'

'You started caving, didn't you?'

'Guess so.' Stephanie chewed a fingernail.

'Hey, your birthday is coming up.'

'Gee, that was a subtle change of subject.'

Tabbie giggled into the phone. 'What are you planning?'

'Can I come to Sydney to celebrate?' Stephanie asked with unrealistic hope.

'Yeah, why not! Hey, just jump on the next plane!'

If only.

Stephanie turned fifteen on the nineteenth of May. She kept her birthday a secret at school, to avoid drawing more unwanted attention. As her family sat around the dining table to share a roast, her father seemed tired and didn't talk. Her mother and April discussed the next gymnastics competition. *Hello? Whose birthday is it today?*

Stephanie left the table after dinner. 'This would have to be the worst birthday I've ever had.'

'What about the cake?' April called.

They could eat it without her. Two months ago, she would never in her worst nightmare have thought she'd be this lonely on her birthday. She still had Tabbie, her ever-encouraging friend. But Tabbie was too far away. Stephanie's shoulders slumped as she fell into bed, still fully dressed. Under the doona, the darkness swallowed her.

In the following weeks, Stephanie pulled every bit of courage she could find to continue greeting the boys at the gate. With each, 'Hello,' they became a little more polite and a little less rude—to her face. But the whistles and comments about her body never escaped her hearing as she climbed the stairs. Daily, the older boys hung out just beyond the gate. Stephanie watched the ground as she passed them, knowing her face would burn with embarrassment if she looked up.

One morning, she was watching her feet while passing the second group. Someone fell in stride with her. The scent of fresh soap and Rexona sent her heart instantly into a spasm. Her hands shook with fright until she grabbed her skirt seam. Had Wolf Whistle Boy decided to take his harassment one step further?

Stephanie regained enough poise to speak. 'Think you'll get to class on time today?'

'I do alright, thanks.'

The voice was deeper than expected. Stephanie turned to see who was walking with her. She clenched her teeth to stifle a gasp when she saw he wore a senior's uniform.

'Sorry.' The word scratched through her dry throat. 'I thought you were someone else.'

'No worries.' He smiled. 'I've been watching you.'

Yeah, and probably laughing at rude comments from the other idiots. Stephanie bit her lip. Why was *he* talking to *her*?

'What's your name?'

'Stephanie.' She swallowed a smidgen of saliva.

'I'm Jason.'

Stephanie smiled. The whole school knew who he was. Jason Hobbs, the senior all the girls swooned over in class. Monica's crush.

'I'd love to hang out with you sometime.' His voice wavered.

She tilted her head to see him straight on. 'What? What do you mean?'

'Like go out sometime.'

'Oh, I suppose.' *Is he for real?*

'Great. There's a party on this weekend, one of the girls in year twelve. A big group of us are going. Not really a party, just a hang-out thing.'

Stay cool. 'And you want to take me?'

'Well, I thought we could meet there, but ah … I could pick you up?'

'Um. Okay.'

She gave him her address. He said he'd see her at seven on Saturday night.

Did I just invite him to pick me up? Did he want me to just turn up by myself? What does he want with me anyway? She struggled to believe he'd show.

For the rest of the day, she walked around school in a daze, her mind clouded with possibilities. She kept replaying the Jason-conversation in her mind. Her heart flipped with the prospect of going on her first date. She kept it to herself, fearing it might not happen. If some of the girls from school were at the party and saw her with Jason, it just might be her pass in.

On Saturday night, she hoped Jason would turn up but didn't really expect him to. She pulled on some jeans and a snug-fitting top, tying a scarf around her neck in case the temperature dropped. Then she flicked her light off and waited beside her window to watch the traffic pass below.

Oh no, oh no! What? A car pulled up right in front of their house. It was him! *And his mother?* Oh, of course he mustn't have a licence.

She ran downstairs. 'Mum, a guy, Jason, asked me to a party tonight and I didn't think he'd turn up but he's here. Is it okay if I go?'

'How are you getting there?'

'His mum is driving.'

'A party, you say?' Her father entered the room.

'Yes.'

'You won't be drinking, will you?'

Stephanie shuffled her feet to hurry him up. 'Of course not.'

'How do I know this boy won't be drinking?'

'Dad, is it okay? He'll be at the door in a second.'

'Steph—' He was interrupted by a knock and turned to open the door.

Jason's hand was still raised, as if to knock again. His mouth was half-open and his tongue rested on his teeth.

Why is he looking so young and dumb? He's a senior. Shouldn't he be more confident?

Her father shook Jason's hand. 'I'm John. You must be Jason. Is there going to be alcohol at this party?'

'Pleased to meet you, John. Yes, there will be alcohol at the party, sir.'

Stephanie's jaw dropped at Jason's polite honesty. He already seemed so different from the boys in her class.

'Will you be drinking?'

'I might have one.'

Wrong answer, Jason. Stephanie stopped her hand from slapping her forehead as she edged towards the door.

'You trust your daughter, don't you?'

Her father looked shocked by Jason's boldness and turned to face Stephanie. 'No alcohol, okay. Remember your curfew is ten-thirty. Take my mobile and ring us if you need to be picked up. Okay?'

'Sure, Dad.' Stephanie kept her cool and grabbed the phone.

The drive with Jason's mum was unexpectedly quiet. Stephanie breathed deeply to calm the knot in her chest. *I can't believe I'm going to my first party in Toowoomba, with a bunch of seniors.* Stephanie couldn't form words in her mind to speak. She stared at Jason and then turned to his mum, willing one of them to make conversation or at least ask her a question—anything to choke the ten minutes of extreme silence in the car.

'Thanks, Mrs Hobbs,' she said when the car stopped.

'Stephanie has to be home by ten-thirty,' Jason said as he climbed out of the car. His mother drove off without saying a word.

'Is she always that quiet?' Stephanie asked.

'Yeah, mostly. She was probably thinking about something else.'

As they walked towards the door Stephanie couldn't believe her nerves. Her knees banged together. *What if everyone sees me shaking?*

When the group saw Jason they erupted with a cheer.

What do I do? Do I run and hide? Do I follow him? Do I talk to the girls? Argh, I'm so awkward!

Music played, almost drowning the chattering voices. Stephanie focused first on the people, then the floor. The girls sat inside on couches and the boys leaned against the railing on the veranda. Jason walked straight past the girls and headed outside. *What? Has he forgotten I'm here?* She was sure he had. She took a couple of slow steps to follow him, but lingered between the couches and the veranda.

'Was she invited?' one of the girls said.

'Well, she walked in with Jason.'

'Did he bring her?'

 Spiralling Out of Control

What, am I invisible? Not worth talking to? The heat rushed upwards from her neck to her cheeks. It was the same as school. *Maybe I should just ring Dad.*

She reached for the phone in her handbag.

'I thought you were following me.' Jason grabbed Stephanie's hand. 'Hi, Crystal. Hey, happy birthday, Jess. You all know Stephanie, don't you?' He didn't wait for them to answer before he led her onto the veranda.

It's a birthday party? Did he tell me that? She wanted to shrink into the decking.

'Want a drink?'

'Um …'

'Coke? Your parents would probably kill me—and you—if I took you back *intoxicated.*' He spoke with an awkward pommy accent.

'Thanks, Coke would be great.' Stephanie smiled as he reached into the ice-filled esky. He flicked ice off the can before holding it towards her.

His hand seemed to linger on hers as she went to take the can. Their eyes met in a moment that was over before it started. One of his friends yelled for more beers. Jason, being close to the esky, answered their call.

Stephanie pulled the ring to open the can. The ting echoed in a moment of silence. Jason's friends looked at her with polite nods, then accepted their beers from Jason as their conversation continued. After a while, the girls called Stephanie in to sit on the couch. She glanced at Jason as she moved inside. He nodded then smiled. She sat on the couch as a rush of warmth swirled around her heart. *Are they accepting me?*

'Have any of you tried the new hair salon on Herries?' Crystal slid her fingers down her perfectly straight hair.

Stephanie pulled at a strand of kinky hair that hung over her shoulder. Hair appointments had never been a priority, as long as she could work it into a ponytail or pin it up to dance.

'Seriously, Crystal, your hair is amazing. Did you get it done today?' said Jess.

Crystal nodded and flashed her nails. 'Got these while I was there.'

Stephanie leaned forward to check out the diamantes stuck on her fingernail tips.

'You look fabulous, birthday girl. Tell us, where did you get your hair done?' asked Lani.

'You won't believe me.' Jess turned from side to side, giving them all a good view. 'It was done by … Mum.'

The whole group erupted with laughter. Stephanie joined them. If only her mother took a slight interest in her hair. The girls continued talking about hairstyles and fingernails. Stephanie smiled and laughed while she kept Jason in view.

Jason returned to the room, turning every girl's head. 'I think Mum will be outside. We'd better go if I'm to get you home by 10:30.'

They all laughed.

Stephanie willed the carpet to swallow her whole.

'10:30! What? Will you turn into a pumpkin?' Crystal looked at the other girls as she spoke.

'Hey, first time I've taken her out. Better do the right thing by her parents.' Jason reached out his hand to help her off the couch.

When she stood, he continued holding her hand. Stephanie blinked with an involuntary eyelash flutter. *He just stood up for me.*

The girls stopped laughing and Jess spoke. 'Nice to meet you, Stephanie. Hope to see you round school next week.'

'Yeah, see ya next week,' Lani called.

'Bye.' Stephanie smiled and followed Jason through the front door, feeling sweat prickle her palm as he clutched her hand.

His mum sat in the car with the engine and headlights on, her face illuminated by the phone in her lap.

'Hope your mum hasn't been waiting too long,' Stephanie said.

'Don't worry about it,' he whispered over his shoulder. 'She'll get over it.'

 Spiralling Out of Control

Jason let go of her hand to open the car door, then slid in the back seat after her. Once again, they drove in silence. He reached across to where her hand rested on the seat and covered it with his. She looked away, attempting to curb her cheesy grin. When the car stopped at her house, Jason jumped out and followed her.

As she raised her hand to grab the doorknob, her father swung the door open. 'Hello. Did you want to come in, Jason?'

'Ah, no thanks. Mum's waiting. See you on Monday, Stephanie.' Jason smiled before rushing back down the front steps.

'A good night?' Dad closed the door.

'Yeah, you could say that.'

'He's a lot older than you, Steph.'

'Only a couple of years.' Stephanie frowned. 'Dad, it was just a party.'

'Were they drinking?'

'Yeah, they were.'

'Did you have any?'

'No.' Stephanie raised her eyebrows. 'You said not to.'

'Good.'

Her mother walked down the stairs. 'Many there?'

'Hmm, average I guess.' Stephanie turned to leave the room. 'I'm tired.'

Her insides bounced. When no one could see her, she sighed, did a happy dance and smiled. *Jason.* She played the night over in her head as she changed into her pyjamas and washed her face.

He was nice. Very nice. School would be better now she'd met him and made a couple of friends. She pulled up her blanket, closed her eyes and let sleep take hold.

Chapter Seven

MONDAY MORNING, STEPHANIE STRODE into school with a little more zest. She looked past the immature boys at the front gate, searching beyond, hoping to find Jason. Her smile fell as she released a breath. He wasn't there. *What if he never talks to me again?* She tried to shake the thought from her mind and continued up the stairs. To her surprise, Jason came from nowhere.

'Did you have a good time Saturday night?' he asked.

'Yeah.' She was consumed with a gush of heart-mushy flutters at the sight of him. *He's the best-looking boy in the world.*

'Maybe we could hang out again sometime.'

'Okay,' Stephanie said. *Oops.* She'd answered way too fast.

Jason turned at the top of the stairs and Stephanie almost followed, but stopped, gathered herself and took her usual route in the other direction. Monica and her posse cornered Stephanie in the hallway as the bell clanged.

'Is it true?'

'What?' Stephanie shook her head.

'My sister said she met someone from school in my year at Jess's birthday party. Someone called Stephanie,' Monica yelled over the noisy bustle. 'Was it you?'

'And what if it was?'

'Did you go there with Jason?'

Monica's friends snickered behind their hands.

Stephanie gave Monica a tight-lipped smile.

'Jason?' Monica rested a hand on her hip. 'As if he's interested in you. He did it for a dare … He thinks you're a … you're an easy sl—'

Stephanie moved forward and dug her elbow into Monica's side as she passed. She clenched her jaw. *I am not—oh!* No one had ever called her that.

'Ha! Look at you, red as a beetroot.' Monica's screeching laugh echoed through the crowded hallway.

Stephanie's head pounded. Blinking, she pushed her way through the crowd, not wanting to give them the satisfaction of seeing her tears.

'As if you'd have a chance,' Monica called after her.

What if it's true? Everything in Stephanie's mind blurred. Monica's sister had been at the party. Stephanie imagined the conversations and jokes flying around the room after Jason took her home. *How could he?* She gritted her teeth. *How could he do that to me?*

Stephanie threw her school bag in her locker, rushed to the bathroom and locked herself in a cubicle. Flipping the toilet lid down, she sat with her feet up, wishing she was invisible.

Her mind filled with scenes from the party and how real and normal it had all seemed. Now she was shattered by the possibility of it all being a charade. She curled into a ball, stretching her arms around her legs. Irregular groups came and went. She listened to the conversations, expecting to hear someone talking about her. But no one did. The lunch bell rang and she stood with a fright and grabbed for the walls for support as her sleepy legs almost buckled under her. Stephanie wanted to stay in the restroom all day, but her groaning stomach drew her out. She splashed water on her face to cool the redness, then wandered through the hallway back to her locker. She pulled her lunch out of her school bag, fixed her eyes on the floor and hurried towards her regular lunch spot.

On the way she was stopped. 'Hey, Stephanie, how's your day going?'

Stephanie jumped.

'What are you doing down this end of the school?' Jess smiled.

'I come here to get some quiet time.'

'Oh, I get it. Were you meeting Jason?'

'No, I've never seen him here. What makes you think that?' *Oh, now I sound nervous and dumb.* Stephanie took a moment to breathe. 'Why would I be waiting for him?'

'Ah, because you were with him on Saturday night.'

Stephanie didn't know how to reply. To say more would make her sound like a young girl infatuated with a senior. Jess looked at her. Stephane cringed at the awkward silence.

'Well if you're not waiting for anyone, do you mind if I sit with you?' Jess pulled out a plastic-wrapped sandwich.

'Sure.' Stephanie didn't move.

'Were you going to sit somewhere?'

'Um, yeah. I usually sit in the courtyard.'

'Let's go then.'

Stephanie walked beside Jess to the wooden plank table.

'Is it you who moved from Sydney?' Jess sat down.

'Yeah.' Stephanie slid onto the bench seat opposite.

'Crystal's sister was telling me about you the other day. I think she's got you all wrong.'

'Like how?' Stephanie lifted an eyebrow. *Was this the conversation Monica was talking about?*

'Don't worry about her. She's a lot of talk.'

'Ya think?' Stephanie squinted.

'Did she give you a hard time about coming to my party?'

'Mm.'

'Monica's been pretty horrible?'

'Yep.'

'So what I reckon …' Jess bit into her sandwich, chewed it a couple of times before swallowing. 'I reckon she's jealous. Take no notice.'

Stephanie shuffled her legs under the table. That was easy for Jess to say.

Stephanie wanted to pour her heart out to Jess, but she didn't. Instead, she bit her lip and listened.

'Jason's one of the nice guys. You're lucky.'

'We'll see.' Suspicion arose under Stephanie's skin. *What if this is just another add-on to the whole scheme of his plan to …*

Even though she was wary of Jess's encouragement, she welcomed the company.

'You'll see.' Jess smiled and sat with Stephanie for the rest of the lunch break.

The next day and every morning that week, Jason fell in stride with Stephanie in the same spot. They walked together for ten metres or so, chatting with ease, then he coolly walked off to his homeroom.

'What about lunch tomorrow?' Jason asked on Friday morning.

'Um, okay.' Lunch sounded pretty innocent. There was safety in daylight.

'I only live a couple of blocks from you so I'll walk around and we can go down to that café on Mary Street.' His smile shone through his dreamy brown eyes.

'Okay,' was all she could get out as she watched him walk away.

Stephanie checked if anyone had caught the invitation exchange. Maybe she should have said no. But she wanted to spend time with Jason again, away from school.

During lunch, she sat with the senior girls.

'Is anyone doing anything exciting this weekend?' Jess asked.

Stephanie shoved more food into her mouth and listened as they talked about parties and part-time jobs.

'How about you?' Jess looked Stephanie in the eye. 'Doing anything exciting this weekend?'

'Nothing special.' Stephanie took another bite. She didn't want to bring her date with Jason to the conversation. She didn't even know if it was an actual date. It was easier to not mention anything. Even if Jason was only a link to making some friends, that was okay. Life was better with someone to talk to.

Lani stood up. 'I'd invite you all over if I didn't have so many assignments due.'

'Yeah, wouldn't it be great to have some more free time again?'

Stephanie nodded. But she already had too much free time. Due dates could wait 'til she was in a better frame of mind.

Stephanie trotted downstairs just before she expected Jason to arrive.

'Mum, I'm heading out with Jason again today. We're having lunch down on Mary Street.'

'Is anyone else joining you?'

'Don't know.'

'Should you take my mobile? I'd wish you'd given me more notice. Have you checked with your father?'

She clenched her teeth. 'I'll be fine.' *How is it I see less of Dad now than ever?*

Jason knocked on the door, saving her from more motherly questions.

'Bye.' Stephanie closed the door, took a deep breath and let his slightly sweaty masculine scent fill her lungs.

Jason spoke first. 'Jess said you've been hanging out together at lunch.'

'Yeah.' Stephanie shoved her hands in her pockets to control her nerves.

'Don't you hang with girls from your year?'

'No.'

Her short answers led nowhere. If she let him talk until there was awkward silence, maybe he'd move on to his next target. *I'm not easy.* Monica had pegged her in the wrong hole.

They entered an old milk bar that had been given an obvious facelift with tall trendy tables and stools.

Jason ordered and paid.

'No, here.' Stephanie pushed some money towards him, dipping her eyebrows. If she let him pay, would he expect something in return?

'Don't worry about it. I have enough cash.'

Jason led her through the back doors where shade sails covered an outdoor eating area. He stopped at a round table and pulled the chair out for her.

During lunch, Jason captured her with his humour. His witty conversation faded the passing of time as she sat listening, wide-eyed and fascinated.

'When I was in year nine, I walked outside my house, and the door blew closed. Our parents were away and my brother had already left for school.'

'What did you do?' Stephanie held her hand to her mouth giggling.

'I went to school in my PJs. Worked wonders with the chicks. They flocked towards me. Striped flannel. But the teachers weren't too happy with my parents leaving us home alone, though.'

She had no funny stories to tell. Everything that came to mind was to do with dancing, and she didn't want to discuss that. So she listened, aware of his eyes focused on her. Aware of her heart fluttering. Aware of heat rushing to her cheeks. The conversation ebbed and flowed until well after they'd finished eating.

She was ready to feed their stats into a compatibility machine if there was such a thing. Jason = Gorgeousness. The way he rested his elbow on the table as he cupped his chin in his hand. The way he looked to the sky when he laughed at himself. The way his eyes danced all over her face as he spoke to her. Stephanie let her walls down. His charm had won her over. If this was a game, he was playing his part really well.

He led her back out onto the path in the direction of her home. Just before they reached her house, he stopped to face her, held both of her hands and kissed her on the cheek. He drew back slowly, allowing his lips to brush across hers. A flush crept into her cheeks. He dropped one hand, and held onto the other as he walked her to the front door. She slipped her now sweaty hand away from his and dried it on her jeans.

Stephanie's mother called from the front room. 'Hi, kids. Jason, would you like to come in?'

'Maybe next time.' Jason lingered in the doorway looking at Stephanie.

She nodded, feeling dreamily crush-struck. *Maybe he is one of the nice guys.*

'See you Monday.' He raised a hand to wave as he strolled towards the gate.

'Okay.'

'He seems nice.' Her mother slid back into the lounge, and binging on whatever series had her entranced.

Stephanie smiled as she ran upstairs to ring Tabbie. 'You won't believe what just happened!'

'You saw Jason again?'

'How did you know?'

'Why else would you be this excited?'

'But?' Stephanie looked at the ceiling, puzzled. She didn't remember mentioning anything about Jason to Tabbie.

'Ha, just joking. I rang while you were out. Second date, hey? Your mum told me.'

Of course, Mum must have blurted the details. Stephanie filled Tabbie in on the party and the morning walks, the way Jason kissed her and how Monica had treated her.

'So you think he's into you?'

'I don't know. How would I know? Lunch and a kiss? Umm...

I don't know.'

'I don't know either.' Tabbie laughed. 'It sounds like he's into you. Do you think Monica is jealous, like that other girl said?'

'Makes sense,' Stephanie said. 'But what if I'm a joke? What if he is planning on using me to win a dare or a bet or something?'

'No sex.'

'Wasn't planning on it.'

'No, you need to make it clear that you're not going to do it.'

'You don't think that's being a bit presumptuous?' Stephanie chewed on the inside of her mouth.

'Steph, you weren't planning on having sex with him, so just be upfront about it.'

'It's not really third date conversation material, is it?'

'Do you want to know whether he's dating you for a dare or not? I reckon if he's playing some sort of game, he won't hang around when he knows where you stand.'

'Okay. Don't know how I'll work that into a conversation on our next date.' *If we have another date.*

Chapter Eight

MUM STOPPED DIRECTLY IN FRONT of the school gate. 'Looks like someone is waiting for you.'

Stephanie bumped the car door shut, and turned to see Jason leaning on the gate, smiling in her direction. Her heart flurried. She relaxed as she walked straight towards him, relieved he had buffered the whistles and comments from the younger boys.

'Hey,' he said with a smile.

'Hi.' She grinned and continued walking.

He led her to her homeroom, glancing into her eyes. She savoured the connection, their gaze locked for a brief moment, until he brushed his hand across her shoulder and walked away. Stephanie smiled, watching him until he was out of sight.

'Dreamer.' Monica sounded like a cat in a fight.

Stephanie's smile dropped.

'Hope he wins his bet on that dare!' Monica shoved Stephanie aside.

Stephanie steadied herself, feeling the ping of disappointment. *Oh, damn. What if it is all a joke?*

Lunch came and she sat with the senior girls, replaying Monica's words in her mind.

'So, Stephanie, did you catch up with Jason again on the weekend?' Lani flicked open a textbook while she ate.

'Yeah, I saw him on Saturday.'

'See.' Jess smiled. 'He's one of the nice guys.'

'Why do you keep saying that?' Stephanie scrunched her plastic sandwich wrap into a ball.

'I've known him my whole life. He's just a true-blue nice guy.'

'Have you met his parents yet?' Lani looked up from her textbook.

'Just his mother.'

Crystal stifled a snort. 'Now, his parents are a worry.'

'Oh, stop it girls. They're fine,' Jess said.

'What's with his parents?' Stephanie chewed the inside of her mouth.

'Nothing really.' Jess twisted her hair and secured it with a butterfly clip.

The conversation ended. What did Lani and Crystal mean? His mother was quiet, but what was so strange about that?

Jason continued to meet her at the gate and walk her to her homeroom. Her hands tingled every time he bumped against her. She held her head up to catch his every word. At times, she would take an extra skipping step to keep up with his long strides. Each day she felt a little more at ease.

One morning, he leaned towards her as they walked, brushing his arm against hers. 'How are you going with your assignments?'

'I haven't actually looked at them for a while.'

'It gets that way, doesn't it? Fun always comes before study.' He gave a little chuckle, though she was sure he was joking.

Surely he'd be pushing for another date or something by now if he was being nice because of a dare. But he hadn't invited her out and she was clueless as to how to bring it up. She wanted to see him again—off school grounds.

As they walked into school Friday morning, Jason rested his arm across her shoulders.

A warm shiver rushed to her chest. 'Where do you go at lunchtime?'

'Why?' He smiled. 'Aren't you seeing enough of me?'

'Just wondered, that's all.' She reached to link her fingers through his.

'Footy. On the oval.'

'Oh.' She blinked over and over, too many times, looking into his deep dark eyes.

'What if I come around this afternoon?' He pulled back his arm to check his watch.

'Okay.' A tingle of warmth hit her cheeks.

'Gotta go. See you at four.' Jason's deep warm eyes smiled as he turned to walk away.

Stephanie melted inside, but was snapped back to reality when Monica shoulder-barged her.

'It's all a game,' Monica whispered, curling her lip.

Stephanie ignored her, pushing the idea of a dare out of her mind.

Later that day, Jason knocked on the door just before four o'clock. Stephanie heard her mother open the door. 'Jason, come in.'

'Thanks.'

'Jason's here.'

Stephanie hoped Jason hadn't seen her in the window, waiting for him to arrive.

'Okay, okay.' She ran downstairs. 'See you later.'

Once outside, she held the door for Jason to follow.

'Where would you like to go?' he asked. 'Do you want to go to the café on Mary again?'

'I don't mind.' She was already ahead of him by a couple of steps.

'Let's just go for a walk.' He brushed her arm as he caught up with her. Walking with Jason sent a warm rush through her veins. He strode close enough for Stephanie to bask in his body heat and breathe in his fresh scent. The afternoon shadows sent zebra markings across the road. Crisp, signs of winter air shivered through her body. When they turned the corner, Jason took her hand and led her into a grassy park. They strolled over a slight rise and sat in a sunny spot out of view from the road, his hand firmly wrapped around hers.

Jason didn't speak. Stephanie kept silent as she soaked in the leafy surroundings. The pure, smog-free slivers of light flickered through the trees. Jason leaned over and kissed her, breaking the awkward silence. It was warm and comfortable and Stephanie willingly pressed her lips to his. When he wrapped his arms around her, the bulge of his biceps restricted her movement. Her brain kicked in. He could overpower her in a second.

Stephanie slid her hands between their chests and pushed him away. Turning her face to the side, away from his kiss, she forced out the words, 'I don't do sex.'

Jason stood and backed off. 'Who said we were going to have sex?'

'I just wanted to be clear. It's just not going to happen. O-okay?' She tried to stay cool, keeping her voice bright. Thin shafts of light shot through the tree like swords. 'I just don't want to lead you on, if that's all you're after.'

'Okay. Yeah, I get it. You want to wait a bit.'

She couldn't read his expression. He took another step backwards, his mood now different. *Distracted.* She hadn't expected him to react like that. What if Monica was right? Stephanie pushed herself up off the ground and walked in the direction of home. Jason followed. She shivered, the breeze between them hit her like shards of ice. Neither of them spoke. She followed the path through her gate.

'See you later,' Jason said.

'Bye,' Stephanie said to his back. He'd already turned and was jogging away.

Were they over before they were officially on?

'Steph, it was only your third date,' Tabbie told her over the phone five minutes later.

'I know, it's just—'

'You've fallen for him, haven't you?'

'But ...' Stephanie sighed, a sudden surge of tears streaming from her eyes.

'How did you fall so hard for a guy in three dates?'

'Plus every morning at school. He's just … really nice. But I think it's over.'

'Did he say it was over?'

'No, but I'm sure it is.'

'You're thinking Monica was right, aren't you?'

'Mm. Maybe.' Stephanie looked out her window, in a vague hope that Jason might return.

'Try not to think about it. See what happens next week.'

It seemed like a throwaway phrase from her best friend. But Stephanie knew Tabbie meant well and tried to look forward to the week ahead. She spent most of the weekend in her room listening to music, staring at the ceiling. A tiny seed of hope held the tears away.

Monday morning she walked into school, hoping to see Jason. But he wasn't at the gate. *I wasn't expecting him anyway.* He wasn't waiting for her on Tuesday either, but Monica lingered nearby.

'So what happened, Stephie? You did it and now he's dumped you?' Monica's smile was smug. 'Hey, boys …' she called out to their classmates, pointing to Stephanie, '… if you like them easy.'

The boys whistled and laughed, their usual response.

Monica cackled.

'Come here, baby!' Wolf Whistle Boy called.

Stephanie couldn't face any more. She took off along the path, up the stairs and into the building. Walking so fast, she tripped on the top step and only just saved her footing before landing on her face. Everything had been going so well, and now it was going haywire. Thankful that Tabbie's parents had paid for her flight, Stephanie couldn't wait to spend the school holidays in Sydney.

On Friday, the sight of Jason standing at the gate took her breath away. But the thrill was swiftly crushed when she saw Monica hanging off his arm. Jason was laughing.

'Hey, Stephie!' Monica called. 'Want to walk us in?'

Stephanie breathed out purposefully to calm her face, hoping to hide the pain screwing around in her heart. She stormed into the school grounds without waiting for them. Jason caught up to her and fell in stride alongside her. Thrilled that he'd left Monica to walk with her, Stephanie looked up and smiled. Until she saw Monica hanging off his other arm, beaming a huge grin. Stephanie looked at Jason, wondering what was going on. His chest rose like he was pleased to have a girl on either side.

'So, Stephie, we're going to the movies this afternoon. Want to come with us?' Monica winked at her.

As if I'd go anywhere with you. She eyeballed Monica. 'No thanks. I'm having dinner with my family.'

'Maybe I'll see you over the weekend then?' Jason's deep brown eyes glistened as he nodded towards her, leaning away from Monica.

'Okay.' Stephanie smiled, aware of the way Monica pulled her arm away from Jason, pouting.

Jason turned at the top of the stairs and left Monica and Stephanie facing each other.

'He's over you.'

'We'll see.'

'He knows you're a cow.'

'Why?' Stephanie tightened her ponytail. *Why is she speaking to me like that?*

'Now that you've given him what he wanted, he's moving on. When are you gonna get it? He's not into you.'

Stephanie clenched her teeth and pressed her fingernails into the shoulder straps of her backpack to prevent slapping Monica. Stephanie turned and walked away, blinking. She refused to show Monica her swelling tears.

It took until the first break for her to calm down. The last thing she wanted was another run-in with Monica, so she found refuge in the library for the short break.

At lunch, the senior girls discussed their movie plans. 'Why don't you come with us?' Jess said.

'Mum and Dad have a family dinner planned. But thanks for asking.'

Are they all going together? Why hasn't Jason invited me?

She tried not to think about it. But that night, while eating dinner with the family, images of Monica nestling herself beside Jason and cuddling into him at the cinema invaded her mind.

Stephanie's mother chattered on about starting work part-time and the wonderful friends she'd made volunteering at April's school. Her father was still at work.

'Isn't it wonderful how the church is attached to the school? It's just like it was when I went to school,' her mother said.

Stephanie rolled her eyes.

'You know, I met a lovely lady called Meryl at April's school who has a daughter in your year and one who's a couple of years older.'

'Yeah, who?'

'Monica is the one your age. Have you met her?'

Stephanie nodded, her neck and shoulders tightening.

'Meryl is so friendly. I bet her daughters are just as lovely.'

Sour sickly bile crept up her throat. 'Urgh! Monica is far from lovely.'

Mum shrugged and moved away from the table.

Stephanie left her half-eaten dinner, grabbed the phone and trudged to her room. 'Tabbie, today was the worst. I think Monica was telling the truth.'

'So forget him.'

'But I don't want her to be right.'

'If she was right, then Jason isn't worth it,' Tabbie said.

Stephanie realised it was too hard trying to work out who was right and wrong. During the weekend she stared at the phone every time she walked past, willing it to ring. But it was silent. She looked out her window every time footsteps sounded on the concrete footpath, hoping they belonged to Jason. But he didn't turn up.

On Monday, Stephanie spoke to her mother before breakfast. 'I want to go to school early today. Do you mind?'

'We can leave now if April is ready.'

Just as she'd hoped, the school entrance was almost bare. She went straight to her homeroom, pulled out some books and worked on an assignment.

Monica followed the bell into the room and stood in front of Stephanie. 'I was waiting at the gate for you.' Monica leaned in a little closer. 'Did you hear? Jason and I had the best time at the movies.' She flicked her hair and pranced to the other side of the classroom, sat down and glared at Stephanie.

Stephanie wondered if she'd been dumped without being told. Could you even get dumped after three dates? Her confused cluelessness gave her no answers.

For the next two weeks, her lunchtime friends disappeared along with Jason. It seemed odd until she discovered the seniors had block exams. Another difference between Sydney and Toowoomba. She tried to focus on her schoolwork but struggled to understand most of the concepts.

The end of term arrived like a sigh of relief. Stephanie needed to leave it all behind. Leave the hole of a town, the lack of friends and Jason for a few weeks. With her bag packed, she flew to Sydney, looking forward to her holiday.

Chapter Nine

Tabbie's mum, Francine, picked Stephanie up from the airport and drove straight to a dance rehearsal.

'Come on, Steph,' Tabbie said on the drive home. 'You'll pick up the steps.'

'I don't dance anymore.'

'You *are* a dancer.'

Stephanie clenched her fist and lightly punched the seat. 'I was a dancer, past life.'

'And now you are back, living in your past life for the holidays. We need someone to fill in for Jaya. Just this once. Please.'

'You didn't tell me this was on.'

'Please?' Tabbie tilted her head like a lost puppy.

'You didn't tell me you had a performance coming up.'

'Please, please, pretty please with sparkles and pink sugar on top. Just for rehearsal. Jaya will be fine by next week.'

Stephanie moaned, squinting. 'Okay. Just this once.'

The girls Stephanie used to dance with rushed to greet her with arms open wide. Her body awakened when the music played. After

    Spiralling Out of Control

watching once, she knew Tabbie was right. The moves came with ease. She enjoyed every minute of the new routine.

Tabbie nudged her as they left rehearsals. 'You loved it, didn't you? Come on, admit it.'

'Yeah, it was fun.' Stephanie allowed the smile that had formed inside to illuminate her face.

'You *are* a dancer. You have to get back into it.'

'Maybe one day. Just not while I'm in Toowoomba.' 'So, are you moving back to Sydney?' Tabbie asked.

'I haven't asked yet.'

'Why not?'

'Not sure.' Stephanie bit her lip.

'Jason?' Tabbie's eyebrows rose.

'Mm, but I guess that won't matter if he goes to uni. I'll ask Mum and Dad when I get back.'

'You've had a whole term to ask.'

'I'll ask when I get back. Promise.'

Tabbie shrugged. 'I went to a youth group last week. I thought it could be fun to take you tonight.'

'Like, at a church? Can we catch a movie instead?' Visiting a church youth group was the last thing in the world Stephanie wanted to do.

'We can see a movie next week,' Tabbie said.

'But won't it be full of religious mumbo-jumbo?'

'No, it's heaps of fun. You'll love it.'

Stephanie chewed a fingernail. 'I really don't want to.'

'Please? I'll never ask you again if you don't like it.'

'You don't accept *no* for an answer, do you? Will it be on again next week? Can we go then?' Stephanie wanted a quiet night after the flight and excitement of dancing for the first time since she'd left Sydney. 'I'm tired and sore. I'd just prefer a night in tonight.'

'Sure,' Tabbie said in an unpleasant tone, then ran upstairs.

The two girls shopped all day Saturday and went out to dinner with friends. It was surreal, like Stephanie had stepped into her past life. She caught up with other friends through the week, keeping the conversation on all things Sydney to avoid telling anyone how miserable she was in Toowoomba. A warm tingle swirled through her. *This is my real home. I have to move back here.*

Later in the week Tabbie went for a run and Stephanie enjoyed a moment alone, knowing she'd have to endure a night out at Tabbie's church youth group later.

She bounced off the couch when Tabbie's older brother, Peter, popped in.

'Hey, Stephanie. Good to see you. Tabbie sure does miss you.' He flashed his crooked smile and flicked his fingers through his hair.

The secret crush reignited hearing his voice and seeing him in the flesh. 'Are you hanging round for dinner?'

'No. Just dropped in to grab a few things and say hi.'

'It'd be good to catch up. Are you sure you can't stay?' She did everything she could to stop her hand from reaching out to touch his arm. *What's going on with me?*

'I can stay for a few minutes.'

They stood just inside the door. He offered small talk while Stephanie wondered if she'd matured enough to compete with his girlfriend. She pushed the thought away. She couldn't go there.

'Pete!' Tabbie barged in and gave her brother a hug. 'Did I interrupt something?'

'No, of course not.' Stephanie pulled a sliver of hair between her fingers.

'Love to stay, but I have to get going.' Peter smiled, jingling his keys.

The girls both waved Peter off, then Tabbie bumped Stephanie's arm. 'Were you flirting with my brother?'

'No. As if.' She had to change the subject, and quick. 'Should we start getting ready for youth group?' Stephanie ran upstairs, hoping Tabbie hadn't seen the blush rise in her cheeks.

As she was applying her make-up, Tabbie pulled on a little black dress.

'Who are you trying to impress?' Would she be underdressed in jeans?

'Just want to look nice.' Tabbie pouted.

'You look fantastic in a pair of jeans. What's with the frock?'

Tabbie laughed. 'Do you want me to get changed?'

'No, just tell me why you're wearing a dress. Should I be more dressed up?' Stephanie smoothed out her T-shirt.

'One of the girls told me tonight will be different. They have a band coming in and I guess it'll be more like a concert.'

'A concert … at church? Why didn't you tell me that?'

'It's not like the churches you know.'

'Not like my school church?' Stephanie shuffled through her suitcase.

'No, it's modern.'

'Okay.' Stephanie closed the suitcase. 'It sounds strange to me. Jeans would be fine for a concert.'

'You're right, jeans would be fine. And if you're happy in jeans, go for it.'

'I didn't bring anything nicer than jeans.' Stephanie faced Tabbie, confused.

'Here. Try this.' Tabbie pulled a teal knee-length dress out of her wardrobe.

Stephanie eyed the dress. 'I love the colour. You know, I haven't bought a dress since I moved. I live in jeans in Toowoomba.'

'The colour is you.' Tabbie pulled the dress off the hanger. 'Try it on.'

Stephanie changed into the dress and stood in front of the full-length mirror. The scooped neckline almost plunged too low, while the fabric hugged her figure.

'Perfect!' Tabbie clapped.

'The length is a little odd. You don't think it's too tight?'

'You look stunning. It looks way better on you than it does on me. Why don't you keep it?' Tabbie reached into her wardrobe again and pulled out a loose beige cardigan. 'Here throw this over the top. It'll look great with your boots.'

Stephanie slipped the cardigan on. It fell just above the length of the dress. It would be fun to have a dress to wear. Jason might like it. *Jason, gah!* She shook her head, flinging him from her mind.

'I still can't believe you get so dressed up for youth group.'

From the entrance, there was nothing churchy about the place. Stephanie stayed close to Tabbie, not wanting to lose her in the crowd. As they walked down the side of a large building, flashing lights lit the way to an open-air stage. Thankful for the cardigan, Stephanie pulled it in a little tighter.

As she looked around, she didn't recognise anyone. Many unknown faces smiled warmly at her. Tabbie introduced her to Shelly, who seemed welcoming. There was a nice buzz in the atmosphere, but it didn't feel like church.

In fact, there was nothing church-like about the whole night, except the band sang, 'Jesus,' a few times in their songs. How could they call the whole set-up church?

The next day, Stephanie sat beside Tabbie's mum in the Eisteddfod audience, watching her friends perform their dance routine. It was fun, even a thrill to be on the other side, but it was nothing compared to the adrenalin rush she'd enjoyed while performing and competing.

Friday afternoon, Stephanie read the open page on Tabbie's computer. A party invitation. She sighed with relief. *Great.* An excuse not to go to youth group again. The people there were nice, but a party was more her style.

Tabbie reluctantly agreed to take her.

When Francine dropped them at the party, Stephanie looked wide-eyed at the number of empty bottles already lying around. 'When did everyone start drinking?'

'Probably when they got here.'

'I mean,' Stephanie rolled her eyes, 'no one drank before I left

   Spiralling Out of Control

town. Now it looks like everyone's getting drunk.'

'We're not. Guess they'll have a headache tomorrow and we won't.'

'Can we go now?' *Why's Tabbie so blasé?* 'Being here feels weird.'

Tabbie grabbed Steph's hand. 'Relax. They're just having a bit of fun.'

'Tabbie,' She pulled her hand away. 'They're being stupid.'

'Hey, you're the one who wanted to come.'

'But—'

'It's not like you to be so easily offended.'

What does Tabbie mean by that? Girls flirted with boys and spilled drinks while another group played spin the bottle.

'Everyone was drinking when I hung out with Jason's friends, but no one was being stupid like this.'

'Okay, okay. I'll call Mum.'

Stephanie dragged Tabbie to the kerb outside the house until Francine returned. Tabbie spoke in hostile bursts all the way home, then went straight to bed. Stephanie hoped her friend would get over it by the morning.

Tabbie's mum offered Stephanie a hot chocolate. She accepted then tiptoed into the bedroom ready to apologise. She sat on the mattress beside Tabbie's bed.

'Tabbie?' Stephanie sipped her hot chocolate.

Her friend breathed deep sleeping breaths.

'Tabbie?' Stephanie finished her hot chocolate and let the silent reply lull her to sleep.

'Sorry if I made you take an abrupt exit last night,' Stephanie said.

'Forget about it. You were right. They were being silly.'

Stephanie packed her bag. *Time's up.* The return flight was booked.

'I can't believe you're going home already,' Tabbie said.

'I know.'

'I still want you to move down here.'

'Me too.' Stephanie pulled at her fingernails.

'Make sure you talk to your parents, okay?'

'Okay.'

'What do you think will happen with Jason?'

'I think it's over.' A tear swelled in Stephanie's eye. 'He hasn't called. I haven't spoken to him for over three weeks.'

It was fun for a while—having a boyfriend, or at least the thought of having a boyfriend. He'd never said they were a couple. Stephanie told herself she could release Jason without too much pain if she knew the girls she'd met through him would continue to be her friends.

At the airport, she turned to wave goodbye one more time and saw a tear run down Tabbie's cheek. Then her own tears began to flow. On the flight home, she put her nose into the airline magazine to distract herself. When the plane touched down, Jason was all she could think about.

Chapter Ten

Stephanie plastered on a fake smile to greet her mother at the airport. She'd half expected her mother to do the usual drive-through-pick-up like she did for her father, but she'd obviously parked the car.

'Welcome home! You look good. I bet you had the best time.' Mum headed towards the baggage carousel.

'More than you could imagine, Mum. Where's April?' Stephanie looked around the crowded airport.

Mum stood back, leaving Stephanie to pull her own bag off the conveyor belt. 'She had a sleepover at a friend's house. We'll pick her up on the way home.'

'Good. I was starting to miss her.' *My pesky little sis.*

The clear roads through Brisbane seemed to put her mother in the mood for a chat. 'We went to church while you were in Sydney.'

'What?' Stephanie turned briskly, flicking her hair. 'The one at school?'

'Yes.'

She raised her eyebrows. 'Why?'

'We used to go—'

'Like, back when I was six?'

'Gosh, is it that long? I guess we just got out of the habit since your father got so busy at work and moving here, and—'

'But it's so boring.'

'Stephanie!' Her mother glanced at her with furrowed eyebrows. 'Look, we're going again next week. It's something we can do as a family.'

'Why? Because Dad's at work as much as he was when we lived in Sydney?'

'Now, don't go saying that. At least he doesn't have to stay away like he did then.'

'Do I have to go?' Stephanie put her headphones back on.

'Yes.'

Turning the volume up, she listened to music, reliving her holiday in her thoughts. Yes, Tabbie was still her best friend, but their friendship seemed a little strained during the holiday. Hopefully they'd fall back into sync again. But she couldn't see that happening until she moved back to Sydney. She'd talk to her parents soon. Just not today.

When Jason wasn't at the school gate on the first day of term three, Stephanie decided to change her routine and arrive early to miss the abusive gate dwellers. She ate lunch alone, wondering where Crystal, Jess and Lani had vanished to.

On Saturday, Stephanie found a quiet moment to talk to her mother. Something had to change. It was time to be direct. 'Mum, I've been thinking. I'd like to move back to Sydney. I think I belong there.'

'Really? I'm sure you're feeling like that because you haven't made any friends here to replace Tabbie.'

'I'm not about to replace Tabbie.'

'You know what I mean. You'll find another friend like her in time.'

'Not likely.' Stephanie shook her head. 'I sit with a group of girls at lunch, but it's not like in Sydney.'

'Maybe you'll find some more friends at church tonight.'

Unlikely. Stephanie shook her head again.

Her mother expected everyone to be ready by six for the Saturday night service. Stephanie pulled on an old pair of jeans. She wore a grudge that intensified when she arrived at the church and saw Monica. Stephanie's ears began to burn. She looked behind her. Monica sat a few rows back, staring at her.

Without thinking, Stephanie followed her family out to take communion just as she did in Sydney, years ago. Back then she went forward for a blessing, but this time she decided to take the bread and the wine along with everyone else. She returned to the pew and knelt down, watching through vague eyes as people walked past.

Monica sauntered up the aisle. 'Jason's been round to my house nearly every day,' she whispered into Stephanie's ear.

Go jump, you stupid cow. Stephanie closed her eyes and gritted her teeth. *That's it. It's over. I have to move on.* The night's darkness seeped through the church windows and fell on her shoulders like a heavy blanket.

After the service, her father started the car and chuckled to himself. 'That was great, wasn't it?'

'No, boring as.' Stephanie looked out the window to see Monica standing against the church wall. She wanted to tell her where to go, but didn't have the guts.

April pulled her seatbelt on. 'It was boring, but Lucy and Samara were there so that was fun.'

'That's great, April,' her father said. 'Steph, you do realise you shouldn't have taken communion, don't you?'

'Um …' She tried to remember why not.

'You haven't been through the first communion … what do they call that process?' Her mother shook her head. 'Perhaps we should look into it. I'll make a note so I don't forget. Was that a friend who stopped to say hello after communion?'

'No!'

'Why would she stop then?' Her father flicked a questioning look to the backseat.

'Was that Meryl's daughter?' Mum tapped on her phone, her favourite way of keeping notes.

'Yes.'

'We could have waited for you to stay back and talk to her.'

'No way.'

'Why not?'

'Don't worry about it.' *I already told you she wasn't my friend.*

The next morning, Stephanie's sleep-in was interrupted by a knock on her bedroom door.

'Steph, Jason is here,' Diane called.

'What?' Stephanie thought she must be dreaming.

'Jason's at the door. Should I tell him to go away?'

'Ah, no.' Stephanie blinked a couple of times. Her stomach flipped. 'I'll be down in five.'

She'd spoken before thinking. *I should just tell him to go away. He hasn't rung or spoken to me for weeks.* She threw on a pair of jeans and a thick jumper, raked her fingers through her hair and brushed her teeth before strolling downstairs.

'Hi!' His beaming smile melted her. 'How was Sydney?'

'Great.' Now he was there in her doorway, she wanted to do anything but send him away.

Stephanie walked past him, through the front door, accidentally brushing against his arm. She tingled all over as she moved to the front steps and sat.

'How's Monica?' The words slipped out. She hadn't planned to blurt it like that. She wanted to pull the words back, but it was too late. Her gaze lowered, to avoid his.

'I don't know. Why are you asking me?' He sat beside her and scratched the side of his head, messing up his already unruly hair. 'Why don't you call her?'

'She said you'd been at her house every day.' The words escaped and she clenched her jaw. *Shush*.

'Yeah, I'm working on a group assignment for biology with Crystal, Jess and Matt.'

'Why there?'

'Are you jealous?' Jason smiled and nudged her shoulder with his.

'I hardly saw you before I went away. I didn't see you at all last week. The last time I saw you, Monica hung from your arm. You haven't called.' Stephanie stood and walked away from the house, hoping her mother wasn't listening.

'Do you want me to leave?' Jason headed towards the path.

'If you want.' Stephanie tried to sound like she didn't care.

He turned to face her. 'There's nothing going on with Monica or Jess or Crystal. I just got caught up with end of semester exams and assignments and everything.' His hand gently rested on her shoulder.

'Oh.'

Jason slid his arm around her neck to draw her closer. 'Where were you last week? I waited at the gate every day except Monday.'

'I went in early.' She took a deep breath. 'Do you want to go for a walk?'

Jason looked at her for a moment. 'You really were jealous…' his voice trailed off. 'Did you really think there was someone else?'

'Monica—'

'As if.' He scrunched his nose, snuffing a laugh.

'But she said—'

'I'm guessing she spun a story. She does that—so does Crystal. Lying is practically normal in their family.'

Stephanie shook her head, looking towards the street.

'She's just a silly young high school girl.'

'Yeah? We're the same age.' She glanced at him as a car passed by.

'But you're different. You're mature and beautiful. I like you, Steph. Really.'

Stephanie smiled, knowing her cheeks were glowing.

'Let's go get a milkshake or something.' Jason took her hand.

'Okay.' Stephanie laughed. A nervous shudder echoed through her voice. 'Guess I was kind of dumb.'

'Yeah, kind of. You need your own phone. Then it would be easier.'

Stephanie shook her head. 'Tell me about it.'

They enjoyed lunch together at the Mary Street Café, and sat chatting until dark clouds rolled in and the frosty air made Stephanie shiver.

Jason held her hand, drawing her out of the chair and smiled into her eyes. 'I hope you can drop the jealous girlfriend act. I've got a pretty heavy workload until the end of the year.'

'Is that what I am?' she asked. 'Your girlfriend?'

Jason nodded and led her out of the café, onto the footpath. 'But don't go getting all serious. I've got uni next year.'

'Where are you going?'

'I'm hoping to get accepted into Melbourne. But I'm applying for Sydney and Brisbane as well.'

'What do you want to do?'

'Engineering.'

'Why not go to uni here?'

'USQ? Because I want to get out of this hole.'

'So do I.' She thought of Tabbie's invitation to live in Sydney.

'Where do you want to go?' he asked.

Wherever you go. 'Back home. I love Sydney. I hope to move back. It gets colder here than Sydney. I didn't expect that.' She walked close to feel his warmth.

'Mum and Dad are planning a white Christmas. They want my brother, Brett, and me to join them.' His hand opened and closed, playing with her fingers as they walked.

'Where? How long will you be gone?' She relaxed, enjoying the sensation of his fingers on hers.

'They want to go to London in October. I'd get back just in time to start uni. But they've just started talking about it. It's still a fair way off being organised.'

'Sounds like fun.'

'I'd rather go to schoolies.'

'They want you to go before you finish?'

'Mum reckons she could push someone to let me do some exams and assignments earlier.'

'Can you do that?'

'No.' Jason laughed. 'Mum just thinks she can have her own way with everything.'

'So what'll you do?'

'I'd rather finish school first, then meet them there.'

'You'd fly there by yourself?' She looked up as he combed his fingers through his dark hair.

'With Brett. He doesn't want to go that early either.'

'Will you and your brother be okay without your parents around?'

'Yeah, of course.' He shook his head. 'It's not the first time we've been home alone.'

Stupid! Of course he's done it before.

'They aren't home much even when they're here. We're used to it. Plus, I'll have you if I need company.' He smiled raising his eyebrows, but then looked forward again. 'Not that I'll have much time.'

In the covering of an old bottle tree, just metres from home, Jason pulled her close and kissed her full on the mouth. The heat of his passion infiltrated the kiss. It was nothing like the kiss on the grassy bank. Blood shot through her veins like electric currents, sending flashes to her eyes. *Is this what the movies mean by seeing fireworks?*

Jason brushed a strand of hair out of Steph's eyes while they stood embracing until a car shone its lights on them. Stephanie pulled away, embarrassed. She caught her breath and rushed to her front door.

'Hello, kids. Dinner is ready. Jason, would you like to stay?' Stephanie's mother asked. 'Or does your mum have dinner waiting for you?'

'No, she's out tonight. That'd be great, if you've got enough.'

Warmth like molten lava oozed around inside Stephanie. She watched and listened as Jason talked to her parents over dinner. In between sentences, his eyes landed on her and lit up. She enjoyed the glow of admiration he showed her.

After dinner her father stood up. 'Jason, it's getting late. I'll drive you home.'

'No problem, Mr Stronge. I'm used to going for night jogs. Won't take me long.'

'Well, keep safe.' Dad left the table.

Jason stood tall, puffing out his chest. 'No worries.'

Stephanie couldn't keep her eyes off his muscles—even relaxed they looked flexed beneath his clothes. She drooled over him a moment too long, then stumbled as she followed him out to the gate. He wrapped his hand around the back of her neck and kissed her again. She accepted the kiss like a drink of water after running a marathon. Breathless.

Stephanie rang Tabbie as soon as Jason left. She told her about the starry fireworks in her eyes and lava running through her blood.

'You're falling in love,' Tabbie said. 'Careful or you might break your rule.'

'Remind me about the rule.'

'Are you saying you want to?'

'I just felt this crazy urge to wrap myself around him and oh …' She closed her eyes and let her mind wander.

'Yep, you'll break it!'

'But I don't want to. You need to remind me why I made that rule.' Stephanie moved the phone to her other ear.

'Because you wanted to wait 'til you were married. Because it's been our pact since we were twelve. We both said we'd wait.'

'Do you think I should wait?'

'I think it's what God wants us to do.'

'How do you really know that?' Stephanie looked up to the ceiling.

'I just know.'

'So you don't think I should.' She chewed on the inside of her mouth.

'You have to make that decision yourself.'

Chapter Eleven

THE FOLLOWING WEEK, EVERYTHING cruised along seamlessly for Stephanie. Monica continued her spiteful ways, but Stephanie didn't flinch. She knew things were good between her and Jason. *Better than good.* Jason had even invited her to an official family meal.

'You can see Jason tomorrow,' her mum said on Saturday afternoon.

'But he told his mum I'm coming for dinner tonight.'

'Well, you shouldn't have told him you were going without asking me first. We're going to church tonight and you're coming with us.'

'Mum, I'm fifteen.' Stephanie clenched a fist, pushing it into her thigh.

'I know.' Mum raised her eyebrows, passing Stephanie the phone. 'You are fifteen and not yet an adult. You'd better let him know you can't make it this time.'

Stephanie trudged into church behind her family. She allowed the priest's words to fill the silence.

'For out of the heart proceeds evil thoughts. Adultery, fornications, thefts, and blasphemy. Yes, we are all sinners…'

Stephanie shut off and lived in her mind, dreaming about Jason until the final hymn.

'Stephanie,' her mother called, soon after they'd arrived home. 'There's a message here from Jason.'

'What'd he say?'

'I'll replay it for you.'

Stephanie ran downstairs and listened. 'Hi, it's Jason here. Steph, you can come over tomorrow. I don't have anything on in the morning.'

Her heart beat a little faster as she walked back to her bedroom. What would a priest know about real life anyway? *We're all sinners. Can't change it.* Her mind wandered, drifting to the possibilities of breaking her rule. *Lust!* She could almost hear the priest's voice as she fell asleep.

Stephanie woke at eight, rushed to the kitchen to find something to eat and set off to Jason's house. It was the first time she'd walked there. Only two blocks away, like he'd said. Her feet took control, speed-walking.

She arrived at his door, her heart swaying between guilt and the anticipation of her dreams being played out sometime in the near future. After she knocked three times, Jason opened the door in boxer shorts.

'Oh, sorry,' she said. 'I woke you, didn't I?'

'Yeah, but that's okay.'

'Where's your Mum and Dad?' she asked.

'They left early. Gone to Melbourne for a couple of days.'

'How often do they go away?' Stephanie looked past him, into the house.

'It's irregular.'

'Is your brother home?'

He leaned against the doorway to let her in. 'No. Brett stayed out last night.'

She stopped for a moment. *Should we be in here alone?* But she squashed the concern under her feet as she walked inside.

Jason led her past the lounge and upstairs. Her heartbeat synchronised with her footsteps.

'You use that equipment?' She nodded towards a room set up like a gym.

'Yep. Let me give you a tour of our upper level.' He spoke in a formal tone. 'Opposite our home gym is where my older and only brother sleeps, when he isn't out partying all night. Then walk this way and you'll see the ever-tidy parents' retreat. That brings us to my ...' He walked inside the dark messy room, picked up some clothes and threw a couple of pairs of shoes into the wardrobe. 'Sorry.'

Stephanie swayed. *Should I sit or stand?* Jason kicked the door closed then moved towards her until his breath tickled her cheek. He wrapped his arms around her and kissed her passionately. They connected like north and south magnetic poles. He sat on the bed and pulled her down to his lap. With their lips touching in soft kisses, he lifted her shirt.

'You must be hungry.' She pulled away.

'Only for you.'

'Ah… breakfast?' She slipped off his lap and shuffled along the bed, away from him.

'No, thanks.' He leaned in to kiss her again.

'Jason.' She groaned.

'Too much? Too early in the morning?'

'Maybe we should go downstairs.'

'We *should*, but we *could* stay up here.' He wrapped his arms around her and pulled her towards him.

'Jason. Stop!'

'Okay, breakfast time it is, then.'

Before he left the room, he turned to flash his heart-melting smile. *Wow, that was full-on.* Stephanie didn't know if she'd be able to stop him if he did that again. She didn't know if she wanted to stop him. Falling back on the bed, she stared at the ceiling fan before following him.

She sat with Jason on the couch as he ate breakfast, still in his boxer shorts. His eyes were fixed straight ahead, watching a music channel. She stole glances, noticing how his facial muscles moved as he chewed his food. When he finished, he caught her watching him.

He smiled and leaned towards her, playfully pecking light kisses on each cheek, then down her neck. Goosebumps popped up on her arms. She shivered, enjoying the moment. They canoodled until Brett arrived home.

'Sorry, don't mind me,' Brett said. 'Just walking through.'

'I'd better get going.' Stephanie touched her warm cheek.

'Yeah, I have assignments to do. Don't know if I'll see you much again this week. Can you come over the same time next week?'

'I have to wait a whole week to see you?' She edged towards the door.

He smiled. 'Absence makes the heart grow fonder.'

Her father towered over her. 'If you don't pick up your grades, we'll have to get you a tutor.'

'It's too hard. It's all different here.'

'It can't be that different. You need to put in more effort.'

'Why can't I just leave school and get a job?' Stephanie chewed on a fingernail.

'To start with, you're too young. And anyway, you need to go to university. You'll have more choices in life if you get a degree.'

Whatever. Stephanie shrugged, hoping the argument was over.

But her father hadn't moved. 'Just try harder, okay?'

'Okay, okay.'

After lying in bed all afternoon with period cramps, Stephanie escaped the torture of going to the Saturday night service. The thought of spending the following morning with Jason kept her awake until after midnight. She awoke in a daze when her alarm sounded at eight. Drinking a cup of coffee, she set off on her morning walk.

This time she only knocked once. Jason's mother opened the door. 'Hello, Stephanie.'

'Morning, Mrs Hobbs.'

'I think Jason is still asleep. Come in and sit down. You can turn the TV on.'

Jason's mum stood at the base of the stairs and yelled for him to come down.

Stephanie found the remote control and flicked the TV on. It was on the same channel as last week.

After a couple of songs, Mrs Hobbs returned with her handbag slung over her shoulder. 'He hasn't surfaced?'

Stephanie smiled, fidgeting as she looked up the stairway. 'No, not yet.'

'Go up and wake him.'

'Are you sure?'

'Fine by me,' she said. 'I have to go out. Behave, okay?'

Stephanie nodded, annoyed at the heat seeping into cheeks. Jason's bedroom door was closed. She tapped quietly with her fingernails. He didn't answer. She opened the door slightly to see him in a peaceful sleep. She thought of waiting downstairs until he woke up, but sighed and walked in anyway. He stirred when she sat beside him.

'Hey, beautiful. How long have you been there?' Jason blinked.

'Just came in.' She smiled, pulling at her fingernails, not sure what to do with her hands.

'Well, now that you're here, come closer.' He held the doona up for her to slide under.

Her heart pounded at the sight of his bare torso. She hesitated.

'Just a cuddle.'

Stephanie snuggled into Jason. His body jerked as if he'd drifted off to sleep again with his arms linked around her. His morning breath wasn't so great, but the warm cuddles were divine. She relaxed and dozed.

After who knows how long, she was woken by Jason nuzzling

Spiralling Out of Control

into her neck, smothering her with kisses. 'Are you sure you don't want to—'

'I've got my period.'

'Does that mean if you didn't have it, you would?'

'Not yet.' But when, she didn't know.

'You're breaking my heart.' He clutched his chest, gasping for air.

'You're hilarious.' Stephanie laughed as she got up and headed to the door. 'And could you put some more clothes on before you come down this time?'

'Scared you won't be able to resist?' he called after her.

'Are you going to the school dance this week?' Stephanie asked over breakfast.

'They're pretty lame.'

She combed her fingers through her hair. 'Do many people go to them?'

'Mainly younger kids.'

'I'm a younger kid, so let's go.' She shrugged, then smiled.

'You're serious, aren't you?'

'You can take one night off study, can't you?' She cupped his cheek in her palm.

'You really want to go?'

Stephanie smiled, nodding.

'Okay, anything for my beautiful girlfriend. But I don't want to hang round if it's as bad as I remember.' He clasped his hands behind his head and stretched. 'Gee, I haven't been to a school dance since year eight.'

Stephanie laughed. 'It'll be fun. I've already asked Mum to drive us.'

Stephanie looked around the school hall. Jason was right, it was full of younger kids. He squeezed her hand as they walked in, sending tingles through her body. She followed him as he led her to the side of the room and sat.

'Don't tell me you're too cool to dance.'

'You go. I'll watch.'

'I'm not going out there by myself.' She grabbed his hand and danced him towards the crowded floor.

'Wow, you really like to dance, hey?'

'It's fun.'

'You sure can move,' he said. 'Why don't you join a dance class or something?'

Stephanie shook her head and danced around him. Jason glued his gaze to her, barely moving. A slow song played and he grabbed her around the waist, rocking her in time with the music.

'You're so hot,' he whispered into her ear. 'Can we leave now and go back to my place?'

'No.' Stephanie giggled as his breath tickled her ear.

'We could get a taxi and be back here by the time your mum comes to pick us up.' His eyes burned into her soul.

'You're crazy.' She had a feeling if she'd gave him any kind of positive response, he'd be leading her out the door.

'*You're* driving *me* crazy!' His arms dropped from her sides. 'I need to cool off. Let's go outside for a while.' He turned and stormed off.

Stephanie followed him but stopped under the bright lights on the hall stairs. *Is this about the dare?*

'Come over here for a bit.' Jason continued towards the darkness.

In that moment, Stephanie didn't trust the shadows. 'No. Come back and sit here, on the stairs.'

'Argh! I'm going for a walk!'

Is he going to come back? Why has he taken off like that? Her breathing was heavy, yet shallow. The hall entrance was busy with kids walking in and out and teachers watching, supervising. She sat on the top step for more than fifteen minutes before Jason appeared from the shadows.

'Where did you go?' Stephanie stood.

'For a walk, okay!'

'You seem angry. What's…?' Her question stuck in her tight throat.

Jason stood in front of her, close enough for her to wrap her arms around him, but she held back.

'You dance around me like that and then you push me away. I'm getting mixed messages.'

'I told you from the beginning where I stood with *that*.' Stephanie reached towards him, but he stepped backwards.

'You say no, but you sure act like you want it.'

'I'm sorry.' The lump in her throat nearly choked her.

'Yeah, me too. Maybe we should cool it for a bit.'

'What do you mean?' her voice wavered.

Jason turned away.

'Jason!' she called.

But he was already running and didn't look back. Stephanie couldn't breathe the tears away.

'Hey, look who's crying! Stephie and Jason have a fight, did they?' Monica walked out from the shadows. 'Yeah, Jason and I just had a little chat. I told him to dump you. Glad he listened to me.'

Did I hear him wrong? Did he say to cool it or…?

Sitting under the streetlights, she clenched her teeth and pushed her tongue to the roof of her mouth in an attempt to stop more tears. Her mother arrived an hour later and she climbed into the car with blurry, wet eyes.

'Where's Jason?'

'He left earlier.' She wanted her voice to stay calm, but failed.

'Maybe it's for the best.'

How could she say that? She didn't even know what happened.

Chapter Twelve

No. Stephanie was sure she'd heard right. He'd said he wanted to cool it for a bit, not forever. Monica was lying. She had to be lying. Jason had said she was a liar. Stephanie cried into her pillow, hoping it would silence her sobs.

She rang Jason in the morning, but he'd gone for a run. She tried his mobile but he didn't answer. She tried again at lunch, but he was sleeping. Almost out of her mind, she rang before church but he'd gone to a party. If she'd just said yes to him things would be fine! Her mind spun in a fury of worry.

Stephanie crossed her arms and tolerated the priest's monotone voice. The hard, wooden pew held her body as the weight of guilty thoughts pushed down heavily. Sweat clung to her armpits. Sex cluttered her mind. *Stop even thinking about it!*

On Sunday, she woke up late. She rang Jason and again there was no answer. She had to see him. 'I'll be back later, Mum.'

'You're not going to Jason's, are you?'

'Yes.'

'Look, if it's over, it's best to leave it.'

   Spiralling Out of Control

'He didn't actually say it was over.'

'No?' Her mother rested her hands on her hips. 'What did he say?'

'He thought we should cool it for a bit.'

'He was just being polite. In teenage-boy talk, that means it's all over.'

'I need to go for a walk anyway.' Maybe she wouldn't even see him. No one had answered the phone. He mightn't be home.

'Make sure you're back by two. April would be disappointed if you missed her gym competition.'

'Yeah, I'll be back by then.' She left the house before she had time to think about it.

She stood outside Jason's house. *Should I knock or continue walking?* Now she was there, she didn't even know if she wanted to see him. She decided to walk on, following the path. She wove her way through the bottle trees, only to return in fifteen minutes and stare at his front door. This time, she wanted to see him more than anything else. *Be brave*, she told herself, taking a deep breath before knocking.

Brett opened the door with bed hair and keys in his hand. 'Think Jason had a big one last night, but go and wake him anyway. I've gotta go out. Make yourself at home. No one else is here.'

'Thanks.' She glanced around the quiet house as she walked upstairs. The slam of a door made her jump. Turning around, she realised it was just Brett leaving. The house was silent as she moved along the hallway. All the bedroom doors were open. All except Jason's.

Stephanie paused for a moment outside his room then knocked. He didn't answer. She clasped her hands, then wiped away the dampness on her jeans. When she didn't hear any movement, she knocked again, louder.

'What do you want?' he yelled.

'Jason, it's me.' Her voice squeaked in a strained toned she barely recognised. 'Can I come in?'

'Why are you here?'

Because I want to see you. She opened the door. 'Can we talk?'

'I thought we talked the other night.'

She wedged the door open a little more with her foot. 'Did you have a big night last night?'

'Do you have a problem with that?'

'No. Brett mentioned it as I walked in.'

He pulled the doona to cover his head.

'Can I get you something?'

'The Berocca is on the kitchen bench.'

Stephanie took her time in the kitchen. What was she doing there? He didn't even want to see her. She pulled her fingers through her hair, scratching her scalp. *Oh! I'll just give him this and leave.*

She returned to his bedside and inhaled stale alcohol. 'Here.'

'Thanks. I was at a mate's house, with the boys. Don't remember what time I got home.'

Stephanie looked towards the door, but something held her in the room.

'Why are you here?' Jason rested on one elbow after drinking the Berocca.

'It's just… did you talk to Monica the other night?'

'At the school dance?'

Stephanie nodded, annoyed with herself for asking.

'She grabbed me when I went for that walk. She's so annoying.'

'She's such a—!' She cut herself off.

'Whoa. You sound angry.' Amusement resounded in his voice.

'Well… oh!' Stephanie balled her fist and punched her leg. 'Can we just go back to how we were last week?'

'Maybe you shouldn't dance like that near me again. It was way too much to handle.'

'So can we try again?' She needed to leave her dancing behind. If Jason couldn't handle it, she'd forget it forever.

Jason sat up, looking deep into her eyes. She leaned forward, entranced by his gaze. His mood had lifted. The sudden lightness made her smile, and she forgot her anger and his grumpiness of a moment ago. He smothered her with kisses, from her cheeks to her neck, warming her heart. His mouth hovered over her chin then connected to her lips with hunger. She responded to every move he made. The temptation was too much to bear. She stopped thinking and let her body give way to her desire. Any self-control she'd found had left the house with Jason's brother.

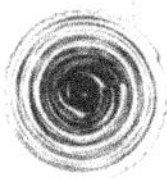

Stephanie lay there, dozing in and out of sleep until guilt consumed her. She rolled off Jason's bed with uneasy awkwardness. The expected euphoria had been overridden by a shameful need to get away without waking him.

But he stirred. 'Hey.'

'Promised Mum I'd be home by now.' Stephanie pulled her clothes on. 'I'll see you later.' She closed the door, leaving without looking at him and ran from his house.

The warmth Jason's kisses had given her earlier was now gone. A shiver pimpled her skin as she chewed the inside of her mouth. She was even more confused than when she'd arrived at his house. Running most of the way home drained the last of her energy. Memories of running with Tabbie in Sydney came rushing back. That was a lifetime ago. She dragged her feet for the last stretch.

She slipped into the shower as soon as she arrived home before she saw anyone. A dirty, sticky, revolting feeling trembled within, baffling her. She needed to wash herself clean. Her hands shook as she shut off the water. *What have I done?* Changed forever. She was scared everyone would find out. *Tabbie will be so disappointed in me.*

'Hi, Steph. Why were you so quick to jump into the shower?' her mother asked as they passed in the hallway.

'Oh, I did a workout at Jason's. He's got a whole room set up like a gym.' Stephanie added some truth to her lie.

'Back on, is it?'

Stephanie nodded.

Her mother shook her head. 'Are you ready to go? It starts in half an hour.'

She'd forgotten why she had to be home by two until her mother mentioned something was about to start. April's big competition.

In the car, Stephanie tried to keep the conversation alive to wipe the morning's images from her mind. 'Will April get into the state team?'

'You know that's what she's hoping for. But that's another year off. This year she's hoping to qualify for State Championships. We should pray for her.'

Stephanie watched her mother close her eyes briefly at the traffic lights. She followed her mother's lead. *Yeah, God, ah, sorry about this morning. I know you're angry with me, but please don't take it out on April. Help her get to State. Amen.*

The morning's incident lay hidden in the back of her mind, while she watched her little sister. She welcomed the distraction. 'Mum, when did April get so skinny?'

'She's training a lot harder now she's level four.'

'Isn't Dad coming? I thought he'd meet us here.'

'He's doing his best to get here.'

'But he's caught at work, isn't he?'

'Yes.' Her mother frowned.

Stephanie ran to congratulate April after they announced the place-getters. 'You blitzed it!'

'Thanks.' April hugged her. 'Would've loved to have come first.'

'Fifth overall is great. The competition was really strong.'

April looked around at the other gymnasts. 'Or maybe I'm just not that good. Don't know if I scored high enough to compete at States.'

'When will you find out?' Stephanie asked.

April shrugged. 'They'll probably tell us at training.'

'Let's get Maccas to celebrate today's comp.' Stephanie swung her sister's gym bag over her shoulder.

April shook her head. 'Can we get something else?'

'Since when have you said no to McDonalds?'

'Have to eat the right foods if I want to make the Olympics.'

'Aiming high! Go for it, little sis.'

      Spiralling Out of Control

Stephanie's over-enthusiastic approach was a bandaid to the rapidly growing pit forming inside her.

Monday morning, Stephanie woke up filled with angst, longing to see Jason. But she doubted she'd run into him during the week. She arrived at the school gates chewing on the side of her mouth.

Monica told everyone we were doing it ages ago. Everyone already thinks we are. Nothing's changed. Except she felt older, but more insecure. Grown up, yet wanting to scream like a child to gain Jason's attention. It shocked her that one isolated incident could cause so many conflicting thoughts. It was no big deal. Heaps of girls her age were doing it.

So why do I feel so crappy? The yearning left an empty hole inside of her. The only thing that could fill it was Jason. Each day, she hoped to run into him. She walked different paths without luck. By Thursday, she was thankful to find Jess and Lani in the courtyard.

Jess greeted her with a huge smile. 'How's things?'

'Okay. Haven't seen you guys for a while.'

'We've been working on assignments in the library,' Lani said. 'Riveting stuff. Would much rather be out here.'

'How's things with Jason going?' Jess pulled out her wrapped lunch.

Stephanie was about to say okay.

But Crystal screwed up her nose. 'I'd be surprised if he hasn't found someone else by the holidays. Monica said—'

'Stop it.' Jess shook her head. 'He's one of the nice guys.'

Crystal laughed. 'I reckon you're silently hanging out for him to come after you.'

'I love him like a brother. You know that.' Jess bit into her sandwich.

The jovial banter continued while Stephanie's chest tightened. Do they know?

'So tell us, are you seeing much of him?' Jess asked.

Stephanie found her calm voice. 'We're keeping it pretty cool. He's full on with school too.'

'Had a chance to talk to his parents?' Lani raised an eyebrow.

'Not really. I haven't met his father, and his mum doesn't seem to talk much.'

Lani laughed.

'Stop.' Jess gently nudged Lani. 'Take no notice of her. They're just busy with their business.'

April burst into Stephanie's bedroom. 'I didn't make it.'

'That's too bad.' Stephanie flicked through a magazine on her bed.

'You don't get it! I missed out on going to States.'

'Well, try again next time.'

'You could at least act like you cared!' April slammed the door as she left the room.

'Chill, wouldya?' She had enough on her mind without adding April's problems.

The next day, Stephanie searched every corner of the school for Jason. *What if he hates being with me? Why haven't I heard from him?* Being constantly on edge was affecting her to the point where she jumped at any unusual noise. She couldn't fight against the urge to speak with Jason, and rang when she got home.

His mobile went straight to voicemail. She hung up and rang his home number. 'Hi, is that Brett?'

'Yeah.'

'Is Jason there?'

'No.'

'Can you let him know I called?'

'Who's calling?' Brett asked.

I'm so dumb. Why didn't I just say my name? 'Stephanie. Thanks.' Her hands shook as she slammed the phone back down. Her mind danced in a muddle. She knew she should wait for him to call but was overcome with a craving for his arms to envelop her again.

Chapter Thirteen

'STEPHANIE!' HER MOTHER CALLED. 'Tabbie's on the phone.'

'Tell her I'll call back. I'm in the middle of an assignment.'

Within minutes, her mother appeared at her door. 'Tabbie's rung a few times this week. She sounded annoyed. You'd better call back this time.'

Stephanie flicked through her school books, her mind wandering everywhere except over the information contained on the pages. She closed them and took a shower. Her silent crying trembled as the water washed her tears into the drain. She wiped her fingertips across the foggy mirror and barely recognised the guilty dejected face. It was time to speak to Tabbie. She needed to get this over and done with, even if she was about to disappoint her best friend.

'Hi Tabbie,' Stephanie's voice was soft.

'Hey, I've been trying to ring you all week.'

'Yeah, had a lot on.' *On my mind, that is.*

'You're quiet tonight,' Tabbie said.

'How are you? How's Sydney?' Stephanie tried to brighten her voice.

'Great, that's why I've been ringing you. I've got the lead in the end-of-year concert. You'd be doing it if you were here, of course, but I'm so excited. And you know that dress, the one I've been wanting all year? Mum bought it for me …'

Tabbie didn't stop talking, but Stephanie's mind was elsewhere. She tried to form the right words in her head. *How do I tell someone I've broken a promise, that I feel dirty and empty and that things can get complicated so quickly?*

'… and I'm guessing you've stopped listening because there wasn't a pink rat or an orange poodle performing in last night's rehearsals.' Tabbie laughed.

'Sorry, Tabbie. I'm the worst friend.'

'Forget it. I'm guessing you're quiet because you're trying to work out how to tell me something. And I'm guessing that it's not about those nasty kids, because you would have just blurted that out.'

Stephanie took a breath but couldn't find the right word to start.

'Ahh, you did it?' Tabbie sounded disappointed.

'Are you annoyed with me?' Tears dripped from Stephanie's eyes.

'Why would I be annoyed?' Tabbie's voice wavered.

'Disappointed?'

'No. Are you okay?'

'Yes, oh … who am I trying to kid?'

'When? how?'

'Last Sunday.'

'Was it good or bad?'

'No, oh, I don't want to talk about it.'

'Okay. Is Jason okay?'

'I don't know. I haven't spoken to him. I just rang him, and his brother said he wasn't there.'

'Do you think he's avoiding you?'

'I don't know what to think. After something like that happening wouldn't he want to see me, or talk about it? I know guys are different but how could we do that then … nothing?'

'Did you talk about it? I mean like, plan it?'

'No, it just happened. We started kissing. His parents were out.'

'Steph, what about protection? You could be pregnant.'

'No, he used something. He must have been planning for something to happen.'

'Most guys plan for something to happen. It's good if he used protection, though,' Tabbie whispered.

'No, it's not.' Stephanie's stomach squirmed. 'I want to take it back. I feel different. Empty, hollow, shallow, dirty, cheap, easy.'

'Different I get, but don't take on those other labels,' Tabbie said. 'Don't be too hard on yourself.'

'What am I going to do?' Stephanie heard a knock on her bedroom door.

Her mother's voice came through the crack. 'Hey, Steph, I need the phone.'

'Gotta go, Tabbie, Mum wants the phone.' Stephanie opened her door and handed Mum the phone without making eye contact.

How long was she at my door for? What if she heard? Urgh!

'Everything okay?' Mum asked during dinner.

'Yeah, fine.' Stephanie wasn't convincing.

'Everything okay with Tabbie?'

'I said everything was fine!' Stephanie scraped the chair across the floor as she stood, and ran upstairs.

She expected to be followed and be given another lecture, but no footsteps came. She closed the door, turned her music on, then buried her head in her pillow. Ten minutes had passed, no one was coming to rescue her. She was alone. *Lonely.* The desperation to see Jason gripped her. She tiptoed out into the hallway and grabbed the phone. 'Hi, is Jason there?'

'Yeah, I'll put him on,' Brett said.

'You didn't return my call.' Stephanie attempted to keep her voice calm despite the tears rolling down her cheeks.

'I didn't know you rang.'

'I left a message with your brother.'

'Why didn't you call my mobile? Brett never tells me who's rung.' A muffled scratch sounded through the phone, 'Brett, the phone message?'

He's annoyed… that's good. I think… oh, I don't know what to think.

'I tried your phone, but it went through to voicemail.'

'Sorry, I didn't check my missed calls. Maybe leave a message next time. Hey, can we meet up again this Sunday?' The warmth in his voice sounded like he was smiling.

'Maybe at the café or movies?' She wanted to avoid his house.

'Mum and Dad will be out again. I thought we could—'

'What? Is that all you want?'

'No—'

'We need to talk.' Stephanie looked out her window.

'Yeah, sure.'

'You haven't told anyone, have you?' She swallowed, hoping he couldn't hear the gulp through the phone.

'No, but what's the big deal? Everyone thought we were already.'

'But we weren't.'

'You sound upset.'

Her head pounded. *Why did I let it happen? The first boy who takes any notice of me and I give away my most intimate moment, the one thing I made a pact to keep for marriage.*

She could hear the priest's voice ringing in her ears. "Those appalling teens who think that they can run around doing as they please? God will not be happy with them. Those relationships are only meant for the marital bed."

'You haven't called all week. I don't know what's going on.' Stephanie couldn't contain the rasp in her voice, nor could she control the flood pouring from her eyes.

'Hang on, I told you I'd be caught up with school stuff. I thought you understood.' His voice was a little deeper than usual.

'But after last weekend, I thought maybe we … maybe you would want to … that maybe, we needed to talk.' She couldn't find words that made sense. 'I just don't know!'

'I don't either. I thought we were cool. It was natural, you know, what happened on Sunday. What exactly do we need to talk about?'

'I don't want to talk now,' Stephanie whispered. 'Someone might be at my door.'

'I've got a lot on tomorrow but I guess I can meet you at the park on Sunday. Around ten?'

'Okay, see you then.' She hung up, sobbing. He didn't get it, didn't think it was a big deal. *Am I stupid for thinking it is? What's wrong with me?*

Stephanie slept through a jumble of frightful nightmares. In her dreams, Jason dumped her because she was making it a big deal. Then the boys at the gate yelled at her asking when she was going to give them some. She dreamed Jason and Monica were together. She dreamed about Tabbie's wedding, where she stood in the church as Tabbie's bridesmaid, feeling deplorable and unworthy, knowing Tabbie had stayed pure. She dreamed of the church roof lifting up and dark shadows coming to take her away. She woke up exhausted.

Chapter Fourteen

APRIL BOUNCED IN FROM TRAINING like a chattering bubble. 'I made it! I'm going.'

'Didn't you tell me you missed out?' Stephanie looked up from her biology textbook.

'Jenna fractured her ankle and the coach said I can go.'

'Great for you but wasn't it a score thing?'

'Yeah, not sure. Maybe they changed the minimum score. But Jenna is gutted.'

'Bet she is.'

Their mother poked her head through the doorway. 'I've put us down to do the offertory tonight.'

'What does that involve?' Stephanie wrinkled her nose.

'You know, take the gifts—the bread and wine—to the altar and hand them over to the priest one at a time. We've been going for a couple of weeks now. Are you taking any notice of what goes on?'

'Do we have to?' Stephanie rolled her eyes.

'Why wouldn't you want to do it?' Mum looked puzzled.

'I just don't want to.' Stephanie pushed out her chin.

'Stephanie. We'll all do it together.'

'Okay.' She groaned.

Having to walk down the aisle plagued her thoughts all day. It was one thing knowing she'd done the wrong thing, but taking part in the service? Did that make her one of those religious hypocrites?

Inside the church, nightmarish flashes stung her eyes every time she blinked. Stephanie stood between the pews and shoved her trembling hands into her pockets to dry off the sweat. She wondered if God would strike her down with a bolt of lightning.

On schedule, the family walked to the back of the church in single file to complete their task. Her father lit the candles and passed the girls one each. The organ droned with the choir singing a harmonic hymn. As they proceeded towards the priest, Stephanie's gaze fell upon Monica, sitting on the end of the row. She focused straight ahead, avoiding eye contact as she walked past.

'Girls like you shouldn't do that,' Monica hissed as she walked past.

Heat as hot as fire rose up her neck. Her face burned. If she fell over she would blend right into the royal red carpet on the floor. After handing the candle to the priest, she ran through the side door and down a flight of stairs. She leaned against the outside wall of the building, breathing deeply. Before her heart had stopped racing, her mother stalked towards her as the final song began, shaking her head. She grabbed Stephanie by the elbow and marched her to the car. John and April followed closely behind.

'How could you do that to us? Our first time and all,' Diane hissed. 'I was so embarrassed. I couldn't get away fast enough.'

'I didn't want to do it in the first place.' Stephanie slammed the car door. 'Don't make me do it again!'

'There's no need to take that tone.' Her father steered the car in the direction of home as they drove in tense silence.

'Why wouldn't you want to do a simple task at the church?' Mum walked from the car into the house. 'You know God wants us to do good work, don't you?'

'Yes, I know.' A pang of shame ripped through her. 'If we have to do something at church, can we find something else?' *I'd rather do nothing. I'd rather not even go!*

Her mother shook her head and dragged her father into the kitchen, closing the door. Angry, muffled whispers seeped through to her. Stephanie went to her bedroom and turned her music up loud. The heavy beat shuddered through her body. It blocked her emptiness, but as soon as the music stopped, she longed for something to fill the hollow again.

Stephanie slept with unexpected peace that night and awoke at ten with a fright. She grabbed her clothes, pulling them on in a rush, and left without checking herself in the mirror or telling anyone where she was going.

'I didn't think you were coming.' Jason stood up from the park bench and wrapped his arms around her.

'I slept in.'

'You feeling any better today?' he asked.

'Better than what?'

'You seemed upset Friday night.'

She tugged a wispy stray hair into place. 'Yeah, I'm fine.'

'What do you want to talk about?'

'You know.'

'Yeah, but I don't really get why we need to talk.' He shook his head.

'I said I had a rule.'

'Aren't rules meant to be broken?'

'Is that what you think?' she asked.

'You mean you really didn't want to break that one?'

'No… yes… no… oh, I thought I did in the moment but…' her voice trailed off.

Jason's face was blank. Maybe it really wasn't a big deal to him.

'I still don't get it. Is it because you're fifteen?'

'It's not meant to happen 'til—'

He smirked. 'Don't tell me you were planning to wait until marriage?'

'Well… yes.'

'That's a bit old-fashioned, don't you think?' He stroked her hair.

'It's what God wants. It's our belief.'

'Yeah, I'm religious too. Doesn't mean I believe that crap.'

'You think it's crap?'

'Most of it.' He nodded. 'The whole going-to-church thing. I stopped years ago.'

She looked up, squinting with the sun behind his head. 'But you go to the school services.'

'Only because it's part of school.'

She paused for a moment, wondering if what he was saying was right. Maybe she had it all wrong. 'Is it okay if we just keep our relationship like this for a while?'

'Like this, as in?'

'Like this.' She smoothed down her clothes.

'Oh, as in with our clothes on?'

'Yes.' She forced a laugh.

'That's what you want?'

'Yes.'

'Really?'

Her gaze darted around the park to trees, grass and a dog and his owner. 'Are you going to dump me over this?'

'No. But maybe you'll feel different in a couple of weeks.'

'Maybe I'm not the right girl for you.'

'I didn't say that. I just think we'll be missing out on a lot of fun, but if that's the way you want it, I can wait a bit. But not 'til marriage… hang on, I don't even want to talk about that. Just don't make me wait too long. I'll go crazy.' He grabbed her into a warm hug.

Stephanie sighed with relief.

For the rest of the day, it was like they'd stepped back in time. She was able to block the bedroom incident from her mind. They walked and talked and laughed in the warm sun until it burned, then they found the shade of a tree. Jason was wonderful and normal again, and she enjoyed his company. Overshadowed with happiness, she relaxed.

Mid-afternoon, Jason walked her to her door where they pashed goodbye.

'You've been gone a while. Are you and Jason getting on well?' Her mother stood in front of the sink.

'Yes.'

'Careful you don't get too close. You're only fifteen.'

'I know, Mum.'

Why did I get myself all worked up? Maybe it wasn't a big deal. She couldn't quite work out the empty feeling that sat heavy inside after she'd said goodbye to Jason. Later on, she rang Tabbie. 'Everything's okay. Jason's okay with not doing it again.'

'That's great, Steph.'

'Are you still annoyed and disappointed with me?'

'No, I told you I wasn't. I just thought you wanted to wait.'

'I guess God is angry with me, hey?' Stephanie lowered her voice.

'Are you sorry?'

'Yeah.'

'He's a forgiving God.' Tabbie cleared her throat. 'Steph, you know that youth group I took you to?'

'Yeah.' Pretty hard to forget.

'I've started going to that church on Sunday.'

'Why?'

'Because I really like it there.'

'I thought it was a bit weird. Does your family go?'

'No.'

'Mum reckons it's a church for those who don't have a religion.' Tabbie didn't speak.

'I'm starting to think church and God are ancient and outdated anyway.' Stephanie flicked lint off her jumper.

The line was silent until Tabbie spoke. 'Can I pray for you?'

'Whatever.' Stephanie couldn't shake the hollow pit growing inside her. 'See ya.'

She expected to feel warm and at ease after sorting things out with Jason, but her insides surged with discontent. She couldn't put her finger on what was wrong.

Chapter Fifteen

The following Saturday, Jason rang to invite her to a family dinner. 'Mum and Dad are heading to China on Monday. It's something they like to do before they leave. It's the only time we eat together.'

'Then shouldn't it just be your family?'

'Mum asked me to invite you.'

On Saturday night, Stephanie held her stomach and groaned until her parents said she could miss church. *Wonder how I can get out of going next week. Oh please!* She never wanted to go to church again.

By Sunday night, nerves knotted her insides, almost as severe as the illness she'd invented the previous night. Stephanie changed her clothes five times wanting to make a good impression. Would jeans and a T-shirt be okay?

'No more cramps?' her mother asked.

'Nope.'

Her mother nodded, agreeing to drive the short distance to the Hobbs home. Stephanie stood at the front door and knocked.

A female voice boomed through the door. 'Would you stop watching that idiot box and help out for a minute!'

Jason opened the door. 'Did you hear that?'

Stephanie nodded.

'Sorry.' He hung his head.

'Have you been a naughty boy?' Stephanie smirked and winked at him.

'Always.' He gave her a cheeky grin then led her into the house. 'Dad, this is Stephanie.'

'Pleased to meet you, Mr Hobbs.'

Jason's father glanced up from the TV. 'Yes, hello.'

The formal dining room walls were darkened with outdated wallpaper, and the room was lit with four small lightbulbs on curly brackets. One wall housed hundreds of books, and another wall proudly displayed family photos. Stephanie drooled over every photo of Jason. He was drop-dead gorgeous.

Mrs Hobbs served an oven-baked meat pie, too perfect to have been homemade and a simple salad. The room would have been warm and inviting if it wasn't for the icy Antarctic atmosphere that swirled as they took their seats.

'So, are you going away on a business trip?' Stephanie asked.

'Mm, yes.' Mr Hobbs shoved another forkful of pie into his mouth.

'Do you enjoy working together?'

Mr and Mrs Hobbs glanced at each other, grinned and nodded.

Jason and Brett didn't utter a word. *Why did they make a big deal about having a formal dinner and not even talk to each other?* Mrs Hobbs stood when they'd finished eating and began to clear the table.

Stephanie pushed her chair out. 'Can I help with the dishes?'

'No, stay there. I'll bring dessert out.' Mrs Hobbs spoke without any facial expression. She opened a boxed chocolate ripple cheesecake on the table. Stephanie enjoyed the delicious dessert so much she forgot about the company until the deafening silence drew her back.

Mrs Hobbs stood as soon as she'd finished.

Stephanie offered to help.

     Spiralling Out of Control

'No, Jack and Brett can do it tonight.' Mrs Hobbs pushed her chair in. 'Right, that was lovely. I have to go and check a few emails before bed. Goodnight.'

Jason's father and Brett cleared the table like programmed robots and took the dishes to the kitchen.

'Do you want to watch a movie?' Jason led Stephanie to the TV room.

'Will that be okay with your family?' She couldn't shake the awkward feeling.

'They'll get over it if it's not.' Jason pulled out *Terminator II* and pushed it into the player.

'Do you have anything newer?'

'Than *Terminator?* Probably. Have a look.' He pointed to the cabinet beside the TV.

'It's fine. I'm happy to watch that.'

Stephanie's mind wandered during the movie, aware of his muscle-rippled body beside her. Instead of seeing the TV, she visualised Jason in front of her, shirtless. She blinked to shut down the thoughts and tried to focus on the movie. Jason mumbled the movie lines. She cleared her throat, hoping he'd stop, but he continued.

'Do you have to do that?'

'What?' Jason's eyes stayed focused on the movie.

'Can you stop saying their lines before them?'

'Oh, didn't realise I was.'

'It's irritating.' She forced a smile to soften her words.

Jason turned the TV off. 'That better?'

'You didn't have to stop watching it.'

'I've seen it a hundred times. You weren't really into it, were you?'

'No.' Stephanie realised she was now looking at the blank TV screen.

'It's getting late anyway. I'll walk you home.'

'Where are your parents? I didn't thank them for dinner or wish them a good trip.'

'They wouldn't have even noticed. They're upstairs. I'll pass it on.'

Jason held her hand as he walked her home. She glanced up into his relaxed brown eyes before they said goodbye, and was sure everything was okay. He didn't follow her inside when she opened her front door. 'I'd better get back home. Might see you tomorrow at the gate?'

'Are you back to regular mornings?' She smiled.

'For a while, yes.'

'Okay, see you then.' She closed the door.

'Tabbie rang a while ago,' her father said as she turned around. 'She said to call back any time.'

'Okay.' Stephanie took the phone to her room. 'Hi, Tabbie.'

'You sound happy.'

'Yeah, just had dinner with Jason's family.'

'What are they like?'

'They're a little strange.' Stephanie laughed. 'They don't talk to each other. We ate dinner in complete and utter silence. He made this big deal about having a special family dinner before his parents go away on business, but they just sat there, eating in silence.'

'How did you cope with that?'

'Silently.'

They both erupted with laughter.

'If dinner was strange, why are you so happy?'

'Because Jason's parents leave tomorrow.'

'Careful.'

'Why?' Stephanie grinned wider.

'Home alone, is he?'

'With his brother.' Stephanie pulled a pair of socks onto her cold feet.

'Temptation might get the better of you.'

'No way! He knows where I stand.'

When she returned the phone to the hallway charger, she mulled over their conversation. Tabbie was right. She just wouldn't go to his house while his parents were away.

Three weeks passed, with Jason meeting her at the gate most days. She ate lunch in the courtyard with Jess, Crystal and Lani a couple of times each week. Though she managed to avoid visiting

          Spiralling Out of Control

Jason's house, emptiness ripped at her insides whenever she was away from him. His parents returned from China in September, the week before spring holidays began.

'So what did your parents do while they were away?' Stephanie asked on the walk into school.

'Business.'

'What business are they in?'

'Several. It's confusing. I'd rather not try to explain.'

'Oh.' She looked at the ground.

'I'm heading away with some of the boys.'

'Where? When?' Stephanie looked at him out of the corner of one eye.

'Next week. I'll miss schoolies because I'll be in the UK with Mum and Dad, so it'll be good to hang out with my mates for a week now.'

'What about your assignments?'

'I'll take some with me.'

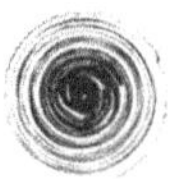

Stephanie attempted to fill the lonely-no-contact-with-Jason-void by calling Tabbie.

'What if he does what a lot of boys do when they go away in groups?' Tabbie asked.

'What? Get drunk? I'm sure he will.'

'Doesn't that bother you? You didn't like it when we went to that party where everyone was drinking.'

'It doesn't bother me because he's not stupid.'

'Have you seen him drunk?'

'No.' She half shook her head.

'Then, how do you know?'

Stephanie held her breath.

'What if they all pick up girls?' Tabbie asked.

'He won't.'

'Did you talk about it?'

'No, didn't think of it. As if he would.' Stephanie clenched a fist.

'You know guys do dumb things when they're drunk?'

'He's sensible with alcohol.' But the fact she'd never seen him drunk hung in the air.

Tabbie was silent.

'Don't you believe me?'

'Sure. It's just that I've read articles about groups of boys going away for holidays. I've seen —'

'I'm sure they make it sound worse than it is.'

Stephanie made an excuse to get off the phone, but couldn't shake the conversation. *What if he's getting drunk and... oh no.*

Her mood spiralled downward. While she slept, she saw Jason with other girls in her dreams. When she woke, the images sat at the front of her mind. She couldn't get it out of her head. *How could he? How could he cheat on me? After we...* Her thoughts swirled in a frenzy until — she wanted to scream.

The next day, Stephanie's heavy heart kept her tucked up under her doona. Just before midday, her mother walked in and sat on the bed beside her. 'Everything okay?'

'Yeah.' A tear rolled onto her pillow.

'Is it that time of month?'

'Yeah.' It was easier to agree than tell the truth.

'Are you missing Jason?' her mother asked.

'Yeah.' This time Stephanie couldn't control herself and sobbed uncontrollably until she snorted.

'He'll be back on the weekend, won't he?'

Stephanie nodded.

'Are you okay to talk?'

Do I look okay? Stephanie wiped her nose with her wrist. It was easier to just nod and listen.

'I guess you and Jason are getting pretty serious.' Mum smoothed the doona.

Stephanie couldn't get any words out from under the snot.

'You know, you might start getting feelings. Like you want to take it further.'

You don't say.

'It's just… well, it's important that you don't. You don't want to fall pregnant before you get married.'

What? The be-careful-don't-get-pregnant talk? Oh, please!

Her mother leaned over to look into her eyes. 'If he pressures you or anything, make sure you let us know.'

Stephanie nodded. *Sure thing, Mum. We already did it! I'm weak. I couldn't say no. Like you'd understand.*

Her mother walked away, the corners of her mouth turned up in a smile.

Stephanie pulled the pillow over her head to muffle a groan.

She doesn't get how hard it is. If Jason were there, Stephanie knew she'd run into his arms and say, 'Yes. Whatever—wherever!' Anything. Anything to stop worrying about him with someone else. Anything to fill the hole inside. She wished he was back in Toowoomba.

The week dragged on slower than the last hour of school on a Friday before summer holidays. Every day, Stephanie hoped the phone would ring. But there was nothing. No phone calls. No email. No postcard. Nothing. Shadowed by misery, his return seemed too far away. Assignment due dates lurked, but when she opened the books, she could only think of Jason. Every other minute she checked the street through her window, hoping he'd come back early and want to see her straight away.

Conflicting thoughts plagued her mind, every minute of her day lacked lustre. Then she began to dread the chemistry she knew would be present when he returned.

Chapter Sixteen

WHEN SATURDAY CAME, STEPHANIE was in a state of panic. Her fear of acting like the jealous girlfriend again pushed her to regain control, to keep calm and not scare Jason off.

After losing another 'must attend' argument with her parents, she trudged into the church. The wooden pew pressed hard against her as she ignored everything going on around her. *God, can you forgive me?* She crossed her arms tight. *If I promise I won't give in to temptation? But those lustful thoughts—I can't keep Jason out of my mind. I'm sorry.* It sounded right in her mind, but would God have heard her thoughts?

When she returned home to find a message on the answering machine, her heart swelled. 'Hi Steph, heading out to a party. Sorry I missed you, babe. You could've come. I'll drop by tomorrow.' She chewed on the side of her mouth. He'd never called her 'babe' before. *Interesting.*

She slept lightly, waking every time she rolled over, eager for tomorrow to start. It was two in the afternoon by the time Jason arrived. Stephanie's insides had knotted up again.

'Hey, babe, ready to go?' He waited at the door.

As Stephanie walked away from the house beside him, the scent of stale alcohol leached from his skin. 'You smell.'

'Yeah, what of?'

'Alcohol.' She twitched her nose.

'So?' he said. 'I went to a party last night.'

Stephanie bit down on her tongue.

'What have you been up to?'

'Not much.' His firm grip on her hand gave her a sense of security.

'Let's go to my place.' He smiled and arched his eyebrow.

'Okay.' The emptiness inside her wanted to be filled again.

His dark eyes melted her insides, and she knew the pull of chemistry had won before she stepped through his bedroom door.

Stephanie pulled her clothes back on while still in Jason's bed, trying not to get tangled under the covers. 'Let's go for a walk.'

Neither spoke again until they were out of the house. Then Stephanie broke the silence. 'So what was your week like?'

'Lots of drinking.'

'I didn't think you drank much.' She didn't want to sound bothered, but her voice let her down.

'I hope you're not about to lecture me.'

Stephanie glanced at him. His jaw clenched, eyes open slightly.

'But—'

'I needed some time out. Don't think I could handle the rest of the year if I didn't take a break.'

'So that's all you did? Drink?' She chewed on the side of her mouth.

'Is that so bad?' He smiled. 'I guess we swam a bit. Yeah… and ate.'

'Were there any girls?' Stephanie knew jealousy resonated through her words.

'Ooh yeah, there were girls!' He laughed. 'But not for me.' He turned and kissed her. 'I have you.'

Stephanie laughed and nearly tripped on the flat ground. His attitude caught her off-guard. Something was different. He wasn't the same. *Is he still drunk?* She couldn't quite work out what the change was.

'I have you, and I love you,' Jason sang.

Stephanie heard the words but didn't want to acknowledge them. *Not yet.* She looked straight ahead, trying to think of something other than repeating those three little words back to him. *What do I say? What do I say?* Her palms tickled with sweat.

'I need sleep.' Jason yawned. 'I got nothing done on my assignments while away. I'll be flat out all week working on them. Okay if I meet you for lunch at school next Monday?'

'Sure.' Her shoulders sank. She had to wait a whole week. She turned and walked towards home. Jason caught up to her and draped his arm around her shoulders. At her fence they kissed goodbye.

'Gotta get some sleep.' He yawned. 'So, so tired.' He turned and left.

It caught her off-guard again. *Not clean. Dirty.* The emptiness sat even deeper this time, like a hollow cave inside. Sure, they'd made plans to see each other in a week, but what if something came up? She hated how he put schoolwork before her.

Tabbie rang the next day after school. 'This term looks crazy. I've got so much to fit in before the end of the year. How are you going?'

'Been really distracted, falling behind. I wish the school system was the same in both states.'

'Distracted? Jason, I bet.'

'Yeah.'

'Did you talk to him about… you know?'

'Yeah, he said he doesn't need other girls. Tabbie, he told me he loves me.'

'Wow. Guess he's really into you then. Have you got round to talking to your parents about coming down here next year?'

Huh? That was a subtle change of subject. Not. 'I brought it up, but Mum shrugged me off, telling me I'd find friends here.' Stephanie

     Spiralling Out of Control

sighed. 'Mum suggested you come up for the week before Christmas. Can you?'

'We're going to our house on the Central Coast that week. Steph, are you going to ask them, or should I tell Mum and Dad it's not going to happen?'

'Guess I've been waiting to find out which university Jason gets into.'

'You're starting to sound obsessed. You need something else in your life other than Jason.'

'Why?'

'Because you can't base everything around him. You need to live your own life.'

'But he said he loves me.'

'Oh, I get it. Now that he's said *that*, he comes first.'

'Tabbie, don't be like that. You're my best friend.'

'Just not your boyfriend. It's okay, I get it.' The disappointment in Tabbie's voice stung.

'I miss you and Sydney more than you can imagine. I'm just … really confused at the moment.'

'I know. Let me know soon okay?'

'Okay.'

It wasn't like Tabbie to act like a jealous friend. Had Stephanie really offended her? She'd have a talk to her parents soon.

Jason was sitting at the courtyard table when Stephanie came out of class for lunch on Monday. 'Hey, babe, glad you could join me.'

'What's with calling me "babe" all of a sudden?'

'I don't know. You're my babe, I guess.' Jason's manner was overly relaxed and cool. *Again.*

'You seem different.' She skewed an eyebrow.

'I'm chilling. I'm on the home run.'

'Do you know which uni you'll go to next year?'

'No. The universities don't send offers 'til…' He stopped and thought for a moment. 'Not sure if it's the end of December or beginning of January.'

'You don't know?' Stephanie laughed.

'It's slipped my mind,' he snapped at her.

'Okay, okay. I was just wondering.' She blinked and looked away. Something was different.

'Sorry. I'm just tired. I ended up going over to Jess's last night to work on an assignment with some others. It was late by the time we finished.'

When they met again for lunch the next day, he'd returned to his normal self. 'Mum and Dad rang last night.'

'I didn't know they were gone again.'

'They left on Saturday.'

'Where are they now?' Stephanie unwrapped her sandwich.

'Europe.' Jason bit into a cold sausage roll. Stephanie cringed at the thought of meat scraps rolled in pastry.

'And?'

'They're organising for Brett and me to meet them in London. They're not coming back for Christmas.'

'Are you really going?' A tear swelled, blurring her vision.

'They've booked the flight, so I guess I have to.' He rested his head on his arms.

Stephanie focused on a tree, willing the tears away.

'I asked if you could come with me.' His words were muffled by the table.

'You did?' She smiled.

'But you don't have a passport, do you?' He didn't wait for an answer. 'Mum said she didn't have time to wait and find out, and booked the tickets for Brett and me.'

'Oh.' Stephanie paused, listening to the hum of students. 'When do you leave?'

He lifted his head. 'Four weeks from Thursday.'

'For how long?' She swallowed.

  Spiralling Out of Control

'We get back the week uni starts.'

'Oh.' Tears fell through her lashes.

Jason lifted his hand and smoothed the wet streams away. 'Why are you so upset? I told you weeks ago that this was the plan for the holidays.'

'I know. It's just that… How am I going to cope with you away?'

'Guess we just make the most of the time we have.'

Jason stood, pulling Stephanie to her feet and into his arms. 'We could taxi it back to my house now. No one will notice we're gone.'

'Okay.' Stephanie blinked away the tears and followed where he led.

She couldn't say no. She wanted him to fill the emptiness that reverberated within. But twenty minutes later, she was filled only to her shallows.

Jason called her a taxi so she could make it back in time for her last class. A dark cloud of judgment shadowed her all the way.

Too soon, Jason was in study mode again. She had never struggled to complete assignments on time in Sydney. But in Toowoomba, everything she attempted fell in a useless mess of words on paper. Any formula in mathematics or historical date fled from her memory. She refused to talk to her family and locked herself in her room, letting her music drain her, deep in her soul, until she felt a release.

Jason stood at the lockers after lunch break. 'Brett and I are catching a bus to the airport early on Thursday.'

'That's in two sleeps.' Invisible shards pierced Stephanie's heart.

He cupped her face in his palms. 'Mum's asked me to do some stuff in Brisbane before the flight. Will you meet me at home after school, tomorrow?'

Stephanie looked into his heart-melting eyes. She had no words, only a bobbing head, nodding. The second bell rang and Jason peeled off down the hall.

The next day Stephanie asked her mum to drop her off at Jason's.

'You shouldn't go to his home while his parents are away.'

'Mum!' Heat exploded into Stephanie's cheeks. 'Brett's there.'

'It's dangerous for a young girl to spend time alone with her boyfriend.'

'It's not like it's the first time I've been there without his parents.'

Her mother gasped. 'You haven't told me this before. What else should I know?'

'That I'm not going to see him until he gets back and, even then, I may never see him again.'

'It's just a teenage romance. You're being far too dramatic.'

'But he might go to uni in Melbourne or somewhere.'

'No high school relationship lasts forever.' Her mother's words cut like an axe.

Stephanie did everything she could to hold back from begging. 'Can you just take me so I can at least say goodbye?'

'How about if I come with you? That way I can say goodbye, too.'

'Mum!'

'It's just not the right thing to do. You're not going to his house.' Her mother shook her head. 'Ask him to come here. He can stay for dinner.'

'He's got too much to do. They leave early tomorrow.'

'Well, you can ring him and say goodbye.'

Stephanie clenched her jaw, knowing she had lost the argument. She fumed until the car stopped, stomped upstairs, grabbed the phone, and took it to her room. 'Mum won't let me come over.'

'Please, babe, I really want to see you before we leave.'

'What if you come over here?'

'Yeah sure, and come straight to your bedroom and…'

'Can't we just *say* goodbye?' she whispered.

'Okay, if that's the way it has to be. Goodbye. Love you, babe. Hopefully we'll run into each other again someday. It was fun while it lasted.'

Stephanie drew in a short breath. 'It's over? Is that what you're saying?'

'We knew it wouldn't last forever. I'll probably be off to Melbourne next year.'

'I'm coming over anyway.'

Stephanie turned the music up in her bedroom, leaving her door closed. She pulled open her window and scanned the side of the house. *Clear.* She held the window frame and stretched, reaching for the downpipe. She hugged the pipe and eased herself down until her foot found a ledge. From there, she jumped, stumbling as she landed. She quickly glanced over her shoulder to see if anyone was watching. No one in sight. *Good.* She ran, hoping she would return before her family knew she was gone.

Jason's front door was closed. She knocked, then quickly glanced over her shoulder in case anyone was watching.

'Glad you could make it, babe.'

'Please tell me we'll see each other when you come back.'

'Sure we will. Wasn't thinking when I said that before.'

'I can't stay. Mum doesn't know I'm here.'

'Sneaky.' He smiled, leading her upstairs. 'Can you stay for a bit?'

A shudder ran down her spine as she followed him to his bedroom without resisting.

Upon her return, Stephanie's mother stood in the doorway, holding a broom like a wicked witch.

April stood behind their mother. 'Big trouble. Huge trouble,' she mouthed.

'I just went to say goodbye, okay?' Stephanie's face contorted, streaked with tears.

'No, it's not okay. I told you not to go over there.'

'Shut up!' Stephanie pushed past her mother, giving April a shove before running upstairs to fall apart in solitude.

Chapter Seventeen

STEPHANIE MOURNED JASON'S DEPARTURE for days before ringing Tabbie.

'I'm a mess.'

'Did you break up?'

'Why would we?'

'Did he ask you to pine after him while he's away? Did he tell you he'd be faithful?' The edge in Tabbie's voice came through loud and clear.

'No. Why?'

'Aren't you scared that it won't last over the holidays?'

'No. He said we'd be okay and we'd pick up where we left off when he comes back. He's hoping to get into a Sydney university. So, if I move to Sydney—'

'Didn't he say Sydney, or Melbourne or Brisbane? Anyway, you know how big Sydney is. You really think a uni student would want to date a high school girl?' The comment was mean, but Stephanie knew Tabbie was just worried about her.

The next day, Stephanie walked through the school grounds with her eyes fixed on the path. Unable to cope with the workload, she knew she'd come close to failing every subject and was now waiting to be told she'd probably have to repeat the year. The tension had been thick at home, but at least they were talking again. That would probably only last until her parents received her report card.

On the final school day for the year, Monica shoved Stephanie against a wall. 'Give me a break.' Stephanie wriggled to free herself.

Two girls from Monica's posse stepped in, grabbing Stephanie's arms, and another handed Monica two eggs. In one smooth swipe, she cracked them on Stephanie's freshly washed hair.

Stephanie stood frozen. Stunned.

'I went round to Jason's the night before he left.' Monica smirked. 'I'm so glad he dumped you. He's mine when he gets back! Got it?'

'But we... he... I...'

Monica stalked away, laughing.

Stephanie, immobilised against the wall, watched as the group around her stared and laughed. Then someone she'd never seen before splashed a drink into her face. Ice-cold red slurpee. Snapping into action, she ran out of the building and down the street, in the direction of home. It was only minutes until the final bell would ring anyway.

'What's happened? Jump in.'

Stephanie looked up to see her mother edging along the kerb with the car window down. She climbed into the front seat.

'Oh Mum, she's horrible. I know you like her mother, but Monica's just horrible!'

'You're all wet. Is that egg? Did she put that on you? What's that red—'

'Slurpee—the stupid cow.'

'I'll talk to her mother about this. It's unacceptable, and at a school like this.'

'That'll just make her worse. She hates me.' Stephanie was beyond tears. Anger seethed through her veins.

Her mother merged back onto the road. 'She can't go on doing that sort of thing—it needs to be addressed.'

'Mum, what if I move to Sydney?' *Oh, bad timing!* But once she'd started, she couldn't stop. 'I could live with Tabbie. Her parents are okay with me moving in and I could go back to Hill Top—'

'Hold on, hold on.' Her mother cut her off. 'You mean you've discussed this with Tabbie's parents?'

'Well, no.'

'Stephanie?'

'Well, it's just … Tabbie asked them.'

'If Tabbie has asked her parents, why haven't you spoken to us about it? Why did you wait until you got egged?'

'I've tried to talk to you,' Stephanie squeezed the words through her narrowed throat. 'I guess I didn't want to leave Jason.'

'But now he's gone.'

'Well?' Stephanie hoped her mother would give in to her pleas while she saw her dripping with red crushed ice and egg.

'Well, what?' Mum glanced at her. 'We moved here to be together, all of us. I don't think your father would be happy to hear you're even thinking of leaving. We don't have the money to be flying you off to Sydney. Just leave it.'

'But Mu-um.'

'Leave it.'

'But—'

'Stop.'

Stephanie clenched her teeth and sat quietly, watching the grey sky thicken. She was cold, miserable, and sure the whole situation was hopeless.

Her mum turned into their driveway and switched the engine off. 'I know we said to wait until you were sixteen, but why don't you see if you can find a part-time job? One of the fast food places might be hiring.'

'Okay.' Maybe it would be a good way to take her mind off Jason.

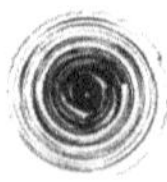

 Spiralling Out of Control

Stephanie visited every business in the surrounding streets, asking if any jobs positions were available. Some asked her to apply online and others suggested she drop in a resumé, but no one seemed interested in hiring. She was about to head home when she saw an ad in the window of the corner store beside the café on Mary Street. They employed her on the spot. She couldn't wait to start, dreaming of all she could spend her money on. Maybe she'd be able to save enough to visit Tabbie. Even buy a mobile phone.

The following night Stephanie sat in church, letting her eyes linger on the stained-glass windows. She looked to Jesus on the cross and stared into his eyes, wondering what purpose his statue had in anyone's life.

Jason's departure escalated her lonely emptiness to a depth too dark to comprehend. No one in Toowoomba understood her turmoil. Maybe moving back to Sydney would be the answer. And maybe, just maybe she could save enough money to fly down.

Jason wouldn't be living in Toowoomba next year. She hadn't heard from him and knew she wouldn't. He was slack at keeping in touch. Too slack to be bothered with postcards or a phone call. She'd discovered that when he went away with his mates. Yet the Jason-sized hole inside her remained.

Stephanie received her first pay like it was a ticket to freedom. 'Mum, I could pay my own way to Sydney after Christmas.'

'It'll be more than $300 return, it's peak fares.'

'I forgot about that. But I was thinking a one-way ticket. Is a bus cheaper?'

'Not a lot. Look, I'll talk to your Dad, maybe we can come up with something. But I'd rather not hear any more talk about moving away, not at the moment.'

Stephanie smiled. 'Okay.' *Not at the moment.* Maybe she'd ask again in a couple of weeks.

Being away from boys ogling her and not having to see Monica every day lifted Stephanie's spirits. She even began to enjoy not having to say yes or no to Jason's bedroom invitations. But it was bittersweet. Jason had filled a void. During the school year, he'd been a friend when no one else had. He'd introduced her to the older girls who were kind to her. But having him fill that void also brought feelings of regret.

When Stephanie's mum told her to get ready for church, she was determined to win the battle to avoid a torturous hour on the pew.

'Mum, it's bad enough that I had to put up with Monica being an absolute cow at school, but why should I have to put up with her during the holidays at church?' Stephanie hated begging.

'I guess you're old enough now to decide for yourself if you want to go or not. But you should really still go. Don't become one of those people who only turn up at Christmas and Easter and live sinful lives throughout the year.'

She nodded and walked away, considering what her mother had just said. *Haven't we been those people for the past few years?* She pushed the thought away. Now was not the time to get honest with her parents. If she could stay away from that steepled building, the guilt of how she'd given in to temptation might leave her.

Stephanie enjoyed the general chatter with customers and found the monotonous task of restacking shelves therapeutic.

'Mum, can I leave school now and just work?'

'You mightn't feel that way after a couple of months.' Her mother laughed.

The following Monday, Stephanie walked towards work and found Jess and Lani sitting at one of the tables in the café beside the corner store. Stephanie waved hello tentatively, wondering if she should stop.

'Hi, Steph! What are you up to?'

'I work next door.'

'Have you heard from Jason?' Lani asked.

'No. He's really bad at communication when he's away.'

'Have you got time to sit down for a bit before you start?' Jess asked.

Stephanie shook her head. 'Unfortunately not. But thanks for asking. Maybe another time?'

'Sure. A few of us are meeting here at nine every Monday morning. Just something to do during the holidays. Come earlier next week and join us,' Jess said.

'Okay.' Stephanie rushed inside the corner store, glowing.

Joining the girls next Monday gave her something to look forward to.

Over the week, Stephanie's boss increased her hours. She added up the amount she'd earn by Christmas, a little more hopeful of change in the coming year. The following Monday, Stephanie had more bounce in her step as she headed to work early to meet her friends. She found Crystal sitting by herself.

'Hi, Crystal. Are you waiting for Jess and Lani?' Stephanie asked.

'Yeah, why? Are you joining us?' She said *us* like it was a private *us*, not a 'you're welcome' *us*.

Stephanie nodded and sat down.

Crystal focused on filing her nails. 'I see the guys are having a great time in the UK. Loads of drinking and partying. Jason uploaded some photos online. Aren't you worried he'll cheat?'

'I don't own him. If he wants me when he comes back, he'll stay true to me.' Her words sounded more confident than she felt. *Yeah, that's it. If he wants to keep me, he has to treat me right.*

Jess bounced in and slid onto a chair. 'Hey, Stephanie, glad you could join us! Hi, Crystal. Lani has some part-time work with her father, so she won't be coming today.'

'Good for her.' Crystal started filing her nails on the other hand.

Stephanie felt silenced by Crystal's glare. She couldn't work out how Jess and Lani had ever become friends with such an annoying person. Jess talked about drinking games and who was dating who, which apparently had changed a lot after one particular party on the weekend. Jess had 'picked up', and was proud of her score. Stephanie knew that if she tried to join in, they'd laugh at her cluelessness. A thought slid its way into her mind. What if Jason was picking up girls while he was on holidays? Or worse, what if he was hooking up?

For the rest of her day, worry rang in her mind like the bell when a customer entered. Momentary thoughts grew into panicking flashes. She could see scenes of Jason playing drinking games and picking up. If a girl threw herself at him, would he even stop to think? As she restocked shelves after lunch, she dropped stock because of her jittery nerves.

'Are you okay?' her boss asked.

'Just a little tired.'

'You want to take an early mark?'

'That would be great.' Stephanie put down the box of canned beans.

'Get a good night's sleep and let's hope tomorrow is a better day.'

'Okay.'

Her hands trembled as she pulled her handbag over her shoulder. Once in her room, she pulled the pillow over her head and hid from the world.

Chapter Eighteen

'Look, do you want to move back or not?' The sharp tone of Tabbie's voice cut Stephanie.

'I thought you were going away this week.'

'We are.' Tabbie giggled. 'I'm overlooking the beach as we speak, checking out the hot boys.'

'Tabbie!' Stephanie laughed. At least her friend had dropped the attitude.

'Have you spoken to your parents yet?'

'I did ask, but my timing was lousy. I'll ask again this week. Promise.' Should she be checking out hot boys too? Just in case? She didn't even want to think about it. Her heart thumped as tears wet her cheeks. If she still danced, that would distract her and she wouldn't miss Jason so much. But dancing was a lifetime ago.

The weekend came, and Stephanie found herself wondering what the seniors were up to. She lay in bed, thinking up smart and witty phrases to fit in with Jess and the girls. But as she filed thoughts that seemed funny, she realised Crystal would glare. Then she'd stuff up and sound dumb.

When her eyes closed, realer-than-real visuals flashed under her eyelids. Jason drunk. Jason with girls hanging off his arms. Jason hooking up with another girl. Her body ached for him. Tears saturated her pillow as she pulled her doona over her head. She left her stereo playing soft music, lulling her into a deep sleep.

Stephanie woke late the following Monday and dashed into the shower. Puffy, red eyes squinted back at her in the bathroom mirror. *Great! Just great!* She arrived at the café to meet the girls, later than she'd planned.

'Did you sleep in?' Jess asked.

'Wow, do you smoke pot?' Crystal leaned forward, examining Stephanie's eyes.

'Yes,' Stephanie said to Jess, then looked at Crystal. 'And definitely not.'

'Sure looks like you've had a night on it.' Crystal laughed.

Stephanie shook her head. 'I've got to get to work. See you next week.'

'Hey Steph,' Jess caught her attention before she slipped inside. 'I got an apprenticeship at Stefan's hair salon, so we won't be meeting here in future. Hopefully I'll run into you round town.' Jess put a finger on her chin. 'You know where Stefan is, don't you? Drop in some time.'

'Sure.' Stephanie forced a weak smile as she blinked her puffy eyes and walked into the corner store ready to work. Jess's hair always looked great. It made sense for her to become a hairdresser. Stephanie wished she could skip the rest of high school and move straight into a career.

During the day it bothered her that she still didn't have Jess or Lani's phone number. Despite hanging out all those lunchtimes, they'd never got close enough to swap details. Maybe Jason knew their numbers.

Jason. The silence was killing her.

Nate, the shop owner, looked up from his computer screen. 'You're early today. Everything all right? Something upset you?'

   Spiralling Out of Control

'I'm fine. Just had a late night.' Stephanie avoided eye contact. Blurting out the details of her life to her boss would be only worthy of the 'Lame Employee Award.'

'It's good you're taking time off over Christmas. Things are getting quiet around here. We might have to rethink your hours when you get back.'

She nodded. *Great. Just great.* She hadn't even saved enough money to get back to Sydney for a visit. Christmas in Toowoomba would mean just the four of them—Mum, Dad, April and her.

Stephanie shuddered inside when she agreed to go to the Christmas Eve service. With her stomach churning, she scanned the church on arrival, thankful she couldn't see Monica. Then she braced herself waiting for more words of condemnation. But they didn't come. The priest spoke of love while she convicted herself of leading a sinful life.

The Stronges drove down the mountain from Toowoomba early Christmas morning to the coast. After checking in for the week, they slapped together a bland Christmas lunch, then lounged on well-worn couches before serving dessert.

Her father reclined, leaning on an elbow. 'Let's take turns in summing up our year in one sentence.'

'Great idea,' April said. 'I've made a new best friend, I competed at States and I think Toowoomba is pretty cool.'

'I'll go next.' Mum sat forward. 'I've made new friends too. I'm enjoying working parttime, and volunteering at school and in the church. I do miss our Sydney friends, but it has been a great year since the move.'

'Your turn, Dad.' Stephanie passed the buck.

'I'm just happy my family is together. I love working and living in the same city. Life has been simpler since the move. That leaves you, Steph.'

'I've made no real friends, I think my boyfriend has dumped me, I got egged on the last day of school, and the job I'm really enjoying is looking shaky because business is slow. The best part of my year was Jason and now he's gone.' She clenched her teeth then swallowed her rage. 'Horrible. My year has been pathetically horrible!'

Her father swung his legs around and sat up. 'Gee, Steph, I didn't realise it was that bad. Why haven't you told us before now?'

Because he'd hardly been around! Stephanie took a deep breath. *Is this my chance? The open door?* 'Dad, Tabbie has asked me to move in with her—'

Her mother shot her a concerned glance as her father spoke.

'What? Move away from Toowoomba?'

'Yes, back to Sydney. I could live with Tabbie's parents. They'll have a spare room, and I could go back to Hill Top. I could be happy again. I'm sick of being miserable! It's like I've been depressed since we moved. I must be horrible to live with. I just want to be happy again.'

'Is that what you really want Steph?' His voice wavered.

'Yes, it really is.' Her mouth held a hopeful half-curled smile.

'I suppose … if you're that miserable here.' He looked to his wife. 'What do you think, Diane?'

'I … I guess we could trial it for the first term.'

'Thank you, thank you, thank you.' Stephanie hugged and kissed her parents, and landed beside April, squeezing her sister's shoulders.

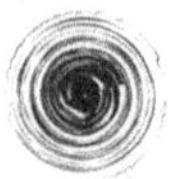

The excitement of moving back to Sydney distracted her from the lingering thoughts of her silent boyfriend who was probably with another girl, or several of them. She knew she had to draw a line in the sand and move on. Her decision left tears streaking her cheeks.

With one phone call, Stephanie was accepted back into Hill Top because she was a past student. When her flight ticket was booked, she tore down her haphazard posters and packed her belongings.

 Spiralling Out of Control

She farewelled her family, boarded a plane in Brisbane and set off to find happiness.

Stephanie floated off the plane into the lounge area. Tabbie greeted her, flashing a 'Welcome Home Stephanie' poster. Tears bubbled up again, joyful tears this time. They happy-danced and hugged.

'I can't believe you're really here.' Tabbie cried.

'I know, I know.' The girls jumped up and down.

Tabbie's mother, Francine, leaned forward. 'You brought more than this bag, didn't you?'

Stephanie nodded. 'Sure did.'

'Then we should head down to the baggage carousel.'

'We've fixed up your room. New curtains, new desk. You are going to love it,' Tabbie told her.

Everything Stephanie saw through the car window made her smile. Everything would be better now she was back.

'Have you heard from Jason?' Tabbie lowered her voice in the car.

'No.' She'd pushed him out of her mind. Just when she was having a moment of happiness. *Sheesh, Tabbie!*

'Maybe it's for the best,' Tabbie said.

Stephanie heard the words, wondering how it could be for the best. She blinked to keep her eyes dry. Her first boyfriend, the boy she was in love with, her first love, her first…

'You didn't really think it would last forever, did you?' Tabbie's voice was soft and gentle.

'Guess that's exactly what I was hoping.'

Tabbie paused, then continued. 'Everyone is going to be so happy to see you again! School just hasn't been the same. Have you got your classes sorted?'

'Yeah. I couldn't get into all the subjects I wanted. Some were full. I'm so glad they aren't making me repeat the year like they were going to make me do in Toowoomba.' Stephanie needed to change the subject. 'Are you going to get part-time work this year?'

'No. Mum and Dad said to wait and maybe get a job next year,' Tabbie said. 'It's good that you'll get the living-away-from-home allowance. You won't have to worry about money.'

'I loved working over the holidays. I loved it so much I'd rather work than finish school.'

'No way, Steph. You've got to finish school and go to university.'

'What if I don't want to? I can't think of anything I'd like to do that needs a degree.'

'You used to want to dance and perform, and you even talked about getting a degree in human movement.'

'I've changed. I told you I don't want to dance anymore.'

'I thought that was just because you were in Toowoomba.'

'No. No more dancing.' Stephanie gently hit the car seat between them with her fist.

Tabbie looked at her with raised eyebrows.

'I'm going to look for a job,' Stephanie said quietly. She returned to the view out her window, not sure why she was so adamant about not dancing again. *I don't deserve that kind of joy.*

Homecoming

Chapter Nineteen

As soon as Francine parked the car in their garage, the girls jumped out and ran upstairs. Stephanie's new room took her breath away. Gold and white curtains matched the doona cover, while pillows and cushions covered half the double bed. She sat in a comfy white swivel chair at the clean desk and slid open the drawers on the right-hand side. Matching lamps framed the bed, and a bookshelf stood against the wall, ready to be filled.

Stephanie jumped up and hugged Tabbie. 'Thank you.'

'You're so welcome, but I didn't do it. Mum organised all of it.'

Stephanie ran back downstairs.

'Thank you, Mrs Moray!' She hugged Francine as her heart swelled.

'You're welcome.' Francine smiled. 'But drop the "Mrs" now that you're living here, please call me Francine.'

Stephanie took her time unpacking and setting up her room, moving things around until she was happy with the way it looked. She smiled at the crisp, white furniture and orderly posters stuck on her wall.

'I feel like going for a walk. Want to come?' Stephanie asked.

'Sounds good, let's go this way. It's really pretty near the parklands,' Tabbie said.

'I was hoping to go down this way.' Stephanie pointed in the other direction and started walking.

'This way it is, I guess.' Tabbie laughed.

Large two-storey houses lined the street. It was relatively quiet even though it turned onto a busy road. They walked several blocks before arriving at a row of shops and cafés. Stephanie looked into every window they passed.

Tabbie cleared her throat. 'Are you looking for a job already?'

'Yeah, I told you I wanted one.'

'Can't we have a bit of fun before school goes back? You know, just hang out together.'

'I'll feel more secure once I get a job, I know it. It'll only be a few hours a week. We'll have heaps of time.' She stopped outside a shop and smiled. 'Bingo!'

Junior wanted
Able to work nights and weekends
Please apply at counter.

Stephanie strolled inside to look around. An intense cloud of incense tingled her nose. She sidestepped carefully to move around unusual pieces of heavy furniture and shelves filled with statues. The back wall housed racks of jewellery and hundreds of candles. A short olive-skinned man pushed aside purple chiffon curtains. Through the gap were tables and chairs in café-style layout.

'Hello, my name is Stephanie, and I'd like to apply for the job.' She was happy with the confidence she exuded.

'Can you make coffee?' He looked at his watch. 'You can have a trial tonight.'

'Okay. And I can learn how to make coffee. It can't be that hard. I'm a fast learner.' Her voice sounded too eager, like her life depended on the job.

'We'll see.' He raised his eyebrows. 'Be back here at five-thirty, and wear black.' Then he introduced himself as someone with a very long name starting with G. He must have read her puzzled glance. 'Everyone calls me George.'

Tabbie faced Stephanie as they stepped back onto the pavement. 'Are you sure you want to work here at night?'

'Yeah, of course.' Stephanie looked back towards the shop. 'Why wouldn't I?'

'It kind of gives me the creeps—thick incense and all those weird things.'

'Don't be silly. It'll be fine!'

After they returned home Steph bounced in to tell Francine.

'I don't like the idea of you working at night. I'm sure your mother wouldn't like it either. Have you told her about the job?'

No, she hadn't, and didn't even want to talk to her mother right now.

Francine seemed distracted as she checked on dinner. 'Now, where was it? Which shop?'

'The Tiger's Eye.'

'I'm really not sure about this. You weren't planning to walk home at night, were you?'

'It's not far. I'll be fine.'

'No, I won't have any such thing. Tom or I will come and pick you up. It's not safe to be out by yourself.'

Stephanie shrugged. 'There's a little café out the back. George is going to teach me how to make coffee.'

'There's a real technique to making a good coffee.'

'I can learn,' Stephanie said.

She raced upstairs to throw on her favourite pair of black jeans and a black T-shirt. The prospect of learning something new gave her walk a slight bounce.

'Hey, Francine, can you drop me down at The Tiger's Eye now?'

'Sure.' Francine laughed. 'I like your enthusiasm. I'm sure they will too.'

 Spiralling Out of Control

When she parked outside, Francine asked, 'Are you sure you want to work here? It's very dark and … I'm not sure about the type of people it attracts.'

'It'll be fine. Don't worry about it.' Stephanie forced a smile. She swung the car door closed with a little too much thrust. It slammed. 'Sorry,' she mouthed to Francine. She'd have to remember Francine's doors closed with one slight push.

This will be great. They'd all see. She was going to thrive now she had a job. The heavy furniture and gift tables had been pushed aside to widen the walkway into the café.

'About time you showed.' George was fussing with the till. He pushed a notepad and pen into her ribs. 'Here, use this to take orders from table eight, eleven and fifteen. They've just sat down.'

Stephanie checked her watch. It was only a quarter past five. She was early, but took the notepad, and kept her head down to keep from rolling her eyes at him.

'Then clear three, twelve and nine. They've just paid.'

'What can I get you?' she asked at the first table. She took orders and cleared tables without stopping. Every time she arrived at the kitchen, George or the chef corrected her order-taking notes. The crowd dwindled until the tables were bare.

'You seemed to do all right. Here's your pay for the night. I'll call you tomorrow after I talk to the kitchen manager. Write your number down here.' George handed her a notepad, thirty dollars and turned away. Stephanie walked outside, working out her hourly rate. 'Argh.' She'd forgotten to ring Francine. She didn't want to go back inside to ask if she could use the phone. Surely she'd be fine if she walked briskly. Plus, once she was outside, she realised what a beautiful night it was. A few paces later, a beeping car horn made her jump.

'Hey, I said I didn't want you walking home by yourself. Jump in,' Francine called.

'Sorry, I was so busy I forgot to ring.' She climbed into the front passenger seat.

'Never mind. I rang to see what time you'd finish. The man who answered was pretty abrupt.'

'Probably George. He's kind of a grump.'

'Well, how was it?'

'Busy.' Stephanie tucked a wisp of hair behind her ear.

'How did the coffees go?'

'No coffee. I just took orders and cleared tables.'

'You don't have to go back if you didn't like it.'

Stephanie sighed. 'It was okay. I'm just not used to it. It was much busier than working in the corner store.' Stephanie took in a deep breath. 'How much per hour do you think that kind of job should pay?'

'For a junior?' Francine paused. 'Around fifteen dollars an hour, give or take a few dollars.'

'I just worked my butt off for five and a half hours and got thirty dollars.' She flapped the money in the air.

'As I said, you don't have to go back.' Francine glanced sideways at Stephanie. 'Plus they aren't doing the right thing if they're paying cash in the hand. You should check if he plans to pay you properly, through your bank account and give you a pay slip. We can look over the employment agreement for you.'

Employment agreement. She hadn't seen one of those. Stephanie sighed and relaxed her head on the headrest.

'Would you like me to talk to him?'

'No, no.' Stephanie would die from embarrassment if Francine spoke to George. 'I'll ask when he rings.'

Steph got out of the car. Tabbie waited in the doorway, bright-eyed. 'Hey, working girl. How was it?'

'I got ripped off. I'm tired. See you in the morning.' Stephanie brushed past her and walked upstairs.

'Steph…' Tabbie's voice echoed in her ears, but she couldn't bring herself to turn around.

'Talk to you in the morning.' Stephanie continued to her bedroom.

'What happened, Mum?' Tabbie asked behind her.

Stephanie paused in her doorway and listened to Francine relay the story before going to bed.

George rang the next day and said she was hired.

Filled with rare confidence, she asked, 'How much will you pay me?'

'Fifteen dollars an hour.'

'Why didn't you pay me that last night?'

'That was your trial. Look, do you want the job or not? There're plenty of people looking for work out there.'

Stephanie squeezed the corded phone and decided on the spot. 'Yeah, I'll take the job.'

'Good. I'll need you at five tonight,' he said.

'What time will I finish?'

'Hours will be five to eleven Tuesday to Friday nights and eight until noon Saturday and Sunday morning.' George hung up before she could say goodbye.

'So, did you get the hours you wanted?' Tabbie asked.

'More.' Stephanie joined Tabbie on the couch.

'More? Like?'

'Like… double what I hoped for.' Stephanie picked at a frayed fingernail.

'How are you going to manage school and work?'

'I told you, I'd rather work anyway. I hate school.'

'Since when do you hate school? Didn't you just hate that school in Toowoomba? Now that you're back at Hill Top, that will change. You'll see.'

Stephanie smiled and did everything she could to stop the sarcastic rebuttal wanting to escape.

'Hey, I'm going to youth group this Friday night. Want to come?' Tabbie asked.

'I'll be working.'

'Can't you take the night off?' Tabbie pouted.

'I don't think so. I can't ask for time off in my first week.'

'What if you give them some notice? What about next week or the week after?'

'They'd be sure to tell me to get another job if I asked.'

'That sounds like a good idea. There are heaps of other jobs available.'

'Okay, okay. I'll look for another job in a couple of weeks.' It wasn't the job she was hoping for anyway. In all honesty, she was happy to change the subject. Stephanie was afraid of going back to Tabbie's youth group, sure they wouldn't be as nice as Tabbie said they were.

After a couple of nights at work, Stephanie lay on her bed and drifted off to sleep as soon as she closed her eyes. Francine woke her, saying her mother was on the phone.

'Hello, Stephanie. Are you enjoying yourself?'

'I am, Mum.' It was good to hear her voice.

'I've tried to ring a couple of times.'

'Francine told me. I was at work.'

'I thought you weren't going to work straight away.'

'But, Mum, I love working.' Stephanie shook her head. 'You know that.'

'How many hours per week is this new job?'

'Six shifts.' She bit her lip. Perhaps now wasn't the best time to start being honest with her mother.

'That sounds like a lot. Are they short shifts?'

'Not really. It's thirty-two hours in total.' Closing her eyes she clenched her jaw, wishing she could shove the words back into her mouth.

'Stephanie! How are you going to get your homework done working that many hours? That's virtually a full-time job.'

'I know… I'll look for something else.' Stephanie stood in the doorway to the kitchen, twirling the phone cord, taking no notice of her mother prattling on. She'd be fine. Not much happened in the first few weeks of school.

'Oh.' Her mother's volume increase caught her attention. 'I nearly forgot to tell you. Jason dropped by yesterday asking after you.'

'Oh?' Her heart pounded. 'What did you tell him?' Her voice rose an octave.

'That you'd moved to Sydney.'

'Whatdidhesay?' she said, running her words together.

'He asked for your number there. I thought he might have rung by now. So he hasn't called?'

'No.' Stephanie swallowed.

'April's missing you, your dad—'

'That's great Mum. I miss you all too, but, I've got to go.' She ended the call to leave the line open for Jason.

Stephanie ran upstairs. 'Tabbie, Tabbie, he's back. Mum just told me Jason's back.'

'So? I thought you'd closed that door. He can't neglect you for over two months and expect you to hang around for him.'

'He's going to call me.' Stephanie bounced on the bed, ignoring Tabbie's comment.

'Steph, careful.'

'Why?'

'Just be careful. I don't want to see you getting hurt.'

'Jason won't hurt me. He's just bad at keeping in touch when he's away. But now that he's back—'

'Steph, he's in Toowoomba, and you're here, remember? Hometown, Sydney.'

'I guess.' For the rest of the night, she entertained the thought of moving back to Toowoomba.

Chapter Twenty

I've drifted so far
don't want to return.
School is …
but an annoyance
in the back of my mind.
Life
Living and being real
is the necessity now.
School keeps kids occupied.
I'm no longer
playing childish games.
A job will keep me grounded.
If only my body
was still in shape …
Professional dancing
shattered
in the forced move north.

Was never meant to be.
Perhaps I wasn't
that good anyway.
Now,
it's part of my life
I need to bury.
Leave behind
like I left Toowoomba
like I first left Sydney.
Sydney, I love.
I have returned.

THE NEXT WEEK, STEPHANIE WORKED the agreed hours, taking naps when she could fit them in. When school started, she missed the naps. Just as Tabbie expected, everyone seemed thrilled to have her back. Girls from all grades welcomed her, giving her almost a celebrity status. That was the only thing good about school.

After not having time to stop and eat on Monday night, she shoved down an early dinner before heading to work on Tuesday. By ten o'clock her eyelids began to droop. The only thing keeping her awake was George, continually barking orders at her.

'How was it tonight?' Francine asked when Stephanie climbed into the car.

'Good.' She yawned.

'How do you plan to keep up with work and school?'

'I'll be fine. I just have to get into a good routine.' But she didn't know when she'd find the time to start that routine.

Saturday morning, Stephanie's alarm buzzed at seven in the morning. She pressed snooze three times but knew she couldn't stop it a fourth time. Her eye lids stuck together and, she pushed herself up from her pillow with a foggy mind.

'You're late,' George's wife, Bridget said as Stephonie walked in.

'Sorry.'

'First and only warning. Next time you'll lose an hour's pay.'

'I'll make it up in my break,' Stephanie said.

'Not good enough. You work the hours we set or get another job.'

'Okay, I'm sorry.' Stephanie pushed the words through her tightened throat. She made a mental note to start looking for another job as soon as she got home.

But when she got home, she fell asleep. She dreamed of Jason walking into her room, of Jason knocking on the door, of Jason on the phone. When she woke up, the phone was ringing and ringing. Was everyone out?

'Got it!' Tabbie yelled from downstairs.

She checked her watch—five o'clock. Stephanie pushed herself off the bed and took her drowsy body into the shower to wake up. The sun was still bright and would have been inviting for someone with more energy. After refreshing herself from the splash of shower water, she wandered downstairs.

Tabbie sat in the lounge and looked up from the textbook. 'That was Jason on the phone.'

'Why didn't you come and get me?'

'You were in the shower. He can ring back. I think you should make him chase you after what he's put you through.'

She hadn't been in the shower when the phone rang. *Why would I want him to chase me? Was it over the top to just want to talk to him?* 'Did he say when he'd ring back?'

'Don't worry about him. Let's go see a movie,' Tabbie said. 'Mum and Dad have gone out to a work dinner.'

'Is there something on TV?'

'Nah, nothing's on. I just checked.'

'Let's have another look.' Stephanie sat on the lounge chair beside her friend.

'How about a walk?' Tabbie stood.

'Do you have any movies here?'

     Spiralling Out of Control

'Nothing I haven't watched a hundred times. Oh, I get it. You're hoping he'll ring back, aren't you?'

'Can you go by yourself?'

'I don't want to go by myself.' Tabbie looked at the clock. 'It's already five twenty. The crazies might be out. I need you to come with me for protection.'

Stephanie chewed on the inside of her mouth.

'We have an answering machine. Look.' Tabbie pressed a button. 'It's turned on. Let's go. I need some fresh air after studying for hours. It'll only take us fifteen minutes to go around the block.'

Stephanie pushed their pace to a speed-walk and was ready to turn around and head back rather than doing a lap.

'Look, no flashing lights, no calls,' Tabbie said when they got back inside.

'What if he didn't leave a message?'

'Our machine tells us even if someone hangs up. See, this light? Not flashing—no calls. Now that you have a job, why don't you buy a mobile phone?'

'Good question. I will when I get some spare time.'

After eating oven-baked pizza for dinner, Stephanie hugged her knees on the couch, anticipating the phone ringing while the movie played in the background. But Jason didn't call.

The next morning, Stephanie woke and went to shower, but Tabbie was already in the bathroom.

'Will you be long? I've got to go to work.'

'Out in a minute,' Tabbie called.

Stephanie looked at the clock. She didn't have time to wait, so she pulled on her black jeans and T-shirt using extra deodorant and perfume so no one would notice.

Tabbie popped her head into Steph's room. 'Shower is free—oh, you're already dressed.'

'Yeah. Why were you in the shower so early?'

'Church.' Tabbie towel-dried her hair. 'Sorry. You've got work, hey?'

'Yep, bye. Gotta go.' Stephanie waved and ran down the stairs.

Work was quiet that Sunday morning. Stephanie found herself daydreaming about Jason moving to Sydney, letting her mind wander to the moments they'd had in his bedroom. She hoped he would call or walk through the door. *As if!* He didn't even know where she worked.

Her mum rang that afternoon. 'You hung up quickly the other day.'

'Sorry about that.'

'How are you managing juggling work and school?'

'Good.' She'd made a promise to herself to only feed positive information to her mother from here on.

'You didn't get too tired?'

'All good. Got through with no problems.' Stephanie thought for a moment as flashes of the week hit her mind. She'd yawned through the day and pushed her eyelids open at night. 'Yep, no problems.'

'Have you been looking for another job?'

'Haven't found one yet.' She hadn't had time to look.

'Do you want to say hello to April?'

'Pass on a big hello for me. I've got to go. Already got a couple of assignments I need to start.'

'Oh, the reason I rang ... a postcard arrived. From Jason. Funny that it arrived after he got home. Anyway, I've redirected it to you. You should get it Tuesday or Wednesday.'

Stephanie's lip quivered as she hung up. She did miss them a bit. Upstairs, she pulled out her school books and stared at them, wondering if she'd made the right decision. What if she'd hung round in Toowoomba for another month? Jason would have come straight to her.

She jumped when the phone rang. She stood, lingering in her doorway.

'Stephanie, it's for you,' Francine called.

She ran, nearly tripping down the stairs. Francine smiled when she passed her the corded phone.

'Hello,' she almost squealed, anticipating Jason on the other end of the line.

'Steph, it's good to hear your voice,' he said. 'Man, how I've missed you!'

'Yeah, I've missed you too.' Her smile so wide she could hardly form the words. She turned away from Tabbie, who was waving to get her attention.

'Did you get my postcard?' he asked.

'Mum told me it just arrived. She's forwarding it to me.'

'When can I see you?'

'I don't know when I'll get back to Toowoomba. I've got a job,' she said unable to stop the bubble in her voice.

'What about school?'

'I'm back at my old school. It's great being there again.' She looked at Tabbie and smiled.

'I'm coming to Sydney.'

'When?' Her heart lunged out of her chest.

'Next week. I got three uni offers but I chose Sydney so I could be near you.' He spoke the words she'd dreamed of hearing.

'Really?'

'Yes, really. What's your address? I'll come around when I get there.'

Her heart fluttered as she gave him her address. Then she hung up, floating around the room like she was weightless.

'What is it?' Tabbie asked.

'He's coming to Sydney.' Her smile broadened.

'When?'

'Next week. He chose Sydney. He had other uni offers but he chose Sydney to be near me. Did you hear that, Tabbie? He's coming to be near me.'

'I was wrong?'

'I think you were.'

'Sorry.' Tabbie shook her head and shrugged. 'But, wow.'

Stephanie bounced on the spot. She almost kicked her leg in the air, dance style, but remembered she didn't dance anymore.

'How are you going with that ancient history essay?' Tabbie asked.

'No go. Can't focus. How are you going?'

'It's hard. I can't find enough information on the internet or in the books I got from the library. Maybe we should work on it together?'

'Great idea. Let's.'

The girls spent the afternoon writing their essays and laughing at their teachers. Between laughs, they managed to get some work finished before dinner.

'Something tells me you won't get that essay finished by Friday if you don't get most of it done tonight.' Tabbie stood to clear the table.

'Thanks for your help, Tabbie.' Stephanie stacked the dishwasher. 'I think I would have failed this one if you didn't help me today.'

Tom and Francine smiled at each other as she left the room with Tabbie. It was a look she'd rarely seen in her family. Her heart ached just a little. Family was family, and she missed them. By the end of the night, Stephanie had completed her essay. She had one of the most peaceful sleeps she could remember. No frightful dreaming, just deep replenishing sleep until her alarm sounded at seven.

'Happy Monday!' Tabbie said, as they passed in the hallway. 'Shower is all yours. Thought I'd get up a little earlier so we weren't fighting over the bathroom.'

'Thanks, Tabbie.' Stephanie sighed. It was good living with her best friend. 'You're one in a million.'

The postcard arrived on Tuesday, and her stomach jumped and churned before tying itself in a knot.

Hi Babe,

Lots going on here, wish you were with us, lots of parties, drinks and you know… stuff.

Got three uni offers, not sure which one I'll take.

         Spiralling Out of Control

See you when I get back.

Luv you,

yours,

Jason.

Jason hadn't called again by Friday and she was getting anxious. Maybe he'd meant he'd see her next week.

On Friday night, Stephanie finished work and crashed with exhaustion in her bed. She was rudely awoken by Saturday, which came before she'd finished sleeping. She rushed into work arriving just before eight, gave Bridget a cheesy grin, and began her daily duties. Weekend mornings had her serving customers in the shop. They'd finally taught her how to make coffee, and she was the main barista on Saturday and Sunday.

Stephanie left The Tiger's Eye and walked home with heavy feet, looking forward to her regular Saturday afternoon nap. As she neared the house, she saw a familiar masculine shape sitting on the front fence. She ran towards him, more certain with every step. He stood before she reached him and caught her as she flew into his arms. She squeezed her arms around his neck. He twirled her around as she savoured his blissful kisses.

Every tiny sliver of pain he'd caused melted away in moments. Her heart swelled with joy as it thumped wildly with passion. She blinked away the happy tears and clung to him a little tighter, never wanting to let him go again.

Chapter Twenty-One

STEPHANIE LINKED HER FINGERS through Jason's and took him inside to meet her surrogate family. She had waited weeks to feel the strong cocoon of his arms again, so she rushed through the introductions. When he gently tugged on her hand, she led him towards the stairs. They slipped away from the Morays and drifted into her room. She kicked the door closed and they pashed, locked at the mouth. After filling herself with his scent and taste, the empty hollow inside opened as Jason's hands began to roam.

'We can't.' She pushed him away.

'Oh, yes we can. I've missed you.' He kissed her on each cheek before melding his lips to hers again.

Oh, stop! No… don't stop. They had to stop. She struggled away from his lips, but he pulled her in again.

'Not here, okay?'

'Alright, where then?' His face contorted, like she'd wounded him.

'Like, can we talk? I've hardly spoken to you. You've been gone forever. Why didn't you ring?'

'Yeah, sorry. It was just so full on, and Mum and Dad didn't want to pay international rates for phone calls. You really need to get online.'

'Yeah, I'll ask. So what did you get up to?' A shiver raced down her spine.

'Did you get my postcard?'

'Yeah.' She glanced at it sitting on her desk.

'That's pretty much it. It's all on the card.'

'What? Nothing else?'

'No, not much. What did you get up to?'

'I worked in the shop next to the café during the holidays. Met up with Jess, Lani, and Crystal a couple of times.'

'Hey, that's great. How were they?'

'Crystal was pretty much her normal self. Lani and Jess nice as always. They were going to a lot of parties, and they talked a lot about picking up guys. I couldn't help wonder if… you…'

'What! If I was hooking up? You've got to be crazy. As if I would.'

'Well, the whole drinking thing at parties often leads to…' She searched for the right words. 'Isn't that what you said you were doing?'

'I told you, you're the only one for me.' He linked his fingers through hers and sparks shot up her arms.

'I know. But it sounded like they were throwing themselves at boys. I just imagined there were probably heaps of girls throwing themselves at you.' She looked up into his eyes.

He twitched and squinted.

Guilt. Not what she wanted to see.

'Crazy. Some girls are just crazy. They're nothing like you.'

'What are you saying?' She stood up, folding her arms.

'Part of it… what you said… was right. Girls just throw themselves at me… Not just me… At all the guys.'

'And what did you do?' She tilted her head.

'I was so drunk—'

'You cheated on me!' She tried to blink away the fury.

'No, Steph, no way.' His eyes pleaded with her.

'What then?'

'There were a couple of times—'

'You did it a couple of times!' She threw her arms in the air and paced to the door and back.

'Steph, wait! Let me talk. A couple of times they kissed me before I could stop, b–but I did my best to push them away.'

Stephanie wanted to believe him. Her doubts were caught in the stagnant silence within the room. Could she drop it and believe him? She yawned as she opened the door. 'I need to catch up on some sleep. It's probably best if you go.'

'I'll come back tomorrow after breakfast.'

She shook her head. 'I'm working.'

''Til when?'

'Same as today.'

He grabbed her, wrapping his arms around her until she had completely relaxed into his body and devoured another kiss. 'Love you, babe.'

She led him downstairs and pushed him out the door without a smile, still feeling the pressure of his lips on hers. She returned to her room and lay on her bed for the rest of the afternoon. *He loves me.* Yet there was a huge possibility he'd been with other girls. *But he says he loves me.*

Dinner started with quiet smiles and glances until Francine started the conversation. 'I think we need some rules if Jason is going to be visiting regularly.'

Stephanie's cheeks flushed. She looked to Tabbie for support, but Tabbie stared at her plate.

'We've never let our kids have boyfriends or girlfriends in their room. It's a rule in our house,' Tom said. 'What was the rule at your home?'

'We never had a rule.'

Francine wiped her mouth with a napkin. 'What do you suggest would be a good and fair rule when it comes to your boyfriends?'

'Well, I only have one boyfriend.' Stephanie smiled. 'Is it okay if he comes into my room during the day but not at night?'

Tom put his knife and fork down with a clatter onto his plate. 'How about only during the day with the door open? Does that sound like a fair compromise?'

'What about privacy?' Stephanie protested.

Francine leaned towards Stephanie, like she didn't want the neighbours hearing their conversation. 'We're not okay with closed-door privacy with a boy in our home. I know you're not our daughter, and you're only boarding with us, but we must make rules while you stay here. Is there going to be a problem with what Tom suggested?'

'No, I can live with that.' She wondered where Jason was living. Hopefully they could find privacy there. So what if girls had thrown themselves at him? He'd moved to Sydney to live near her. He loved her.

Sunday morning at The Tiger's Eye, Stephanie dusted ornaments and shuffled candles between shelves. Customers were scarce so she looked for things to do to avoid Bridget barking orders at her. She checked her watch every other minute until she could leave.

Stephanie ran most of the way home, tripping over her feet to get there, but Jason was nowhere in sight. She looked up and down the street. Just parked cars and leaves scurrying across the path. Deflated, she entered the empty house in search of something to eat.

A thunderous knock on the door pulled her from the kitchen with excitement. She could see his broad-shouldered shadow through the patterned glass in the door. *Breathe... think calm*, she told herself before letting Jason in.

'Hey, sorry I'm late. I've just been moving my things in.'

'Where to?'

'A couple of blocks from your school, I think.'

'Who are you living with?' Stephanie asked.

'Axel. Mum knows his mum. She organised it all. He seems like a dork.'

Stephanie chuckled and walked back into the kitchen.

'So am I forgiven?' Jason followed.

'I thought you said you did nothing wrong.'

'Am I forgiven for being in the wrong place at the wrong time where girls threw themselves at me?'

'I guess so … you did push them away.' She hoped. 'Didn't you?'

He nodded.

Stephanie pointed to the food she was about to prepare. 'You hungry? I was just making some lunch.'

'Yeah, starving.' He stood behind her, linking his arms around her waist while she cut the sandwiches.

After lunch, when the dishes were stacked in the dishwasher, he took her hand and led her upstairs. They were alone. She took a deep breath as a warm rush darted through her veins, her heartbeat increasing every second. He guided her into her bedroom and swung the door closed with his foot as he kissed her.

Oh, no! I wasn't going to do this. Oh maybe, just one more time. No one will know. The front door slammed shut, shuddering her window. She jumped, pushing him back, and flicked the door open in one swift move.

'What's up?' He held his arms out from his sides, palms up.

'New house rule. I have to leave the door open.'

'Are you kidding?'

'Would I have opened the door if I was?'

'When do I get time alone with you?' His hand followed her curves. 'In privacy?'

'Stop it.' She moved away. 'Someone's coming upstairs,' she whispered, hoping whoever it was couldn't hear her heart thumping.

'Hi, Steph.' Tabbie poked her head through the doorway. 'Hi Jason. Sorry, didn't realise you were here.'

Stephanie raised her eyebrows and looked wide-eyed at her friend.

'Okay, we can chat later.' Tabbie turned to walk away.

 Spiralling Out of Control

'Is there something you wanted to talk about?' Stephanie followed her out.

'No, no. Nothing important. Just come and chat when Jason goes.' Tears brimmed on Tabbie's eyelashes.

'Won't be long.' Stephanie smiled and returned to Jason.

'Everything okay?' he asked.

'I think she needs to talk about something.' She tugged on his hand. 'You should go, and I'll see what's up with Tabbie.' She wanted him out before she closed the door and broke the new rules. He was reluctant but she led him downstairs and out to the kerb. 'Can you wait? We could go for a walk.'

'I'd really like to, but I told my flatmate I'd help him. There's some big party on next weekend. I saw a flyer at uni. Love you to come.'

'When?'

'Friday night.'

'I'm working.' She pulled at her fingernails.

'Come after. It won't start until late anyway.'

'Where is it?'

'Close to uni.'

'Can you pick me up? I'm not sure if Francine would want to take me to a party after work.'

'Yeah, I can pick you up.'

'Okay.' She was excited to be going out on a date. Then she frowned when she remembered. 'But I can't. I have to work in the morning.'

'It won't be too late. Don't worry. See you Friday. Love you, babe.' He wrapped his arms around her in a bear hug.

Stephanie was still smiling when she walked into her best friend's room. 'What's up?'

'You didn't have to kick him out because of me.'

'It's okay.' It was best she pushed him out. Stephanie sat on her friend's bed. 'What do you want to talk about?'

'Rhet asked me out on a date.'

'Wow, that's exciting.'

'If Mum and Dad would let me go out on a date, it would be exciting.' Tabbie frowned.

'Who's Rhet?'

'A surfy guy I met at the beach.'

'Why won't they let you?' Stephanie asked. 'I know they're strict, but you'll be sixteen soon.'

'I'm not sixteen for another two months.' Tabbie rolled her eyes. 'They said I have to wait.'

'What if you just go on a date without them knowing?'

'I can't lie to them.' But the sparkle in Tabbie's eyes suggested that she was thinking about it.

'Or tell them … tell them you'll be staying at a friend's house, and go on the date from there.'

'How is that not lying?'

'Do you want to go or not?'

'I do.' Tabbie paused. 'But I don't want to lie to Mum and Dad.'

'Well …' Stephanie let the silence stretch between them like a rubber band.

Tabbie lifted her head. 'Do you think Suzie or Jaya would be okay with me staying at their house for a night?'

'You can only ask.'

'What if you come and stay too?'

'Which night?'

'This Friday.'

'I'm working Friday night, plus Jason has asked me out.' Stephanie saw Tabbie's eyes gloss over. Her friend needed her this time. 'But I guess I could go with you straight after school.'

'How would that work? Would you get Jason to drop you back?'

'Um… I think—'

'You're thinking about staying with him, aren't you?'

'Possibly.' Stephanie shrugged.

'Are you sure? I thought you said you didn't want to do it anymore. I thought you said it didn't feel right.'

Stephanie breathed in. *Urgh!* Tabbie was right. Sex would take her back to feeling horrible again. 'Yeah, okay. I'll get him to drop me off. Probably after midnight. We'll just have to get one of the girls to agree to help you out.'

On Monday morning, Jaya agreed to their scheme.

'Now you just have to ask your parents, and it's all sorted,' Stephanie said to Tabbie. She enjoyed watching her friend act a little disobedient for a change.

The rest of the week was an uphill treadmill of work, sleep, and school. Having no contact with Jason left Stephanie parched.

Tom and Francine were happy for the girls to stay out for the night because they were living it up themselves at a fiftieth birthday party. 'You'll call me any time if you want to come home, won't you?' Francine insisted.

'Seriously, Mum.' Tabbie rolled her eyes.

'Sure, Francine,' Stephanie butted in, 'We will. Won't we, Tabbie?'

'Stephanie, are you sure Jaya's mum is okay to pick you up from work?'

'Yes, it's all sorted.' She tugged at a stray hair.

'If something happens and she can't, make sure you ring me. Have a great time, and be careful.' Francine spoke with more love than Stephanie remembered her own mother speaking. A pang of guilt shuddered through Stephanie. She'd helped create the lie.

After school on Friday afternoon, the girls caught the bus to Jaya's home. Stephanie pulled on her black jeans and T-shirt, ready for work. She slipped her uniform into her school bag and checked that she'd included another shirt to wear to the party. Returning to Jaya's that night was not going to happen. She knew that already.

'Hope your date goes well, Tabbie.' She hugged her friend. 'Thanks for doing this for us, Jaya. You're the best. I'll have to get the next bus to get to work on time. Don't worry if I don't come back tonight.'

'Why? Where will you stay?' Jaya raised one eyebrow.

'I'll work it out. I have to get back to work by eight in the morning.' She ran out, ignoring the torrent of questions Jaya was firing at her. She should have told her Jason would drop her back to the Tabbie's house, but the right words didn't come to mind until she was on the bus.

Work was at its peak in busyness. Stephanie didn't look at her watch once.

George surprised her by saying, 'Knock off now. See you in the morning.'

Stephanie checked her watch. It was already eleven. She grabbed her bag and swung it over her shoulder. She'd hoped to find five minutes to touch up her lip gloss, but hadn't even found time for a toilet break. Dashing into the bathroom, she changed her shirt, applied lip gloss and another coat of mascara before running out to meet Jason. Glancing up and down the street, she realised he wasn't there. She checked her watch. Eleven fifteen.

Come on, Jason. You said you'd be here at eleven. Stephanie's breath was heavy, her smile had fallen from her face. Her school bag dragged her shoulder down. She checked her watch again. *Jason! Eleven thirty. Where are you?* Tears seeped from her eyes. She'd ring Francine. As she put her hand to the shop door, she took one more hopeful look up and down the street.

George stood at the cash register, and gave her a questioning look.

'Can I please use the phone?'

He nodded.

Francine didn't answer. The phone didn't go through to the voicemail. It just rang out. *Now what? What's Jason's mobile number?* If only she'd written it down. She wished she had a mobile phone.

Walking back outside, she faced the direction of her new home. Her feet moved forward, but fear swept over her. Moody shadows shot chills through her body. She shivered at patches of unknown between trees and buildings, fences and roads. Frozen with fear, she couldn't go on any further. Tears bubbled over her lashes and ran down her cheeks. The street lamp cast her trembling shadow on the pavement.

          Spiralling Out of Control

Chapter Twenty-Two

'Hey, babe, jump in!'

A taxi had pulled up without her noticing. 'Jason, you said you'd be here!'

'Hey, cut the waterworks.' He opened the door and pulled her in.

'Have you been drinking already?'

'What do you think? We're going to a party.'

He groped her. He kissed her and it was like he was trying to swallow her whole. He wasn't romantic. He wasn't loving. He was like a hungry animal. Their teeth smashed as he plunged his tongue in her mouth. She struggled with him for a moment, but she was fighting a losing battle and her body went limp until he'd finished.

She hoped the taxi driver was watching the road and listening to the radio. The car stopped and Jason threw money at the driver. Stephanie slid low in the seat to pull her jeans back to her waist. She clutched her bag and stumbled from the taxi, pulling her shirt down.

Jason grabbed her hand and led her through an alleyway, not once turning back to look at her. A disgusting, filthy feeling swept over her as she replayed what had just happened. In the heat of the heavy kiss, she'd allowed him to take another piece of her. Her attraction to him clouded her mind.

To her left, a wall stretched up into a tall building. On the other side, a maze of small shrubs covered the lawn. Through the thick small branches, she heard voices and squinted to see where they came from.

Who'd be so crazy as to hang out in the middle of the bushes? Then her eyes adjusted to the darkness and she focused on bare skin. Embarrassed, she looked forward, smoothed her shirt once more and checked that her fly was up. She fought against the burning tears.

Jason reached into an ice-filled tub and grabbed two beers, pushing one into her hand.

'Jason, I'm too young,' she whispered.

'Don't worry about it.' He took the bottle back and unscrewed the top. 'Enjoy!'

She put the bottle to her mouth. The bitterness shocked her and the bubbles made her cough and sneeze. Jason laughed. Her cheeks burned as she put the bottle to her mouth for another swig.

'Woo-hoo. Jason likes them young, hey?'

'Take no notice. That's just Axel, my flatmate. Such a dork.' Jason led her to another group of people. Introductions overwhelmed her, as each name blended with the music. She forced more beer down her throat and smiled. Another bottle landed in her hands, this one filled with pink liquid. The sweetness swished around her mouth, awaking her tastebuds. It was soon empty, and Jason handed her another, sweet and delicious. She wondered what it was. She pulled the bottle back from her face, but the shadows covered the label.

'Jason.' She held up the empty bottle. 'Yeah, 'nother 'un like t'at.'

Jason focused on his conversation while he handed her another. She sat beside him, watching him listen to a group talking. She swigged another drink as she drank in his good looks. The group burst into laughter, echoing in her ears.

The stars in the sky shone down on her. She stood to meet them halfway. Her world moved. She stepped forward to steady herself and grabbed Jason's elbow.

'Whoa, babe. You okay?'

'Sure.' She put her hand to her mouth when she didn't recognise her own voice.

'Hey, you don't look so great. I think you've had enough.' Jason led her back through the alleyway.

'Oh, 've only been here a li'l while. Do we 'ave t'go?'

Stephanie looked neither left nor right, but only at Jason.

'Yeah, I think we'd better. You have to work in the morning.'

'But—'

'But nothing. I'm taking you home.' Jason laughed.

My man, my strong wonderful man. She looked at him through drunken-dreamy-eyes in the taxi on the way back to his flat. Her mind went blank until she woke in a fright. The alarm blared. Jason was shaking her.

'Come on, babe, you start work in fifteen minutes.'

Stephanie realised she had no clothes on. She cleared her throat. 'Um.'

Jason threw her one of his T-shirts and she slipped it on under the privacy of the doona.

'Can I have a shower?' she asked. 'I haven't got a towel.'

'Sure.' He smiled. 'I'll get you some Berocca too.'

Stephanie turned the shower taps on and jumped in and out before the water ran warm. She downed the sweet vitamin B drink and rushed to work arriving ten minutes late.

'That's the second time you've arrived late.' Bridget shook her finger in Stephanie's face. 'I'll have to talk to George about this.'

Her head pounded all morning and she willed the time to go faster.

'I've spoken to George,' Bridget said at the end of her shift. 'He said to give you the choice, lose one hour's pay, or work an extra hour.'

'What!'

'You could always look for another job.'

'I've got to go home. Take the money off.' Under her breath she added, 'And I'll start looking.'

'What was that?'

'I'm going home. Goodbye.'

Stephanie crashed into a deep sleep until she was disturbed by Tabbie calling her for dinner. *Tabbie!* She'd completely forgot about her big date.

'How did it go?' Stephanie whispered at the dinner table.

'Later.' Tabbie stared at her with wide eyes.

Stephanie mouthed the word, 'Sorry.'

'I noticed a missed call last night. Did you try and ring?' Francine asked.

'Oh, yes.' Stephanie thought quickly. 'Just rang to let you know I got home safely.'

'That's good. I was worried you might have needed a lift.'

Stephanie forced a smile. Maybe she should have tried again and saved herself from the humiliating taxi ride. But the whole night hadn't been totally humiliating. Parts of it were fun. But her head still ached.

'So spill.' Stephanie patted Tabbie's princess doona after dinner. 'I want all the details.'

'Yuck!' Tabbie flung herself face down beside Stephanie.

'Yuck?'

'Yes, yuck. It was horrible.' Tabbie rolled over and aimed her fingers down her throat like she was about to puke.

'Why, what went wrong?'

'We were going to go to the movies, but Rhet got the times wrong. He got there late and the movie had already started and it would have been too late to go to the next one, so we sat in the coffee shop and had a milkshake.' Tabbie took a breath.

'That doesn't sound too bad.'

'The whole time I had to push his hand off my thighs. Eww! It's gross just thinking about it.'

'Oh, no.'

'Then he was Mr Octopus Arms most of the way back to Jaya's. With a block to go I ran away from him, but look what I did.' Tabbie pulled up her jeans to show her purple, grazed knee.

'Ouch! Did you get inside okay?' She should have been there for her.

'After I fell over, Rhet laughed like a hyena. I yelled at him, "Shut up!" He didn't follow any further.'

'I'm sorry it was so horrible.' Stephanie didn't push for more details. She waited, not knowing what to say, while Tabbie took a few minutes to calm down.

'Anyway, how was your night? Amazing, I'm sure.'

'Pretty average.' Stephanie looked towards the ceiling and decided it was better not to fill Tabbie in.

'But you stayed with Jason for the night … somewhere?' Tabbie turned her head away.

'Yeah, slept in and got into trouble at work.' Stephanie directed the conversation to work. 'I have to find another job. George and Bridget are horrible.'

'Steph, did you… you know?'

Tabbie already knew. 'Yeah.' Stephanie stood and moved towards the door. 'I've gotta get some more sleep. I don't want to be late again. They cut my pay today.'

'Oh, that's harsh.'

'Have you got church in the morning?' Stephanie asked before she left the room.

'Yeah. I wish you could come sometime. You'd love it.'

'No thanks, but I hope you have a great day.' Church was for good girls. Part of Stephanie wished she was one.

She lay in bed, rolling from side to side, replaying the previous night in her mind. *I should have stopped him in the taxi. I shouldn't have drunk so much so fast. I should have taken some pyjamas.* She tried to remember, but nothing came up except for a few fuzzy memories. *I'll never know what happened.* Nothing. Hours—vanished from her life.

She charged towards the window, pulling it open, letting the out-of-season cool air calm her. She clenched her fists. *Stupid.* She was too young and stupid to be going to university parties. Stephanie closed the window with cold numbness in her cheeks and found comfort under her doona.

The next day she made it to work on time. People walked through the doorway in a constant stream, keeping her mind occupied and off Jason for a couple of hours. When she arrived home, Tabbie wanted to work on an assignment.

'Sorry, Tabbie.' The quicker she could get away from Tabbie the better. 'I'm not in the right frame of mind.'

She took herself out of the house and walked around the block, meandering down the street, then up the street. She leaned against a bus stop and watched the cars go by. Over and over she searched for memories from Friday night and wondered how she should act next time.

At school, Stephanie was free to act like the innocent girl she once was. Everyone looked at her exactly the same as they always had. Everyone except Jaya, who wanted details of why she hadn't come home.

'So, are you sleeping with him?' Jaya raised her eyebrows.

'That's a bit below the belt.' Stephanie turned to walk away.

'You are, aren't you?' Jaya pinned her down with a glare.

Too many questions. Shh. She didn't want to answer. She didn't want anyone to hear the conversation. 'No, Jaya.' She wanted to run. 'It's not what you think. Just drop it.'

'You ask me if you can sleep over but you don't, and I get no explanation.' Jaya screwed her face up. 'Great friend you are, Stephanie.'

'I'm sorry, Jaya. It was late, so I went back to Jason's. That's it.'

Stephanie enjoyed being known as the person she used to be and not who she had become. But it was a hard act to keep up. It was a mission to get to work each night and even harder to wake up and get to school on time. She was exhausted by exhaustion.

Jason didn't call or drop by. Obviously, he only came when it suited him. A pang of disappointment gripped her chest each day as she arrived home and he hadn't miraculously appeared along the way. She wished he'd contact her through the week.

Friday night, she looked up and saw Jason pushing aside the chiffon curtains at the entrance of The Tiger's Eye café. Stephanie straightened the tray she held, to save the plates. They rattled and clanked.

'Hey, babe.' He followed, leaving an arm's length distance between them. 'You okay to come with me after work?'

'Francine will be here to pick me up.' She removed the plates from the tray.

'Ring her. Tell her we're going out.'

'I don't have any clothes or anything.'

'You look hot like that. Come on. There's a great party pumping.'

'Okay,' Stephanie said without thinking. 'George, can I please use the phone to ring my lift?'

'Make it quick! And if your friend isn't ordering, get him to leave.'

Stephanie was thankful Francine answered on the first ring. 'Jason's here, so you don't need to pick me up.'

'That's great. I'm about ready for bed anyway. See you tomorrow.'

Francine's yawn sounded through the phone as she hung up.

George lingered until she put the phone down. 'And you'd better tell that boyfriend of yours we'll charge him corkage if he opens any of those drinks he's carrying.'

'Did you hear that?' Stephanie raised her eyebrows.

'Sure. Drinks can wait.' Jason twisted the bag in his hand.

'Can I get you a coffee? You have to order, or wait outside.'

'Yeah, coffee would be great, babe.'

Twenty minutes later, she put down the order pad, wiped the bench and grabbed her things. Her only desire was sleep.

'Do we have to go? I haven't seen you all week. Can we just go back to your place and chat?'

'The party is going off. I—'

'I'm just so tired, Jason.' Stephanie yawned.

'I know someone who can fix that.' He waved to signal a taxi.

Stephanie's head nodded as she slipped in and out of sleep with the hum of the engine. She woke up when she heard the rustle of the drinks bag while Jason paid the taxi driver.

'You'll have fun, babe. We won't stay too late. I know you have to work in the morning.'

They walked into a shabby-looking older house. People crowded the upstairs veranda at the front and others spilled out from the closed-in ground level. Jason took her upstairs, wandered through every room, then went back downstairs. Stephanie followed closely behind, not wanting to lose sight of him.

'Matt, gee, I thought you must have left,' he said, as everyone in the corner of the downstairs room looked up. 'Hey, my girlfriend is really tired. Do you have some—'

'Shh.' Matt looked agitated. 'You don't have to tell the whole party. Here.' Matt held out his hand as Jason held out his. They shook formally. *What's this? A drug deal?*

Jason turned and grabbed Stephanie's hand as he walked past her. He pulled her back upstairs and into an empty dark room.

'What is it?'

'Speed.' He opened two drinks, and shook the powder from a small ziplock bag into each bottle. 'Here. Drink up.'

'Isn't that a drug?' she asked. 'Is it dangerous?'

'Don't worry, babe. I wouldn't give you anything bad. Remember, I love you.'

The three little words that made her heart flutter and her mind melt.

   Spiralling Out of Control

Chapter Twenty-Three

STEPHANIE WAITED FOR THE HIGH. With each swig came the same warm-rush-dizziness she'd felt the previous week. Jason had another drink in her hand before she'd finished the first. When she heard a great song playing downstairs, her hips moved to the beat.

'Babe, you wanna dance?' Jason smiled.

'Yeah, love to.' She followed him downstairs, grooving to the music.

'Are you going to get back into it now that you're in Sydney?'

'No. Shut up and dance with me.' She heard the words fumble out of her mouth. Her body moved in an instinctive rhythm. Jason walked away from her. She saw the gap between them grow, and willed her legs to follow him.

'Hey, stay 'n dance.' She heard a voice behind her.

Stephanie spun around to a group of girls.

'Okay.' The echo of her own voice made her laugh.

Song after song played. Stephanie's mouth was dry.

'Jason!' she called.

'You okay?' a girl asked. 'Here, you look like you need a drink.'

'Thanks.' Stephanie didn't recognise her own voice. She sculled the drink and took another, and another, and then another. She was sure the fluorescent light dangling from the ceiling was flashing. When she stopped dancing to breathe, everyone seemed fuzzy. She saw Jason in the distance and made a beeline for him, bumping into shoulders and drinks in hands, before landing in his arms.

'Oh, my goodness!' She laughed when she looked at his watch. 'I have to be at work in three hours. That's hilarious.'

'Chuck a sickie.' Jason wrapped his arms snug around her waist.

'Okay.' She laughed with short manic frenzy.

Stephanie woke with a fright when the alarm blasted at seven the next morning. Her head throbbed and her stomach churned. Taking a sick day was the furthest thing from her mind until she stood. Everything swayed. *Man, I'm way too sick to work.* She fell backwards onto Jason's bed.

'Jason, I feel sick.'

'Huh?'

'I can't go to work. I'm too sick. Can you ring them?'

'No. You. Phone's on the bench.'

She rolled off the bed, grabbing the wall to balance herself as she left the bedroom. 'Can't see it.'

'Check the couch. Axel probably left it there.'

'Yep, found it.' She picked up the phone and punched in the number. 'Sorry, Bridget, I'm too sick to come in today.'

'Would it have something to do with going out last night?'

'What do you mean? I'm sick.'

'Self-inflicted, I bet,' Bridget snarled though the phone. 'Be here tomorrow or you won't have a job to come to!'

The line went dead.

'Stupid cow!' Stephanie threw the phone on the couch.

'What's up?' Jason called from the bedroom.

'Silly cow gave me a hard time. Saying I'm sick because it's self-inflicted.'

'Well, she's got a point.'

'Whose side are you on?' Stephanie returned to the bedroom and burrowed her head back into the pillow.

She slept until after midday. *Francine! Tabbie!*

'Jason.' She rocked him. 'Jason, I've got to get home. Can you come with me? I'm not sure which bus—'

'It's not that far. You can walk.'

'I still feel horrible.'

'Bus.' Jason grabbed a pillow to cover his face. 'It leaves from the end of the street.' His voice was muffled by foam.

Annoyed that he wouldn't even see her to the bus, she grabbed her bag and slammed the door without saying goodbye. She walked the whole way home to let off steam.

'Was everything all right last night?' Francine asked as Stephanie entered the house.

'Sure, no problems.'

'I didn't hear you come home. What time was it?'

'I…' Stephanie looked at Francine. *Argh.* She couldn't find the right words to lie. 'It got really late, so I ended up staying at Jason's.' Stephanie rushed her weary body upstairs, hoping leaving the room would stop the questions.

'Are your mum and dad okay with you staying at Jason's overnight?' Francine followed her.

'They trust him. He's a nice guy.'

'He might be nice but, Steph, you're young.'

'What do you mean?' Stephanie tried to look innocent, plastering on her sweetest smile as she tilted her head to the side.

'Are your parents really okay with this?'

'I said they trust him. Look, I really need some sleep. It was a late night.' Stephanie closed the bedroom door in Francine's face.

She couldn't fall asleep, so she opened her school books and stared at the pages for two hours. Her eyes followed the words, but she couldn't absorb any of the information. Tabbie knocked, interrupting her senseless study.

'Come in,' Stephanie said.

'How's it going?'

'Not learning much.'

'How was last night? You stayed at Jason's again, didn't you?'

Stephanie raised an eyebrow. How did Tabbie know everything?

'Your bed was empty this morning.' Tabbie rolled her eyes. 'Steph, I can't stop Mum from ringing your parents. What if they want you to go home or something?'

'I don't know.' She thought for a moment. 'What if next time they ring, I stay in the room with your mum. You know how I usually have quick phone calls with my family? I'll continue the conversation when they hang up.' Stephanie smiled at her brilliant plan.

Tabbie leaned against the wall, just inside the bedroom door. 'Or you could come home instead of staying with Jason.'

'But that would be boring.' Stephanie closed her books. 'I'm living on the wild side.'

'Just tell me you'll be safe. You know Mum is okay with you ringing at any time of night.'

'Maybe they'd be okay with you ringing, but I'd be stretching the friendship if I rang at four in the morning. Anyway, Jason loves me. He won't let anything bad happen.' Stephanie shivered when she looked into her best friend's concerned eyes.

Her mum rang that afternoon while the girls were watching TV, as if on cue.

'Steph, it's your Mum,' Francine called.

Stephanie jumped up almost too quickly and took the phone. 'Hi.'

Francine was preparing dinner in the kitchen, so Stephanie lingered near the kitchen doorway.

'Yeah, school's pretty hard. Work is busy.'

Stephanie looked up to see Francine watching her.

'Ah huh, yeah, mmm, sure.'

She was quiet for a moment while her mother lectured her on getting enough sleep.

'Yeah. Is April there?'

Stephanie smiled at Francine and turned to look out the window. 'Hi, April. How's gym?'

Nodding silently, Stephanie listened as April relayed the story of how she'd just missed out on getting into the gymnastics competition team.

'Will you come visit soon?' April asked.

'Sure, I will. Okay, bye.' She waited for the hang-up clink, and then she continued. 'Oh, April, can you put Mum back on?'

Breathe. Relax. Just get the right words out. 'Mum, I wanted to talk to you about something.' Stephanie quieted her voice, speaking just loud enough for Francine to hear.

'I was out with Jason last night and it was getting late, so I stayed over. Is that okay with you?' She waited a moment, then continued. 'I know. Uh-huh.'

She paused once more. 'So you're okay with me staying again? ...Yeah, I know you trust him... Mm, I am lucky to have found him. Thanks heaps, Mum. Bye.' She smiled while her heart thudded. *Did it! That was easy.*

Stephanie returned to the lounge without looking at Francine. With her heart thudding in her chest, a smirk found her lips as a knot formed in her stomach.

'Steph, how did you go?' Francine walked into the lounge room. 'Did you talk to your mother about staying at Jason's?'

'Yeah, she said it's fine.' Stephanie glanced at Francine, then back to the TV to avoid eye contact.

'Just be careful, okay.'

Stephanie nodded.

'Tabbie, dinner is in the oven. Could you make sure it doesn't burn?' Francine picked up her handbag and keys. 'I have to pop out to see a friend. I'll be back in an hour or so.' The door closed behind her.

'You're getting a bit too good at lying, don't you think?' Tabbie spat the words.

'Don't go getting all judgmental on me now.'

'I'm not judging you, just stating a fact. Lying isn't the right thing to do. Wouldn't it be better to 'fess up and tell the truth?'

A guilty rush came over Stephanie. Her face burned as she stared through the television. When the tension got too thick, she left to find comforting isolation in her bedroom. She turned her music up and lay down, exhausted and still queasy from the alcohol. *How am I going to make it through the week?*

Outside, the blue sky was fast becoming a deep, inky black but she didn't want to leave her room for food. She wanted to fill herself by replaying moments with Jason instead. He'd been half asleep this morning. He would have taken her home if she'd let him wake up a bit.

'Hey, sorry if I upset you before.' Tabbie creaked the door open slowly.

'You were just being honest. Apparently something I could get better at.'

Tabbie smiled.

'I know you're right. I'm stuffing up, aren't I?'

'You need to study more if you want to pass.' Tabbie half-shook her head.

'I'm too tired most of the time.' Stephanie rubbed her eyes.

'Have you looked for another job?'

'Haven't had time.'

'Maybe I could help you find one.'

'I'll get to it, eventually.'

'What are you doing with all that money?'

'Yeah, I do have a bit in the bank.' Stephanie smiled. 'Let's go shopping tomorrow after work. I'll buy you some new clothes—a peace offering.'

'What about school?'

'Stuff school.'

     Spiralling Out of Control

'I can't, Steph. And you shouldn't either. We've got millions of assignments to do.' Tabbie swung the door open further.

'I guess. It was just a thought. You're too good. You do all the right things. I'm going to bed.' She forced a yawn. 'Heaps tired.'

'What about dinner?' Tabbie asked.

'Nah, too tired tonight. Can you tell your mum for me?'

Stephanie's stomach took another dive into a pit of nausea. Was it even possible to change the past and make it right? She pulled on her pyjamas, thinking of Tabbie. How had their close-knit friendship drifted a universe apart? Moving back hadn't brought them back in sync like she'd hoped. Finding no answers, she slid into a tangle of lustful dreams.

Chapter Twenty-Four

'LET'S TAKE IT FOR A TEST DRIVE,' Stephanie suggested.

Jason stood in front of a small red hatchback with $1000 on the windscreen.

'Why? I'd have to get a loan to buy it.'

Today, March the seventh, Jason turned eighteen. He'd passed his driving test before leaving Toowoomba, which led Stephanie to a crazy idea. She wanted to blow him away with the most awesome gift on the planet. A car would be sure to win her the most-fantastic-girlfriend-in-the-world award.

'Surprise!' She clapped then threw her arms out to the sides. 'Happy Birthday! I'm buying you a car.'

'No way! You can't buy me a car.'

'Why not? I love you.' It was the first time she'd said those three words. They rolled off her tongue as natural as a breath. *I am so totally in love with you.*

They took the car for a test drive and after a quick transaction, Jason drove it back to his apartment.

He stopped the car and rubbed the dash. 'Hey babe, you know I really love the car and all, but it's my eighteenth, you know, and everyone wants to take me out clubbing.'

'But I can't come.'

'Yeah, I know. But come up to my room for a while. Let me thank you.'

'What? You want to take me to bed, then you plan to go out and leave me.' She clenched her fists.

'No, I'll drop you home first.'

'It's your birthday. I'm your girlfriend. I want to celebrate with you.'

'We can celebrate now.' He put his arm around her shoulders.

'I mean tonight as well.'

'Too bad you aren't eighteen.'

'Yeah, too bad,' Stephanie hissed through clenched teeth, pushing his arm away. 'Take me home.'

'Oh, babe, don't be like that.'

'Take me home.'

'Come on. Come upstairs.'

'Fine, I'll walk.' Stephanie climbed out of the car and slammed the door.

'See you when you cool down, babe.'

'Don't bother!' Her hands trembled, her face flamed. The path bounced in front of her tear-pooled eyes. *Such an idiot.* She couldn't believe she'd just spent all her money on a boyfriend who'd rather go out with everyone else on his birthday. *It's over. I can't do this anymore.*

Sadness, emptiness, and fear swallowed her. Stephanie concentrated on putting one foot in front of the other, counting the steps to shush her sobs. She crossed the road hearing screeching tyres and a horn blast. Her heart flapped around in the hollow pit of her chest. She was shaking by the time she arrived at the Morays.

'Steph!' Tabbie opened the door. 'Oh my goodness, you look like a train wreck! What happened? What's he done to you?'

'Nothing. Well, not nothing. But Jason hasn't done anything to me. He just doesn't want to be with me. It's his birthday.'

'What? Slow down. Weren't you going to look at cars with him?'

'We did. I bought him one.' Stephanie sniffled.

Tabbie grabbed the box of tissues and handed her one. 'And then he made you walk home? What a creep!'

'No, but I got so angry, I yelled at him and left.' Stephanie sat on the couch.

'Why? What were you so angry about?'

'He's going clubbing.'

'You can't go though.' Tabbie shook her head slowly.

'I know. But I wanted to celebrate with him, and he chose his friends over me.'

'Oh, Steph.' Tabbie wrapped consoling arms around her.

Throughout the following week, Stephanie ignored Jason's phone calls. The constant lump in her throat and thudding in her hollow chest were a reminder of who she'd become. *What was I thinking, dating a senior? Now a university student.* The weekend came and Stephanie clung on with painful hope, wanting Jason to turn up at work. A grey blanket fell over her when he didn't show.

She wanted him to make more of an effort if they were going to stay together. *Oh, who am I trying to kid?* The following week there were no messages, no calls and no visits. She saw Tabbie through bitter, envious eyes, willing her own life to be simple and innocent. She sat her mid-semester exams and handed in half-finished assignments. She even wagged school to avoid the teachers.

By Easter, it had been four weeks since she'd seen Jason.

With threats of Stephanie not having a job when she returned, George and Bridget eventually agreed with her request for time off. She boarded the plane to Toowoomba on her first day of school holidays with counterfeit happiness. Her mother asked about school and Tabbie and Jason. Stephanie shut most of the questions down, avoiding any sincere answers. Even though her father had the week off, he wasn't present the few times he was in the house.

  Spiralling Out of Control

'I've got state clubs coming up.' April beamed with excitement.

'I knew you'd end up getting in the team. You're thinner than you were when I left. How on earth do you have the energy to keep training?'

'But I look good, hey?'

'You look skinny,' Stephanie said, eyeing April up and down.

'Skinny is good.'

'Healthy is better.'

'Maybe you should lose a bit.'

'April!' Stephanie gasped.

'What?'

'I can't believe you just said that.'

'You've put on weight since you left. You shouldn't eat so much.'

'Shut up!' What is her problem?

The few conversations she had with her father felt strained. She thought back to her primary school days when he was her hero. Now a canyon had grown between them and she didn't know when it had happened.

'Here, Steph.' Her mother handed her a small wrapped box.

'But it's weeks 'til my birthday.'

'Only a few. We didn't want you to go without giving you an early present.'

'Thank you. I doubt there'll be a whole lot of celebrating back in Sydney.'

'What makes you say that?' her father asked.

'It's just…' Stephanie ran words through her mind about Jason, but didn't dare speak them.

'Is it time to come back? Remember, we did say it was only a trial. Maybe you should move back.' Her mother nodded.

'It's all fine. Just not the same as celebrating with your own family.' A flush of nostalgia warmed her hollow inside. 'But at the same time, I can't wait to get back to Sydney.'

'Have you forgotten something?' Tabbie asked, as they walked through the airport.

'No, I think I've got everything.'

'I mean…' Tabbie pulled a face and pointed at herself.

'You had your hair done or something?'

'No, it's just—'

'What? Just tell me, Tabbie.'

'Did you forget my birthday?'

'No! No way. I've never forgotten your birthday. How could I have?'

'You really did forget it?'

'Yeah. Sorry.' Stephanie pulled at her fingernails.

'I thought you might have been planning to surprise me or something.'

'So, so sorry, Tabbie.'

'Are those earrings new?'

'Yeah.' Stephanie stopped, knowing her next words were going to fall hard. 'Mum and Dad gave me an early birthday present.'

'Oh.'

Stephanie skipped ahead a couple of steps, turning to face her friend. 'I'll make it up to you. Let's go out tonight.'

'We've got school tomorrow.'

'It doesn't have to be late.'

'No. Don't worry about it.' Tabbie continued walking, leaving Stephanie to catch up.

Stephanie watched the sun dropping in the western sky as Francine drove them home in silence. She'd really let her friend down. She couldn't lose Tabbie's friendship. If she did, she'd be all alone again.

School returned and Stephanie had to take her head out of the sand and face the fact she was failing.

Each teacher gave her some personal input…

'Your grades have slipped.'

So what!

'We need to call your parents.'

No.

'Stephanie, you've always been a great student here. What's changed?'

Whoopee, a lot has changed.

'Would you like us to organise a tutor?'

'Okay.' Stephanie agreed with a sweet smile, having no intention of following through.

Nights of falling asleep on a wet pillow and mornings of puffy eyes filled the weeks that followed. The silence from Jason echoed through her life.

'Happy birthday!' Tabbie burst into Stephanie's bedroom with helium balloons and a small gold foil box. 'Thank you.' Stephanie's eyes welled up and overflowed.

'Here.' Tabbie passed her tissues. 'You've done enough crying.'

'I can't believe you've done this for me when I totally forgot your birthday.'

'Forget it. It's in the past.' Tabbie handed Stephanie a small box. 'Just enjoy yours.'

'Do you want to ditch school for the day with me?'

'No, I can't. I've got a quiz today. Everyone at school knows it's your birthday. You'll have a great time, you'll see.'

Stephanie pulled the lid off the small box. A silver bracelet with a small charm in the shape of a cross gleamed up at her. 'It's really pretty. Thank you!'

Friends with bunches of helium balloons met her at the school entrance. The sudden influx of affection encouraged her. But it was nothing more than a band-aid, temporarily covering the wound Jason had left. Underneath, rejection and abandonment seeped into her mood. She plastered a smile on her face anyway.

Chapter Twenty-Five

'Sweet sixteen, hey?' Jason waited at the gate after school.

'And never been kissed.' Stephanie smiled. The surprise momentarily deleted her memory of how infuriated she was.

'Much.' Jason laughed as he swung her around, kissing her again and again.

'It's been forever since I've seen you!' Her pain rose up and she slammed a fist into his chest.

'Yeah, sorry. Why didn't you return my calls?'

'Gee, you must have tried a total of three times.' Stephanie raised her eyebrows.

'No. It would've been way more than that.'

Stephanie shook her head, focusing on ants carrying a twig along the kerb.

'Guess I've been into partying and clubbing. Time just got away.' He pulled her hand and she followed without resistance. 'Let me make it up to you.'

'Jason! So, you think it's all okay, just like that?' She stopped, and kicked at the paving. 'I thought we were over.'

'Come here, babe, I have something for you.'

Her feet froze, cemented to the path.

'Hop in.' Jason opened the passenger door for her then sauntered around to the driver's side and climbed in.

'Here, happy birthday.'

She was lured into the car by the gift box he held. Sitting beside him, she opened the gift. A pair of long chandelier-style earrings. 'They're beautiful!'

He passed her another gift. 'And I got you this.'

She lifted the lid, 'Oh.' She closed the box immediately, not wanting to pull the sexy red lingerie out while school kids were walking past.

'Do you like it?'

'I guess so. Just wasn't expecting it.'

'But wait.' He reached into his pocket. 'I also got some of this, for both of us to celebrate your birthday.'

'What's that?'

'Es.' He dipped his head. 'Ecstasy.'

'Isn't that dangerous?'

'Only if you get the cheap stuff, or you don't know the dealer—some of them are crooks.'

'So, you know the dealer, paid top dollar and you have the police report to confirm you didn't buy from a crook?'

'Come on, babe, don't stress over it. It's just a bit of fun.' He grabbed the packet from her hands. 'But that's for this weekend. For now, there's one more.'

'What else?' She narrowed her eyes. 'I would have been happy with just the earrings, and a huge apology.'

He looked up. 'Ouch. Felt that.'

'It's been weeks. Plus, Easter back in Toowoomba.'

'Oh, you went back. I didn't. Decided to stay here.'

'I thought we were over.'

'I did too, for a while.'

'So, what's going on?' Stephanie swallowed the lump in her throat. 'Where have you been?'

'Like I said, I've been clubbing heaps. Like heaps.' He shook his head. 'But I really miss you.'

A tear dripped from her face and rolled down her hand.

'Sorry.' He leaned over and pushed his lips against hers. 'Can you forgive me?'

No, but I don't know how to say no to you. Her lips moved in sync with his, returning his kisses.

'I want to take you out clubbing for your birthday. I've got this friend who can make you an ID.'

'You mean a fake ID?'

'Yeah, of course.'

'But that's illegal.'

'Come on, babe. Dress up a bit, and no one will ever find out. I'll get one of the girls to help you.'

'Are you sure about this?' Stephanie flicked the rear vision mirror around, assessing her reflection.

'Yeah, it's been great, but going to the clubs without you is kind of… well, I'd rather you were there with me.'

'You're serious.' Stephanie rested back against the seat.

'Yeah, let's go, they're waiting for us.'

She started to mull over the privileges of having a fake ID. It could be fun.

He parked outside a three-storey building.

'On the top floor.' He led her to the stairs.

'Your friend lives here?' Stephanie followed Jason like an obedient lamb.

'Doubt it. It's just where they agreed to meet us.'

Half the railing was missing on the external stairs, and graffiti coloured the bricks.

'Hi.' A man opened the door. 'You must be Steph?'

'Yes.' There were no more introductions.

Stranger Man guided her towards another room where she met Stranger Girl. Stranger Girl showed her to a room set up like a dressing room without a mirror. 'I'll do your make-up first, then I'll do your hair and we'll pop this top on.'

Stephanie sat in the chair. Stranger Girl fussed over her for twenty minutes or so before handing her the top. 'Here.'

'Oh, ah … can I use the bathroom to change?'

'No, here is fine.' Stranger Girl didn't move.

Facing the wall, Stephanie changed her top. Stranger Girl took her back to the other room where Jason waited with Stranger Man. Steph stood in front of a blue background staring down the lens of a flashing camera.

'Whoo-hoo! You look hot, babe,' Jason said.

Steph blinked away the spots ingrained by the flash, while Stranger Girl sent her back into the dressing room. With the door closed, she changed in privacy and returned to Jason wearing her school uniform. 'Where did they go?'

'They're in the end room.'

'Shouldn't we say goodbye?'

'No, let's go.'

'What about the ID?'

'They'll post it to me. It'll be ready by the weekend.' He draped his arm around her shoulders and led her back downstairs.

'I'd better get to work,' she said.

'You might shock them if you walk in looking like that. They're used to fifteen-year-old Stephanie, not eighteen-year-old Steph.'

'Do I look that much different?'

'You're hot, babe.' He unlocked the car. 'Let's go out for dinner.'

Once in the car, she twisted the rear vision mirror and smiled with satisfaction. She looked eighteen. 'But what about work?'

'Tell them you can't get there.'

'What if they sack me?'

'I'll get you another job. I know heaps of girls working as waitresses and glassys, and they're getting paid way more than what you get.'

George's gruff voice boomed down the phone when Stephanie rang The Tiger's Eye. 'Why can't you come in?'

'It's my sixteenth birthday and I was—'

'We've given you enough warnings,' he shouted. 'If you expect to take a day off for your birthday, you can find another job.'

'My boyfriend wants to take me out to dinner—'

'Are you coming in or not?'

Stephanie looked towards Jason. His eyes filled with warmth. 'No.'

'If you don't come in tonight, don't come back at all.'

'Really?' She bit a frayed fingernail.

'Yes.' The phone slammed in her ear.

She ran into the lounge room and jumped onto Jason's lap, laughing.

'That didn't sound good. What are you so happy about?'

'Where were those glassy jobs?'

'Did he sack you?'

'No.' She smiled. 'But he will, if I don't show up tonight.'

'Is that a yes to dinner?'

'Where are we going?' she asked. 'Are some of my clothes still here?'

'Yeah, your stuff is in the top drawer.'

Stephanie skipped into his bedroom and opened the drawer. He'd shoved her clothes in with his things.

'I've only got this.' She held up a crushed pair of jeans and a top. 'Maybe I should go home first, grab some clothes and tell them what's happening.'

'No, don't go. Those will be fine.'

'Are you sure?'

Jason nodded.

'Okay, I'll give Francine a call.' She smiled looking out the window, as she picked up the phone, filled with anticipation for the night ahead. She left a message and they caught a train into the city. Jason led her to a restaurant with Harbour views. If she'd worn a puffy dress, she would've felt like a princess. It was her first time in a posh restaurant without her parents. Jason leaned across the table. Her heart fluttered, anticipating a kiss at the perfect moment. But there was no kiss.

'Babe, I'm a little short. The ID cost more than I thought. I have to wait for Mum and Dad to return from China for my next allowance. Have you got some cash on you?'

'Gee, thanks for the birthday dinner.' Quick way to ruin a great night.

'Hey, babe, I'm sorry. I'll pay you back.'

'Yeah?'

'Sure.' He reached across the table to cover her hand with his. 'Don't ruin a great night. I didn't realise it was going to cost so much here.'

Guess I'm just overreacting. 'Okay.' She opened her purse and pulled out her card to pay.

Chapter Twenty-Six

Stephanie welcomed the chance to breathe now she didn't have to work each night. Hanging out with her friends and sleeping long nights left her with boundless energy.

She walked out of school on Friday to see Jason leaning against his car.

'Got it.' He flapped an envelope in the air.

'How does it look?' Stephanie bit her lip as she slid into the front seat.

'Great. No one would ever question it. See for yourself.'

She peeled opened the envelope flap and peeked in, then smiled. 'It's good.'

'It's great,' he said. 'Looks like we're going out tonight.'

'What will I wear?'

'You've got time to shop. We won't be going out 'til after eight.'

'I'll get Tabbie to come with me,' she said, thinking out loud. 'She should be out soon. Can we wait for her?'

'Yeah, sure.'

Stephanie jumped out of the car and rushed back towards school fence line, when she saw her. 'Hey, Tabbie,' she called. 'Come shopping with me.'

'Are you asking or telling?'

'Can you?'

'I guess,' Tabbie replied. 'We'll be back in time for youth group, won't we?'

'Sure, Jason's parked up here.' Stephanie pointed.

'So it's all roses again then?'

'Yeah.'

Tabbie screwed up her nose as they neared Jason's car. 'Is he coming shopping as well?'

'I'm sure he'll drop us off. He's not into shopping.'

Tabbie laughed, and climbed into the back seat.

'To the shopping centre, thanks, driver,' Stephanie said.

The girls shared milkshakes and ice creams. They both tried on beautiful clothes, and ugly clothes. Then Stephanie tried on some scanty clothes.

'Eww, that's trashy. Where would you wear it anyway?' Tabbie screwed up her nose.

'It's how they all dress.' Steph didn't want to fill Tabbie in on the whole fake ID and nightclubbing adventure she was about to embark on.

'Who? The girls at those parties you've been going to?'

'Yeah, I just feel so out of place and young.'

'You're sixteen, Steph.' Tabbie pulled out something more conservative. 'Here. What about this, and try this top.'

'Okay.' *Yeah, heaps more comfortable, but not really nightclub worthy.* Steph stepped out from the change room.

'Yeah, I like it,' Tabbie said.

'Me too.' Steph smiled. 'I knew there was a reason I brought you. Why don't you get something too?'

'Ah… not from this shop.' Tabbie looked from rack to rack. 'I don't have uni parties to go to. Where would I wear clothes like this?'

'Maybe you could come with us to a party sometime,' Steph suggested as she paid for both sets of clothes.

'Three's a crowd.'

Tabbie was right. Stephanie knew she'd made the suggestion in a blissful moment. Yes, it would be nice, but it wouldn't be much fun having Tabbie tag along to a party. Plus, Stephanie wasn't ready to let her best friend see the parties Jason had introduced her to.

'Let's find you something. Next shop is your choice.' Steph's insides warmed as she played the generosity game and bought Tabbie some new clothes. 'Do you want to come back to Jason's for a bit? He can drive you home?'

'Are you going back there now?' Tabbie frowned.

'Yeah, we're going out tonight.'

'I'll get the train home.' Tabbie bit her lip. 'I'll be fine.'

'I've had so much fun this afternoon. Please come back and have some dinner with us,' Steph said. 'We're probably getting pizza. Please say you'll stay.'

'Okay. But I do want to get home for youth group. Can we eat as soon as we get there?'

'Sure.'

When they arrived at Jason's, laughter spilled down as they walked up the external stairs. Stephanie spoke to Tabbie over her shoulder. 'He must have some friends over.'

'Should I just go home?' Tabbie stopped halfway up the stairs. 'If I get the next bus, it'll still be light when I get home.'

'It'll be fine, Tabbie. Just come in for a minute.'

'Alright, but if it's not okay, I'm ringing Mum.'

'Okay.' Stephanie opened the door to find a room full of people dressed for a night out. She inhaled, feeling more than a little uncomfortable herself.

'Babe, how did you go?' Jason jumped up, grabbing two beer bottles.

'Is it okay if I use your bathroom?' Tabbie asked.

'Go ahead,' he pointed, 'down there, to your left.'

     Spiralling Out of Control

Stephanie grabbed his hand and dragged him into his bedroom. 'You didn't tell me everyone was coming over.'

'You didn't ask.' He stroked her cheek. 'Did you get some clothes?'

She linked her fingers through his and whispered, 'Yes, but please don't say anything to Tabbie about nightclubs or fake ID.'

'Sure, babe.' He passed her a half-full beer, holding her close until her anger settled. 'Have a drink, babe.'

She took a mouthful, heard the toilet flush, and rushed out to meet Tabbie in the hallway. She turned back to Jason. 'Are we still getting pizza?'

'Yeah, we'll order them later.'

'Can we get some now?' she asked. 'I invited Tabbie to hang around for dinner.'

'Great, Tabbie, grab a beer from the fridge,' he said, and walked away.

'Steph, are you drinking?' Tabbie stared at the beer bottle.

'It's only a beer.' She twisted the bottle in her hands. 'And Jason's had half of it.'

'But, you're only sixteen. I didn't think you liked it.'

'Tabbie, don't get so stressed. I'm careful. Like… it's just one.'

'Hi, I'm Jules.' A girl introduced herself as she pushed past them.

'I'm Steph, and this is Tabbie.'

Jules waved and kept walking.

'I think I'll ring Mum,' Tabbie said.

'You won't tell her about the drinks, will you?'

'Are you trying to hide it?'

'No.' Stephanie shook her head and put the bottle down. 'Just rather your parents didn't know.'

'Okay, I won't tell them.'

'Thanks.'

Tabbie rang her mum while Stephanie took another swig of the beer.

'Can we wait downstairs?' asked Tabbie. 'Mum's only ten minutes away.'

'Sure. You don't want a cuppa or a soft drink?'

'Stephanie.' Tabbie's voice hit a higher pitch than normal. 'I want to get out of here.'

'Okay, okay. I'm coming.' Stephanie sculled the rest of the beer, grabbed one of the shopping bags from Tabbie, and walked her downstairs.

'Promise me Jason doesn't drink and drive.'

'No, he gets a taxi if he goes anywhere after a couple.'

'Promise me, no matter what time of day it is, if you are ever in trouble, you'll ring us.'

'I'll be fine,' she insisted.

'Promise me.' Tabbie held Stephanie's hand and stood so close their noses almost touched.

'Okay.' She wanted to back away.

'Mum and Dad would rather know that you're safe than have anything happen to you. You're like one of our family now.'

'Okay, okay. I'll call if I need them. But everything will be fine.' Stephanie's head tingled, her mind wandered, and she hoped Francine was close.

Woah. It must have been a heavy beer.

'Are you okay?' Tabbie asked.

'Yeah, just thinking about what you said before.' Stephanie sidestepped to steady herself. 'Oh good, here's your mum.'

'Yeah.' Tabbie squinted. 'Be careful!'

'Bye.' She hugged her friend, waved and ran back upstairs before Francine stopped.

'Hey, babe.' Jason met her in the doorway. 'How are you feeling?'

'Great!' She laughed.

'It's good, isn't it?'

'What?'

'That feeling. We're going to have the best night.'

'Steph, this is Jules. She's going to help you with your make-up.'

'We met in the hallway,' said Jules.

Stephanie smiled, sure she looked like the prize school dork. Heat rushed up her neck at the sight of Jules' giraffe-like legs. Could she learn how to grow legs like that as well as learn make-up tips?

'It'll only take a minute.' Jules drank from her stubbie. 'Do you wanna grab another drink before we start?'

'I'll just get a water.' The beer had gone straight to her head. 'Jason will probably bring me another soon.'

She followed Jules into the bathroom with flying-floating-fuzzy-dizzy steps. Watching in the mirror, she was enthralled by every minuscule detail in the reflection. Everything fascinated her. Jules' words echoed as she explained her way through applying make-up and showed how easy it was to style hair in minutes. It was all new and different to how she'd worn make-up for dancing.

'Wow, that's really cool how you do that. Thanks for making me up.' Stephanie laughed.

'Easy as. You'll be able to do it next time.' Jules packed up her make-up. 'See you later. I've got to get to work.'

'You aren't coming out?'

'No, not tonight, but I'll be there tomorrow if you can face up for two nights in a row.'

'You're so beautiful. See you tomorrow night.' Stephanie hugged Jules goodbye with a beaming smile.

She found her new clothes and watched herself in the mirror as she changed. An extraordinarily wonderful sensation rippled through her body, like she could walk on water. She laughed, looking at everything with a new never-seen-it-before kind of amazement.

'What's so funny?' Jason walked in.

'Let's go!' she said, shaking her head. 'I'm ready.'

'Yeah, me too.' He laughed, looking down at his shorts and T-shirt. 'Okay, maybe I'll get changed.'

'I'm so in love with you,' she cooed.

They fell onto the bed snogging, until Stephanie's stomach groaned. 'What about pizza?'

'We'll get some out. You look hot.' He looked into his wallet. 'Hey, babe, have you got some cash?'

'Yeah.' She grabbed some money from her purse and handed it to him.

She wrung her hands then shook them like they were burning up. 'Can you carry my purse for me? I'd rather not carry anything.'

'Sure, babe.' He shoved her small coin purse containing her cash, cards and ID into his pocket and joined the crowd in the lounge room. 'Okay everyone, let's go. Party time!'

Chapter Twenty-Seven

THE BUS PULLED INTO AN UNKNOWN DESTINATION. Steph relaxed, confident her ID would work. She looked through adoring eyes at all of Jason's friends. She linked her arm in his, unable to hide her excitement. This was going to be the best night! She had the best boyfriend in the world.

'Still feel great?' Jason asked.

'Yes! Better than great. I feel amazing!'

He laughed. 'It's the Es.'

'But I didn't take any.' She leaned away from him.

'I put it in your beer.'

'You drugged me?' She spat the words in his face.

He covered her mouth with his hand. 'Shh, babe, it's not like that. I wanted to surprise you for your birthday. Let's celebrate!'

Her anger dissolved in his smile. She laughed and hugged him. When they arrived at the nightclub, the bouncer looked carefully, shifting his eyes from Steph to her fake ID over and over. He nodded and handed the ID back, stamped her wrist and let her walk through. *Piece of cake!*

'Gee, this place seems quiet,' she said.

'It won't be in an hour or so. Wait and see,' Jason said.

'Why did we come so early?'

'To save money,' he said. 'They charge you to get in later.'

'Here, can you put my ID in my purse?' Steph linked her arm through his. 'I'm hungry.'

'Yeah, me too.' He took her to the bar and slipped the ID into his jeans. 'Want some corn chips?'

'That'd be great. But right now, I need to dance.' Steph moved to the music and found her way to the dance floor.

She danced and grooved first with Jason, then with anyone who'd dance with her, then she danced alone. She loved the lights flashing, the pounding music and the amazing rush from the Ecstasy. The floor filled within a couple of songs. She continued to dance, bumping into people in every direction.

'Having fun?' Jason came to dance with her for a song.

'I'm having the best time!' She threw her arms around his neck. Nothing mattered more than kissing him full on the mouth right there and then.

'Hey, hey, cool down a bit.' He pulled back. 'Wait until we get home.'

'This place is wild!'

'Steph, I'm hungry. Want to come outside for a bit and get something to eat?'

'No, I just want to dance.' She twirled away from him, out of control, and continued to dance ecstatically with anyone on the dance floor.

She blinked. It seemed as if a blanket had been lifted. Steph shivered. She looked for a familiar face, but she saw a sea of strangers. The dance floor was nearly bare. Her mouth was dryer than a desert. She asked for water at the bar.

'Three dollars, thanks,' the bartender replied.

'Oh, I'll go and get some money.' Steph turned around, searching for Jason. He was nowhere. She waited outside the men's toilets, but the only faces that appeared were strangers.

He's left me! How could he leave her there? She walked out of the nightclub and into the street. Fear crept into her thoughts. She looked up the street and saw blank, unknown faces. She turned and walked the other way.

'Hey, baby, looking for me?' asked a greasy-unbuttoned-heavily-gold-chained guy smoking a cigarette.

Steph trembled, turning to run, not knowing the area or where Jason would have gone. *Jason, where are you?* A tear seeped from her eye.

Maybe she should go back to the club. She turned and ran back, but the street was full of neon-lit nightclub entrances and she had no idea which club they'd been in. Steph walked towards one entrance, taking short breaths and showed her wrist stamp.

They laughed and asked for a twenty-dollar cover charge. She hung her head and backed out onto the street again. Steph tried again at the next door, but they also asked for a cover charge and ID.

'My boyfriend has my money and ID.' She pulled a finger to her mouth to chew a fingernail. 'He might be inside. Do you mind if I check?'

'Good story, love. No entry,' replied the bouncer.

Steph walked away, shaking her head. Perspiration dripped under her arms and a pit of nausea churned in her empty stomach. She sat on the pavement, leaning against the brick wall with her head resting on her knees, and cried.

'Hey, babe.' She looked up. It was Jason. 'Let's go.' He grabbed her by the hand and ushered her into a taxi.

The wild time, the buzz, the excitement all seemed hazy now.

'I'm hungry,' she said.

'Can we go through the next Maccas drive-through?' Jason asked the taxi driver.

Stephanie began to cry again.

'It's okay, babe,' he soothed. 'I'm here, you're okay.'

She rested on his shoulder. 'I'm tired.' She nestled in and gave way to the fatigue that pulled her.

Stephanie woke up in Jason's bed, fully clothed, unable to swallow. 'Ahh, yuck. I'm so thirsty.'

'Here.' Jason passed her a bottle of water.

'Gah. That was horrible. Really needed that water. What time did we get back?'

''Bout five.'

'What time is it now?'

'Midday.'

She sat up and thought for a moment, trying to sequence the previous night's events.

'You left me there.' A sliver of memory came back to her.

'You were dancing. You didn't want to come with me.'

'I didn't know anyone there.' She began to cry. 'Where were you?'

'I would have come back in if you'd waited.' He rolled over. 'You were having such a wild time.'

'Anything could have happened to me!' she shouted.

'Shh, you'll wake Axel.'

'I'm going home.' She sat up.

'What, back to Toowoomba?'

'No, back to Tabbie's.'

'Hey, don't go all psycho on me. Stay with me, babe.' He grabbed her hand. 'I've got another round ready for tonight.'

'Again?'

'Yeah, it's your birthday weekend.' He pulled her back onto the bed. 'Come on, babe. You've got nothing else on today. It was fun, wasn't it? You looked like you were having a ball.'

'Promise you won't leave me again.'

'I promise,' he said with a smile. 'Am I forgiven?'

She sighed and shook her head, but caved. 'Yes.'

'I loved having you there with me last night.'

Once again, his charm had melted her good judgment. He said, 'Jump', and she asked, 'How high?'

 Spiralling Out of Control

They drifted off to sleep again, tangled in each other's limbs. Steph woke up, craving hot potato chips. When she stood, every muscle in her body pulled.

'Ouch, my legs.' She collapsed on the couch.

'That's what happens when you dance all night.'

'Argh!'

'Tell me more about your past life, when you were a dancer.'

'No.' Steph snapped. 'I don't want to talk about it.'

'Why not?'

'Because it…' she thought for a moment. 'I don't know. I just made a decision that I never wanted to dance again or talk about it again.'

'Why?'

'Can't remember.' Steph's mind whirled as she tried to remember why she stopped dancing. It all seemed fuzzy. It happened because of the move to Toowoomba.

Jason moved to the couch and channel-surfed. Steph sat beside him, easing her legs onto his lap. 'I had such a horrible time in Toowoomba. Most of the time, I wished Mum and Dad never moved there. But if I hadn't moved there, I would never have met you.'

'Huh? What was that, babe?' Jason murmured.

'Don't worry.' She winced as she shifted her legs forward.

'Yeah, I think you should dance. You could make some good money dancing.'

'You think?' The scent of night air drifted through the windows.

'Yeah. I might grab a shower. We'll leave in half.'

'I'm still half asleep.' Steph yawned. 'Can we stay in?'

'Come on, babe. Everyone is going out again. They'll be waiting for us.'

'Okay, okay. Why do you get to make all the decisions around here?'

'I don't. But I make the best decisions.'

Steph looked in the mirror and applied her make-up the way Jules had shown her. When she finished, she tilted her head in every direction, not sure if she was satisfied.

'How do I look?'

'Hot,' he said, eyeing her up and down. 'Babe, you always look hot, with or without all that stuff on your face.'

'But Jason…' She played with her hair. 'What if I don't look eighteen?'

'Babe, you look fine. They'll only ask questions if you look nervous. Walk in there with the confidence you had last night, and you'll be fine.'

'Okay, okay.' She turned back to the mirror and applied more eyeliner and another coat of mascara.

'Here.' He handed her a small tablet.

'Are you sure it's safe?'

'We've been through this, babe.' He placed it in her hand and opened two beers.

She swallowed, breaking out in a nervous sweat. That was the last she'd take. 'I don't want to take any more, okay?' Stephanie stood close to Jason, looking up with wide eyes.

'Are you serious?' he asked. 'You'll have as much fun tonight as you did last night.'

'I'm serious, Jason,' she said, with an assertive voice.

'I'll never force you to take anything. I love you.'

'That means no more spiking my drink, okay?'

'Okay. Let's get some KFC on the way. I was starving last night.'

Stephanie poured a large glass of water before they caught the train. The same incredibly amazing buzzing feeling swept over her again. Her steps sprung. She couldn't wait to get to the nightclub to let the beat move her body again.

It was déjà vu, except for a new security check to get past. Steph exuded over-confidence. She stood looking through the door as the bouncer took his time to check her ID, before letting her in. This time she placed her ID and some cash in her pocket—she didn't want a repeat of last night. A large group of Jason's friends were already at the club. She spotted Jules on the dance floor and ran out to meet her.

'I love this place,' Jules shouted over the music. 'They play the best dance mix here.'

'Yeah, it's great,' Steph said.

They occupied the dance floor song after song. Steph focused on Jules' glassy eyes. She was the only one who out-danced Steph.

'Need a drink?' Steph asked.

'Great!' Jules said.

'I'm getting a drink. Do you want one?'

'Great!' she said again.

Stephanie returned to the dance floor with two bottles of water, but Jules had disappeared. She spun around with the lights, looking in between the flashes, searching, hoping Jason was still there. She spun around again. *Ah, there he is.*

'Jason, thank goodness you're still here. Did you see where Jules went?'

'No.' He pulled her onto his lap. 'Come here for a bit, babe.'

They canoodled in between drinking water.

'Oh, get a room you two,' said a passer-by.

'Come and dance with me.' Stephanie dropped the empty water bottle on the table.

'No,' he said. 'I'd rather watch you dance.'

'Come on,' she pulled his hand. 'Just one.'

He smiled and followed her. After a while he retired to the table, but returned again within a few minutes. 'It's boring over there. Everyone else has gone. You want to keep dancing or go home?'

'I want to dance all night!'

'Couple more songs, then we'll go.'

They danced until the crowd started to dwindle. This time Steph stayed awake on the drive home and was shocked when Jason asked her to pay the sixty-five-dollar taxi fare. She handed over the money and said nothing.

That night, intimacy brought pleasure. *Why did I used to feel so dirty after making love with Jason, when now it feels like the most wonderful and natural thing to do?* She tucked the pillow under her head and sleep came immediately.

They were snapped awake by the phone ringing.

'Leave it.' Jason covered his head with the doona.

The phone stopped and then started ringing again.

'Ignore it,' he rolled over. 'Axel! Can you get that?'

After a brief silence, the phone began to ring once more.

'Someone really wants you,' Steph said. 'Don't think Axel is going to get it.'

'They can leave a message.' He squashed the pillow over his head.

Jason's mobile started ringing. He reached down to his jeans on the floor and pulled it out of his pocket, turning it off without looking at the caller ID.

Steph was now wide awake. Pain shot up her legs as she walked to the shower. Her muscles pulled worse than the day before. Her feet stung as the water washed her blisters. It had felt great to be in Jason's arms and in his bed. But now, standing in the shower, she wanted to wash away the familiar uneasy, disgusting feeling. The conflicting feelings confused her. *I have to get out of here.*

'See you later.' She kissed Jason and watched him fall asleep again before she left.

   Spiralling Out of Control

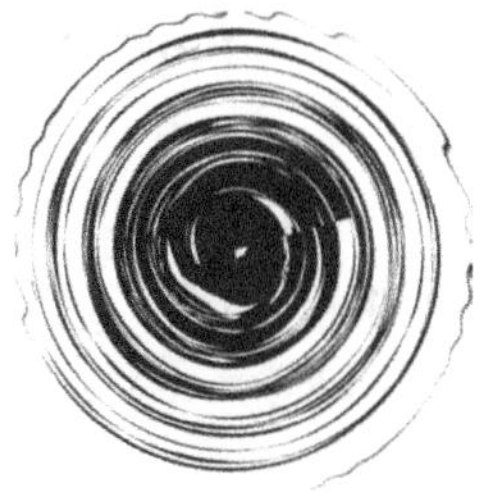

Chapter Twenty-Eight

STEPHANIE WALKED IN, closing the door behind her. Francine and Tom looked up from the TV.

'Hey, nice to see you,' Francine said. 'We've missed you the last few days.'

'Is Tabbie home?'

'She shouldn't be far away. Church should be finished by now.' Francine walked into the kitchen and turned the kettle on. 'Would you like a cuppa?'

'That'd be great. Coffee, please.'

'You look tired,' Francine said. 'Maybe you should spend a couple of nights back here.'

Steph sat on the couch and focused on the TV to avoid any pointed questions about her social life.

'How's work going, Tom?' she asked, to change the subject.

'Pretty good. It's a busy time of year.'

Steph was staring at the TV when the news headline caught her attention. Words flashed across the screen: "GIRL DEAD—VICTIM TO CLUBBING DRUG."

'Last night, the eighteen-year-old university student took the pill known as Ecstasy, leaving her family to swallow the bitterness.' The newsreader went on, but Steph focused on the photo, in the top corner of the screen. *Jules.*

'What are your plans for today?' Francine asked.

'Sorry.' Steph stood with trembling hands. 'I've just remembered something I've got to do.'

'Are you coming back for dinner? Do you want a lift?'

'No, I'll catch the bus. But thanks.'

'Will you be at Jason's. Do you want us to pick you up? Or should I get Tabbie to ring you later on?'

'Yeah, oh um, no.' Steph stopped in the doorway. 'No, don't worry about it. I'll call her.'

Steph took her aching legs and sprinted down the street to catch the next bus. She climbed the stairs at Jason's flat to find the door locked. No one came to quiet her pounding on the door. Her eyelids dropped, heavy with emotion. Leaning against the door, she drifted in and out of an abnormal slumber. Minutes blinked into an unknown amount of time.

'Hey, babe.'

She opened her eyes to find Jason's hand reaching towards her. She took it and let him pull her to her feet.

'How long have you been here?'

She snapped back to reality. 'Did you see?'

'What?' He unlocked the door.

'Jules—'

'What about her?'

'On the news…' She followed him inside.

'Was it on?' He mumbled a few choice words under his breath.

'You know?'

'Yeah, I got sick of the phone ringing. I answered it soon after you left.'

'I can't believe she's… gone.' Steph looked to Jason for comfort, but his face was blank.

'Me neither.' He slammed his fist against the wall.

'Jason,' she said in a small voice. 'Did Jules get hers from the same dealer you got ours?'

He looked at her with dark eyes, nodding.

'It could have been one of us.'

'Yep.'

'You said it was safe!'

'I thought it was.' He slammed the door closed. 'I believed them. I'm so glad we're both okay. I know that sounds horrible. I am sad she's gone, but—'

She pushed her hand on his mouth, smothering his words, wrapping herself around him. She needed comforting. He hugged and kissed her. Then he tightened his grip and lifted her up, continuing to kiss her as he carried her into his room. She knew he was comforting himself as much as he was comforting her.

Stephanie didn't go to school the next day. The pain in her legs, similar to a thousand stabbing knives, kept her on the couch. Grief consumed her. She didn't want to tell anyone she'd known Jules or how she'd known her. She had to hide it from Tabbie. If Tabbie found out, she'd accuse Steph of taking drugs as well. It was all too hard. On Tuesday, she decided to look for a job instead of going to school.

'What you up to? Are you thinking about leaving school?' Jason asked.

'No, I'm nearly out of money.' Stephanie opened the free local paper. 'But there's not much in here.'

'Here.' He passed her his mobile. 'Might be easier to search the internet.'

'Thanks. We spent so much on the weekend. Maybe you could get a job too, rather than spend all my money.'

'I've got too much study to get through to worry about a job. Just don't go getting one that makes you work crazy hours like The Tiger's Eye.' Jason lay back on the lounge, staring at the TV.

'Yeah, I don't think I could go back to that again.'

'Hey, hang off looking for a bit. I might be able to get you a job as a glassy.' He ambled into the bedroom and fished his hand in the pocket of a pair of jeans on the floor.

'Yeah?'

'Here, I got this cut for you.' He handed her a front door key.

She looked at him puzzled. *Is he asking me to move in?* She was too scared to ask.

'So you don't have to sit at the door if Axel or I are out.'

Stephanie gave up scrolling through jobs listed and went for a long walk. The glassy job was fast becoming an option. Disillusioned and hit by an exorbitant sorrow for Jules' family, she wound her way around the streets with no goal destination. Eventually she made her way back to Jason's as the sun was retiring and her stomach ached for food.

'Where have you been?' Tabbie was sitting on the top step when she returned.

'What are you doing here?'

'Mum said you came by on Sunday. But you haven't returned anyone's calls and you haven't been at school. Your mum and my mum want to know where you are. Mum knows you haven't been at school and wants you to ring her ASAP.'

'Whoa, hold on.' Stephanie opened the door. 'Back to Sunday.'

'You have your own key to Jason's now?' Tabbie's voice flounced with surprise. 'Have you moved in?'

'No, no—'

'Well, you haven't been home much.'

'Don't get all weird on me.' Steph was hit in the face with a wall of stale, musty, alcohol odour. She rushed to open up the windows. 'There's just been stuff going on because of my birthday—you know?'

'No, not really,' Tabbie lowered her head, glaring through her eyelashes. 'Mum said you ran out after the news came on TV. It was Jules that I met the other night, wasn't it?'

Stephanie clamped her mouth shut.

'And she's dead?' Tabbie opened her eyes wide. 'Who are these people that you're hanging out with? What are you doing with them? Are you really going out with *that* kind of guy?'

A clammy sweat hit Steph's body.

Tabbie gasped. 'Did you take that drug too?'

Stephanie looked at her best friend and swallowed, feeling her throat narrow. Unable to maintain eye contact, she looked at the floor.

'Are you going out to nightclubs as well?'

That was everything. Steph's gaze darted around the room. Tabbie knew everything. How could she have guessed it all?

'Oh, Steph.' Tabbie's voice softened. 'There's so much more for you.'

'What do you mean? How do you know?'

'I just know God loves you.'

'Don't go getting all religious on me now.'

'I don't think nightclubbing is the smartest thing to do. Come back home with me now, Steph. Please.'

'Jason's expecting me to be here when he gets back from uni.'

'Leave him a note. He can always come over to our house.'

The warmth in Tabbie's voice cradled Steph's guilt and grief. She sat down to write Jason a note.

> *Hi, Jason,*
>
> *How did you go finding me a job? Just popping over to see Tabbie for a while. Come over later if you want.*
>
> *S xx*

Tabbie leaned over her shoulder. 'You looking for work again?'

'Yeah, I'm almost out of money.'

'Have you tried Maccas or Woollies?'

'No, I'm hoping for a higher-paid job.' Stephanie put the pen down.

'Make sure they treat you better this time.'

'Yeah, for sure.' She grabbed her bag.

The girls caught an overcrowded bus home. Packed like sardines, they stood face to face in the aisle, swaying to the rhythm of the bus.

'Are you going to tell your mum anything?' Stephanie asked.

'She probably should know, but I won't say anything. That's up to you.'

'I'll leave it a bit, you know—I need to process it all first.'

'But what about your mum and dad? They're the ones you really need to talk to.'

'No way! They'd make me go back to Toowoomba. I'd rather die than have to go back there.' Steph's shoulders tensed with the sound of her own words about death.

'Well, you've got to call them. Mum might answer the phone instead of me and that conversation—'

'Okay, okay. You're right again. I'll ring. But I can't tell them everything. They'd freak.'

'It's up to you.' Tabbie looked through the window then back again. 'You tell what you want when you want. I may not agree with the way you're living right now, but I am here for you.'

Stephanie enjoyed a quiet night with the Morays. She rang her mother and spun a story about severe period pains and needing time off school to go to the doctor. She slept in her own bedroom, waking through the night in a shiver of sweat. Midweek, Stephanie followed Tabbie to school, but couldn't concentrate. Her mind was still stuck on Jules and the drug they'd all taken. She didn't understand what the teacher was talking about.

It was obvious she'd missed important schoolwork and had no idea how she would ever catch up. She flicked forward and backwards in her textbooks, trying to grasp the information.

By the end of the week, Jason hadn't called or visited. She was ready to give him a piece of her mind.

'Will you come to youth group with me tonight?' Tabbie asked, during their lunch break. 'You aren't working, and you don't have plans with Jason.'

                    Spiralling Out of Control

Steph looked into Tabbie's pleading eyes. This was important to her. 'Okay, just this time. Then will you stop asking me to come?' It would have to be better than sitting at home stewing.

'Agreed.' Tabbie smiled.

After the final bell, Steph saw Tabbie waiting outside her classroom. *She obviously thinks I'll escape and run away if she doesn't escort me to youth group.*

'Let's go,' Tabbie almost squealed.

The girls walked towards the school gates, Tabbie skipping every second step and Steph walking alongside with an artificial smile.

'Jason!' Steph ran to where he leaned against the schoolyard fence.

'Oh. Hi, Jason.' Tabbie rested a hand on her hip.

'Hello, Tabbie,' he said formally, tilting his head. 'Steph, I got you a job.'

'Really?' She jumped on the spot. 'Where? When do I start?'

'At The Groove. You start tonight.'

'Tonight?'

'Only until ten. If you want to try it out, they'll give you a trial tonight if we can get there by five.'

'Well that kind of sucks. I was looking forward to you coming tonight,' Tabbie said.

'I know. I'm really sorry. But I really want to try this job. I'm running out of cash.'

'Isn't The Groove a hotel in the city?' Tabbie touched Stephanie's shoulder.

'Yeah, that's the one.' Jason nodded.

'What will you be doing? Don't you have to be eighteen to work at hotels?'

'I'm sure that's just to serve drinks,' Steph said to Tabbie.

'How about you do a trial another night? Come with me tonight and think about it.' Tabbie looked at Jason. 'Surely they'll let her trial another night.'

'Maybe.' Jason shrugged. 'Or they'll just find someone else.'

'I've already decided, Tabbie. I'm going in tonight. Can you let your mum know about the trial? She doesn't have to know the details — just tell her it's in the city.'

'Be careful, Steph.' Tabbie whispered in her ear as they hugged goodbye.

'I will.' Steph smiled and turned away from Tabbie's concerned expression. When she was sitting beside Jason in the car, she asked, 'So what will I be doing? Is it a glassy job, like you said?'

'Yeah, just clearing glasses and plates from tables. They pay cash.'

'Is that legal? Aren't they meant to do tax and stuff?'

'Babe, don't worry about it.' He started the car. 'This way, you end up with more money.'

She exhaled a breath of excitement. Working again would bring her out of the funk she'd been in since Jules passed. 'What will I wear?' she asked.

'Whatever you want to wear out afterwards. They'll give you a uniform when you arrive.'

'Do they know I'm sixteen?'

'No way. You have to be eighteen to work there. Just tell them you're eighteen. You've got proof if they need it.'

'How did you hear about the job?' A knot formed and twisted in her stomach.

'It was where Jules worked.' His voice shrunk with each word. 'They needed to fill the spot quickly.'

Jules had taken the time to show Steph how to do her make-up. Jules had danced with Steph and considered her a friend. And now she was taking her dead friend's job? She sunk into the car seat haunted with grief once again.

They stopped at McDonalds for an afternoon snack because Jason rarely had food in the house. 'We'd better go home so you can change. They might look at your ID too closely if you show up in your school uniform.'

In Jason's room, Stephanie found some clothes she'd worn out on the previous Saturday night. The lingering nightclub scent brought back the memory of dancing with Jules. Her anxiety compounded in the car, as they crawled along in heavy traffic, bottlenecking towards the city.

'So we're going out after my trial?' She chewed on a fingernail.

'Yeah, they all want to celebrate Jules' life.'

'I'm scared. What if I drop a tray of glasses or something?'

'Don't worry, babe. You'll be fine.'

Jason stopped the car outside The Groove and kissed her goodbye. 'I'll be back at ten. Just ask for the manager, Gav. He's expecting you.'

Chapter Twenty-Nine

THE STREETS LOOKED DIFFRENT in the afternoon twilight. Neon lights had flicked on but didn't yet illuminate the area. Steph glanced up and down the street, took a deep breath, and entered The Groove.

'Is the manager here?' she said with forced confidence.

'Are you Steph?' the girl behind the counter asked. 'You're here to take Jules's place?'

Stephanie cringed. The last thing she wanted to do was to take a dead person's place.

'Just wait here. I'll get Gav.'

'You must be Steph.' Gav only looked a couple of years older than Jason.

He took his time to explain exactly what her job entailed. It was a relief to find she'd be working for someone who treated her with respect. He handed her a black T-shirt and a pair of black shorts with the hotel logo.

'You are eighteen, aren't you?' Gav caught her off guard as she returned from changing into the uniform.

'Yeah, I am.' Her words came out too fast and she expected him to ask for her ID. But he didn't.

'That's good.' He moved away and pointed through the open door. 'You can start by clearing the tables in the beer garden.'

Phew! Stephanie took her tray and started work. Dinner was being served and the outdoor area was crowded with Friday drinks-after-work patrons. She managed to keep all the glasses on the tray and was able to ignore the few sleazy men who gave her a slap or a pinch on her bottom as she walked past. It was mostly an enjoyable first night.

'You did great tonight,' Gav said.

'Thanks.'

'Job's yours if you want it. Tuesdays and Thursdays, nine to midnight, and five 'til ten Fridays.'

'Sounds good. Thank you. See you Tuesday.' Stephanie left with a bounce in her step. She pushed the door open and landed in Jason's arms.

'Are you ready to go out?' He lifted her off the ground in a bear hug.

'Sure.' She smiled. 'Are you?'

'You look happy. Went well, did it?'

'Yeah, it was much better than working at The Tiger's Eye.' She hugged him. 'Thank you for getting me the job.'

'No worries. Let's go.' He took her by the hand and they walked a couple of blocks to meet up with the others.

There were no drugs that night. Each round of drinks was shouted by a different friend. They started with beer, then vodka, then bourbon, then a variety of shots in miniature glasses. Stephanie looked at everyone, alive and drinking, then she thought of Jules lying in a coffin in the grave. Out of everyone there, she'd known Jules for the shortest amount of time.

'I don't feel so good,' Stephanie said.

'Are you going to be sick?' Jason asked.

She shook her head, then shrugged. 'Can we go home?'

'Yeah, you're looking pretty green.' He ushered her out without saying goodbye to anyone.

Stephanie dozed in the taxi and was thankful Jason helped her up the stairs. She fell onto his bed and closed her eyes to stop the room from spinning.

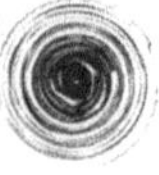

She rolled over and blinked sleep from eyes. *Daylight.* 'Argh. I feel terrible.'

'It was a big night.' Jason yawned.

'What did you put in my drink?' She pulled the pillow over her head.

'Nothing, babe, just alcohol.'

'Then, why do I feel so bad?' Her stomach churned at Jason's stale breath.

'Here, have some water.' He swung a bottle across the bed.

'I don't think I could stomach it.'

'Sleep,' he said. 'Just sleep 'til you feel better.'

She squinted as Jason left the bed to take a shower, then she closed her eyes again. The next time she awoke, the TV blared, but she drifted off to sleep once more. After stirring several times, she woke alert just after two.

'I'm hungry. Got anything I can eat?' She looked in the empty fridge.

'Let's get Maccas.' He grabbed the car keys.

'Ow. My head is killing me.'

'There's paracetamol in the cupboard.' Jason sat back down in front of the TV.

Stephanie found the painkillers and swallowed them with a gulp of water. She was sure the churning in her stomach would only end with puking.

'You'll feel better when we get some greasy food.'

'Why didn't we go to Jules' funeral?' Stephanie asked as she climbed into the car.

'Didn't want to.'

'But she was your friend.'

'Her parents were really angry,' he said. 'Guess I didn't want to face them.'

'But you didn't give her the E.'

Jason was silent.

'You bought it for her too?' Stephanie raised her voice.

'I bought a bunch of them for everyone.' He turned the key in the ignition. 'Can we drop it?'

'Where did you get the money?'

'They paid for their own. Just shut up, okay?' He pulled into the drive through.

'Why did we drive when Maccas is so close?'

'Would you rather get it yourself?'

'No. But we usually walk.'

'I'm feeling too shabby.' He slammed his hand on the steering wheel.

'And touchy.' She looked out the window as he ordered at the drive-through speaker. 'Can you drop me back home? I want to see Tabbie.'

They ate in the car and drove to the Morays in silence.

'We're going out again tonight. I'll pick you up later, okay?'

'I think I'll stay here a couple of nights.' She opened the car door. 'See you during the week.'

Stephanie began to walk but turned back to face him. 'I'm working Tuesday night. Can you drive me?'

'I'll pick you up from school,' he said, looking at the road.

She walked inside without saying goodbye.

'It's good to see you back here,' Francine greeted her. 'Have you had lunch?'

'Yeah, just ate McDonalds.'

'You don't sound very happy. Is everything okay with Jason?'

'Yeah, it's fine. We're just both tired and cranky.'

Tabbie walked into the room. 'How did the new job go?'

'Went really well.' Steph combed her fingers through her hair and felt it stick out in clumps like a bird's nest. 'And it's less hours.'

'Yes, Tabbie told me.' Francine looked up. 'Now, where exactly is it?'

'In the city.' Steph jumped in before Tabbie slipped with a truthful answer. 'I'm clearing tables, three shifts a week.'

'Do you want me to drop you off and pick you up?' Francine asked.

'Jason said he'll drive.' *I hope.* Or was she just assuming he'd be happy to drive her in?

'What are the hours like? Weekends? Afternoons?' Francine folded the newspaper she'd been reading.

'Nights.'

'That's a shame. You get so tired working nights.'

'It's fine, Francine, I enjoy working.' Steph paused. She'd actually enjoyed herself more last week, when she hadn't worked. *No, no. I love working.*

'Have you let your mum know?'

'No … I haven't had a chance to ring her.'

'Phone is free now. You really should let her know.'

'I'll call her tomorrow.' *Or I might forget to call her tomorrow.*

'Do you want a study partner?' Tabbie asked.

'Umm.' Steph realised she'd left her school bag at Jason's. 'I might have to use some of your notes.'

'Leave yours somewhere, did you?'

'Yeah.' Steph checked her fingernails. 'Did I miss much last night?'

'It was fun.' Tabbie's face glowed as she laughed. 'We played poison ball, and one of the leaders tripped over a ball and twisted his ankle. It was really funny—not that he got hurt, but it was just a fun night. Wish you could have come.'

'So you just played games? What about all the religious stuff?'

'We don't do religious stuff,' Tabbie said. 'We sang songs, then one of the leaders preached—'

'About what God expects of you? Like a homily?' Steph rolled her eyes.

'It's different to the churches you've been to.'

'When it comes down to it, churches are all the same—full of rules and full of people breaking them.' Steph glanced at Tabbie expecting her to bite back, but she looked calm.

'Go,' Steph said. 'Teach me all you know.'

'Come on, Steph, I can't do all the work for both of us.'

'I'm so sick of study.' Stephanie closed her eyes and flopped back onto the bed. 'I wish you could finish school for me.'

'You know you'll kick yourself if you don't finish,' Tabbie said. 'We've got a maths quiz tomorrow.'

'I know a formula.' Stephanie laughed. 'Bed plus Steph equals sleepy.'

'What did you do last night?' Tabbie threw her books on the bed.

'Why?'

'You are in one *fine* mood.'

'I'll leave you to it then.' Stephanie sat up.

'I want to study with you. Can you cut the sarcasm and jokes?'

'Okay.' Reluctantly, Stephanie worked on learning each formula with her friend.

She spent Sunday lying on the couch, watching TV in snippets, and dozing in and out of sleep. The next day, she opened her wardrobe to find there were no school uniforms. She went downstairs to check the laundry and found nothing there either. They were all at Jason's. *Stupid!* She ran back upstairs.

'Tabbie, can I wear one of your uniforms?' she whispered. 'I've left mine at Jason's.'

'Steph!'

'I know, I know. I'll remember next time.'

'Look, where are you living?'

'Here.' Stephanie chewed on the side of her mouth.

'But you've been at Jason's—'

'I know. Don't lecture me about it. Can I *please* borrow a uniform?'

Tabbie shoved her clothes at Stephanie, pushing her out of the room. The borrowed uniform hung loosely around Steph's hips but hugged her chest. She walked into school feeling uncomfortable and out of sorts without her school bag. During class she pulled at the fabric to close the gaping buttonholes. Her desk was bare, so she leaned over to read her classmate's textbook.

Stephanie stared at the maths quiz, not knowing which formula to use with what problem. It was nothing but a waste of time. *When am I ever going to use any of this stupid stuff?* She pulled once more at her blouse, unable to stop flashing her chest. It was all too much. She thrust her chair back, stood and walked to the door.

'Stephanie.' The teacher walked towards her. 'What's wrong?'

'I'm sorry, miss, I just can't sit this quiz. I've got to go and get something from home.'

'You do realise this contributes to your final results?'

'Yes. I've got to go.'

'Be sure you stop at administration and get a slip before leaving the school grounds.'

But Stephanie walked towards the bus stop without passing the administration office. She made her way to Jason's and let herself in, not expecting to see him there.

'Babe!' Jason was standing on a chair. He jumped off to kiss her.

'What's happening?' He leaned backwards to catch a ball.

'We're just playing some indoor cricket.' He pointed to Axel.

'Hi,' she said to the guy who was seldom there.

'Wanna play?' Jason jumped back up on the chair.

'No, thanks.' Stephanie wondered what he was on, but didn't ask. She didn't want to know the answer.

'What are you doing here?' He bowled the ball.

'I forgot my school bag and uniform.' She ventured into his bedroom to collect her things. 'I failed a quiz today.'

'Too bad,' he said, as he caught the tennis ball.

'Guess I'll just take this back to Tabbie's.' She held her school backpack against her stomach. *Or I could stay. You only have to ask.*

'Okay.' He laughed. 'You still want me to pick you up for work?'

'That'd be great. I thought you had a full day on Monday?'

'I was too tired this morning. I'll catch up. What day did you want me to pick you up?'

'Tomorrow.'

He didn't acknowledge her response, so she wrote a note:

See you Tuesday after school.
Please pick me up at
the school gate for work.

S xx

Steph dodged the ball on the way out, and left them to their game.

Chapter Thirty

On Tuesday afternoon, Stephanie was ready and waiting at the school gate, but Jason hadn't arrived. Buses drove in and left filled with kids. Steph chewed on the side of her mouth. *Where is he?* At least she didn't have to rush into work. The shadows grew longer and the school became a ghost town. Steph was sick of waiting and moved towards the bus stop when she heard a squeaky car horn. She turned as Jason pulled up beside her.

'You're late,' she said with a clamped jaw.

'I had things to do. You need a mobile phone.'

She climbed into the passenger's seat.

'Hey, babe, how about we go out tonight, after you finish work?'

'I don't finish until midnight.'

'I thought you only worked 'til ten.'

'That's Friday night. During the week I don't start until nine.'

'Bummer.' He paused. 'Let's go out anyway.'

'Can we decide after I finish? I might be whacked by then.'

'Let's go get you that phone.' He pulled out onto the road.

'What phone?'

     Spiralling Out of Control

'I would've texted or called you to tell you I was late, but how could I?'

'I don't have the money for one.'

'They aren't much.' The car in front of them hadn't moved when the light changed to green. Jason blasted his horn. 'You sign up for a plan, and the phone comes free.'

'But what about the contract?' Did she have to be eighteen?

'There's a shop just down the road here.' He parked the car and took her inside. He set her up on a twenty-four month plan. *Why didn't I do that myself months ago?*

By eight Steph was tired. Nine was late to start work when the school day started only hours after she would arrive home. And now Jason expected her to hit the town at midnight. She jumped into the shower, hoping the splash would refresh her.

The Tuesday night crowd was slow, and her shift dragged. She walked outside at midnight, expecting to see Jason. He wasn't there, but at least now she was armed with a mobile phone.

'Hello,' Jason answered.

'I'm finished work. Where are you?'

'Look the other way.'

She turned and there he was, walking toward her. His eyes darted spasmodically, and he looked as if he was about to pop right out of his skin.

'Everything all right?'

'Great,' he said. 'In fact, I've got a surprise for you.'

She knew when she looked into his eyes. *Drugs.*

'You've got to try this, babe.' He took her down a dark alley.

'I thought I told you no more drugs,' she whispered.

'But this is different. It's pure, and there's nothing in it that can hurt you.'

'That's what you said last time.'

'I know. I was wrong last time. This time, I've done my research.'

'What is it?'

'Coke,' he whispered.

'Cocaine!'

'Shh, babe, you'll get us in trouble.'

'No way!' She jabbed at his arm with her fist. 'This has trouble written all over it.'

'Come on, babe, just try it.'

I don't want to try it. She widened her eyes, silently pleading for him to stop.

'Come here.' He grabbed her arm and pulled her into a public toilet for disabled people.

She moved her feet in an awkward attempt to leave. Jason blocked the doorway as he worked the powder on the narrow basin shelf. 'Here, like this.' He snorted a line and then set another up for Steph.

'No!'

'Just this once.' He pulled her closer.

'Jason.' She wrung her hands. *I hate drugs.* She was never going to take drugs.

'Come on, babe.' His grip was firm around the back of her neck, pushing her face down. 'Just tonight. For me.'

He'd won again. *Why can't I just say no and stick to it?*

The cocaine was soon in her blood and she walked back out onto the street, wired. If this was a high, she wanted it to last forever!

Most clubs had free entry on Tuesday night, making it easy for them to wander in and out, club after club. At times they'd dance together and other times Jason would sit and watch her. Steph only stopped dancing to snort more white powder. When the nightclubs closed, they wandered aimlessly around the city until suit-wearing businessmen crowded the streets. With only a small amount of cash left, they caught the train home.

Stephanie was wide awake. She showered and pulled on her school uniform. 'Do you have uni today?'

'Yes!' Jason laughed. 'Will I get there? I don't know…' his voice petered out.

She poured two coffees. 'Coffee's ready, hon.'

     Spiralling Out of Control

Jason was silent.

'Honey?' She took the mug to him, where he'd crashed out in front of the TV. Maybe she should catch an hour before school. She curled up beside him.

Blinking, Stephanie looked at her watch. It was late afternoon. 'Jason!' she yelled when she realised he wasn't beside her. 'Jason, are you here?'

She ran through the flat until she found him on his bed.

'Huh?' He squinted.

'I missed school.' She sat beside him. 'You missed uni.'

'Worth it, wasn't it?' Jason chuckled. 'Last night was great.'

'Yeah, but university is important to you.' She grabbed his hand.

'I can catch up. And you hate school anyway.' He rolled over and closed his eyes again. 'Don't worry about it, babe.'

She clenched her teeth. He'd told her not to worry too many times. She wished he'd just talk to her. Have a straight discussion. She took one last look at him snoring on the bed, and left to catch a bus to the Morays.

'Why didn't you call us?' Francine followed her upstairs. 'It's dark out there. We could have picked you up.'

'It's okay. I'm here now.'

'We've just eaten, but I can reheat some leftovers.'

'Thank you, Francine. That would be great.'

Stephanie ate, then retreated to her room, seeking serenity in her comfortable bed. Anxiety pulled at her chest. She couldn't keep living this way. *How do I stop him?* Darkness filled her night and emptiness sat hollow in her soul. She wanted to spill her heart. Fill the silence with words to someone who would understand, but instead she imploded. All she wanted to do was sleep but the ceiling stayed in her vision most of the night.

When Stephanie finished on Thursday, Jason waited outside the school grounds. He looked at her with clear eyes, standing tall in his freshly pressed clothes. 'Hey, babe.'

It's all going to be okay. She sighed, falling into his arms, as fresh soap and aftershave tingled her nostrils.

That night, Jason came into The Groove before her shift had finished, and sat at the bar with a glass of water. The breath of hope she'd taken in the afternoon was squashed when she watched him tapping his fingernails on the counter, while his leg bounced, and his gaze darted from wall to wall. 'You ready to go?' he said.

'I've just got to get out of my uniform.' She kissed him on the cheek. He leaned away. 'Back in a minute.'

After she changed, Jason stood on the other side of the door in the staff-only area.

'You shouldn't be in here.' Steph looked down the hallway to make sure Gav wasn't nearby.

'Don't get so stressed, babe.' He followed her, rattling his car keys. 'Let's go home.'

'You aren't driving, are you?'

'Yeah. Why not?'

'Have you been drinking?' she asked when they were out on the street.

'Only water.'

'Jason!' She stomped her foot on the pavement. 'What are you on?'

'Nothing for you to worry about.'

No. She cringed at the thought of climbing into the car with him. Maybe she should catch public transport. Steph fumbled with her bag. 'What if we leave the car here and catch a train home?'

'It's fine!' Jason opened the car door and pushed her in.

'Ow!' Stephanie gasped when her arm scraped across a loose panel on the car. She held her arm to stop the blood dripping onto her jeans. Then she froze, unable to force herself back out of the car.

Jason drove erratically, swerving past cars and rounding corners too closely. He bumped a signpost, snapping off the passenger side mirror.

'Stop!' Stephanie's scream seemed to go unheard. Her head flung back onto the headrest when Jason floored the accelerator. 'Jason! That was a red light!'

'It's okay. No cars were coming.'

Stephanie's legs stung with her fingernails clawing for control. The scratch on her arm ached. Nothing slowed him down. He sped through give-way signs. Pedestrians darted for safety, and car horns sounded when he pulled out into a stream of traffic. Steph's heart pounded in her throat as the tyres screeched around yet another corner.

'Jason! Slow down.'

'Nearly there.' He slammed on the brakes, leaving rubber on the bitumen.

She coughed as smoke wafted from the tyres and overheated engine. Trembling, she stepped out of the car.

Her breath was heavy as she forced the words, 'Can you not do that again?'

'Do what?'

'Drive while you are on something.' She slammed the door. 'It's stupid!'

'Don't stress, babe. Nothing to worry about.' He smiled and took her in his arms. She needed him to hold her limp body up. His leg jerked while they kissed, and tears flooded her eyes. Her shoulders slumped and her chest heaved after the ordeal.

Once inside, he held out a small plastic bag. 'Do you want some?'

'Jason! No, I'm going to sleep.' She climbed into bed and pulled the pillow over her head to block out any more drug scenes. A pit of darkness swallowed her into an agitated sleep.

Part 3

— *Steph* —

Chapter Thirty-One

Steph awoke to her alarm, feeling somewhat at ease. Jason snored another breath while she got dressed. He stirred as she was about to walk out the door. 'Hey, babe. Are you going?'

'Yeah, I'm going to school.'

'Rent is due,' he mumbled. 'Can you lend us some money?'

'Oh, man.' She paused. 'You'll pay me back?'

'Sure.'

She tapped her hand on the door frame a couple of times. Maybe her sleeping over without paying rent was annoying Jason and Axel. 'Okay. My pay is in that bag beside the bed.'

'Thanks, babe. And sorry about last night.' He pulled the cash from her purse and shoved it under his pillow. 'It was crazy. I'm so glad you're with me, reminding me to keep straight.'

'Yeah, see you later.' Her fingernails cut into her skin as she clenched a fist.

'Love you, babe.'

His warm eyes penetrated and dissolved her fury. She took a deep breath and closed the door. *Everything will be okay. It will.* It had to be.

Sitting in class, Steph shuddered as the teacher's voice echoed in her mind. She was overwhelmed by the amount of work due and the amount she'd missed. She was different, out of place, somehow more mature than the other girls. No one knew what her life was truly like out of school. She'd even avoided going into details with Tabbie. As she stood at her locker, contemplating what to do, Tabbie appeared.

'Are you sitting with us for lunch?'

Steph swung her locker door backwards and forwards. 'No, I have a few things I need to get done.'

She watched until Tabbie had walked around the corner. In a trance, one by one, she placed all her books and belongings into her backpack. She pulled the heavy, bulging school bag over her shoulder and took one last look at her surroundings. *It's been fun, Hill Top, but I've outgrown you. I'm moving on.*

She lifted her arm to wave as she walked out of the school grounds. With no money or bus ticket, she pondered which direction to take. It hit her front on—leaving the school grounds had cemented a decision to not graduate. Her mind pounded with freedom and fear. *Just breathe. It's going to be okay.* She had a job. She had Jason. She didn't need school. It was going to be fine.

The sun warmed her back as the breeze rustled leaves from the trees. Nature gently invited her to walk back to Jason's. Meandering along the way, she contemplated where she lived. Her bedroom at Tabbie's house belonged to sixteen-year-old Stephanie. The girl who stayed at Jason's was eighteen-year-old Steph. With each step she took, she knew it was time to shut down the sixteen-year-old and let the eighteen-year-old take over.

She saw no reason to go back to the Morays' place and hoped Jason would be ready for her to move in. She tried to find the right words. *Hon, I'm here most nights.* Or… *It's easier to get to work from here.* Or… *Can I move in?*

Nothing sounded right, no matter how many times she played with the words. She sat on a park bench, dreaming into the clouds, imagining what it would be like to live with Jason forever. She thought about their wedding day and what their children would look like.

She wasn't ready for children, and found a clinic on the way to Jason's. She was surprised how easy it was to get a prescription for the pill. A couple of hours later, she climbed the steps to Jason's apartment.

'Hey, you're home.' Jason sat on the couch. 'I was just wondering if you wanted me to pick you up. You should have rung.'

'I needed a walk.' She poured a glass of water.

'You walked from school?'

'Yeah, needed to think.'

'What about?'

'Us. School. Where I live.' She'd slipped. It wasn't how she wanted to bring it up.

'Yeah, Axel asked if we could split the rent three ways—with you here so much.'

Not exactly a 'would you like to move in' invitation. She took a breath. 'Are you asking me to move in?'

'You don't have to get all formal about it. But you are here most of the time.'

Hmm. Maybe moving in wasn't as big a deal as she'd thought. 'Did you get to uni?'

'No. Didn't have much on today.' He surfed the TV channels.

'Ah … Jason.'

'Yeah.'

'I need to check something.'

'What?'

'Are you okay to take me to work and stay sober?'

'Oh, come on, babe. It was just a one-off.'

'It's just that… we haven't spoken about how I'll get there and back, like ongoing. Are you sure it's okay? Three nights a week that you don't get drunk or stoned.'

'It's cool, babe. I've got to meet some people in there tonight anyway. Let's go in a bit earlier.'

'I don't want to get in the car with you again if you're on something.'

'Sure, babe, don't worry. We'll get a taxi next time.'

Steph sighed. *Next time?*

A couple of hours later, they entered a café down the road from The Groove. Jason said hello to several people, high-fiving others as he walked in.

'How do you know everyone?' Steph asked.

'Not everyone.' He laughed. 'I've come in here a couple of times while you were working. Don't go anywhere—I've got to see someone for a minute.'

She sat on the nearest chair and watched him slide into a booth in the opposite corner. Two shifty guys looked up. Jason shook hands with one of them as he sat down, then again before he returned.

'What are you up to?' She raised an eyebrow.

'Nothing for you to worry about,' he said. 'I'll walk you to work.'

Steph had an uneasy feeling while she worked. She expected Jason to turn up high and offer her more drugs. This time she'd have to say no.

Gav told her she was welcome to stay and have a drink on him at the end of her shift. When Jason arrived, he was more than happy to have a beer with her there. Jason bought her another couple of drinks. She let the alcohol warm her insides and relax her body. A couple of hours passed while they laughed and drank.

'I think I need to go to sleep.' As she stood, the room spun. 'It's been a long day.'

'No way.' He led her by the hand. 'We're just warming up.'

Jason led her through an internal walkway. Neon lights flashed through a doorway as music vibrated through her bones. Inside, women were wearing underwear or less. She looked wide-eyed at Jason. The Groove had another nightclub?

'Ha ha, great joke.' She laughed in Jason's ear. 'Now can we go home?'

'Why?' He looked from the girls dancing on stage to others delivering drinks. 'I didn't think you'd be intimidated by a few girls.'

'I'm not intimidated.' Her cheeks burned. 'This is a men's club.'

'But there are heaps of girls here.'

Steph looked around the room. There were, but she was the only one fully clothed.

'Have you been here before?' She pushed on his shoulder.

'I'm only male.' He linked his arm through hers.

'Can we go?' She quivered.

'But look at how they dance. You're way better than them.'

'I'm not dancing here.' She pulled her arm from his and walked out.

'Babe.' He followed. 'Don't be so precious. I was just having a little fun.'

'Can we go home?' She spun on her heel to put distance between her and the men's club.

'Hey, stop!' he called.

Steph turned and waited for him to catch up.

'Look, babe. Maybe you just need a little—'

'I don't need a little anything.'

'Come on, babe, we'll have so much fun.'

'No.' *No no no no no.* She shook her head.

'Come on, babe, just one more.' He led her into the same public disabled toilets, gripping her hand. He pleaded, and she submitted. Soon she was high and having another crazy, wild time with Jason.

The next day she woke after midday. 'I should go and see the Morays this afternoon. Will you be here later?'

'Yep.' He rolled over to face her. 'Hey, babe, why don't you grab the rest of your things? You may as well move in.'

Ahh, finally!

On the way to the Morays, Steph's heart constricted. She didn't know what made her feel worse—that Jason had taken her into a topless bar, that he had been there before, or that he'd compared her dancing to the girls on stage.

No one was home when she arrived at Tabbie's house, so she immersed herself in the solitude. He'd asked her to move in. *What if he changes his mind?* She'd better leave some things here. She didn't want to tell her mother or father—or the Morays, for that matter.

Tabbie pushed open the front door. 'I didn't see you at school yesterday.'

'I was so tired—'

'I thought you said this job was better and less hours. If you can't handle school, maybe you should quit this job too.'

'I'll work it out. I'm just getting used to it.'

'Are you coming to school camp this year?' Tabbie picked up some papers from the table. 'I grabbed an extra permission form for you.'

'Isn't that ages away?'

'It's just after the holidays, but we have to hand the forms in by Monday.'

'I think I'll pass.' Steph screwed up her nose. 'It'll be pretty boring anyway.'

'Boring, how?' Tabbie dropped her bag on the floor. 'Compared to what you and Jason do?'

'I'm feeling a lecture coming on.' Steph turned to leave.

'I'm not going to lecture you,' said Tabbie. 'I'm just concerned. You're making some… bad decisions.'

'Well, don't be concerned.' Steph clenched her jaw. 'I'm doing just fine.' She walked away from the conversation, and filled a bag with clothes to take back to her new home.

Chapter Thirty-Two

Weeks passed.
Unreturned
phone calls.
Mum continues to ring.
I won't answer.
Her tone annoys me.
Frustrating.
Freaking borderline manic.
Her and Dad
argue
about
everything.
I reply
'I'm fine.'
'Very busy.'
'The Morays are great.'
'Yep, keeping up with everything.'

Mum
Dad
Both so self-absorbed
they don't question.
Texting is easy
but to speak to them
would surrender
reveal
the guilt in my voice.
I don't fight enough
I've let Jason
push the drugs
every
night.
Though now
the push has stopped.
I crave the high.
I'm living
my worst
nightmare.
Drinking binges.
Cocaine benders.
Blurring days and nights.
Days
Weeks
Months
Passed

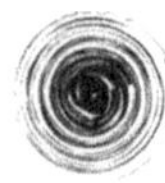

     Spiralling Out of Control

'Morning, babe, how'd you sleep?' Jason asked late one afternoon.

'Pretty good.' Steph was relieved. He spoke in a sober, non-drug-induced tone.

'Did you get paid? I'm all out and I feel like heading out tonight.'

'I was hoping to come straight home after work.'

'I spoke to Gav. You don't have to work tonight.'

'Oh, good. Let's stay home.'

'Did you get paid?' he repeated.

'Yes.' She was slow to answer. 'I did, but can't we have a quiet one? Isn't rent due?'

'Come on, babe, it's Friday night. Everyone's out.'

Steph's phone chimed. She retrieved a text message from Tabbie. 'So if you don't call me back, Mum will ring your parents. We're worried about you!'

'It's Tabbie. I've got to call her.'

'I told you not to hang out with your old friends. You don't need them anymore.' Jason's fist clenched and moved through the air like it was thick mud. 'We're going out tonight.'

Steph nodded and walked outside to call Tabbie straight away. It would be best to fill Tabbie in on the story she'd given her parents.

'Please don't tell anyone, but I'm not going back to school.' She hugged her arms and wished summer was here and not still months off.

'That's pretty obvious. You haven't been there forever, but what about your parents?'

'I forged their signature on some papers. All the letters and phone calls go to Jason's.'

'Surely school is after some answers.'

'I forged a letter from Mum and Dad saying I needed some time off and I'd be back next year.' Steph bit the growing lump on the inside of her cheek.

'They bought it?'

'School rang here, and Jason acted like he was my dad on the phone. Yes, they bought it.'

'Stephanie!'

'Look, I know, I'm not Miss Goody-Two-Shoes like you.' She ran her fingers through her hair. 'I'm sorry I'm failing as a friend. I'm sorry I quit on you.'

'Are you okay?'

'I'm fine, just a little tired. Mum and Dad have got enough on their plate fighting with each other, so tell your mum not to bother them. I'm fine. Really. I was about to have a sleep, so I'll talk to you later, hey?' Steph hung up, went back inside, and fell on the bed.

That night, Steph followed Jason into the little café down the road from The Groove, where he spoke to someone who looked familiar.

'Who is that? Do I know him?' Steph asked when he returned.

'Doubt it.'

'From The Groove.'

'Possibly.'

Steph stared, trying to place him. She couldn't remember the last time she'd been able to think straight. Tonight was no different. She sat at a table while Jason bought them both a drink.

'I think I might have worked it out.' She gathered her thoughts as she sipped.

'Doesn't matter, let's go.' Jason pulled her to his chest and kissed her.

'Same guy you spoke to last time I was here with you, isn't it?' The pieces of the puzzle fell into place.

'Don't worry about it, babe. Come on, let's go. I've got us another treat.'

'No, thanks. None for me tonight.' She clenched a fist. After speaking with Tabbie, she was determined to say no and stick to it.

'It'll be fine.'

'What is it?' She groaned.

'Same,' he said. 'Let's not try any of the nasty stuff when we know we can get the pure, harmless—'

'Jason!' Her protest was unheard, and once again he convinced her to take another line.

     Spiralling Out of Control

Soon she was wild, ready to take on flying monsters. Her mind accelerated. She followed Jason through a maze of alleys and hallways. By the time they entered the club, her eyes were unable to focus. The lights and pumping music toyed with her adrenalin. The dance floor invited her, and Jason followed. Girls danced around them in clothes that looked more like underwear. Dancing with Jason took her high to another level. Song after song, they bumped and swayed to the music.

Her top was hanging around Jason's neck. *What?!* She blinked. A draft swung past her torso. She shivered. Thank goodness she'd worn a full cover bra. Steph took another look around the room. She'd been here before. Jason had taken her to the men's bar at The Groove. She clasped a hand over her mouth and ran to the restrooms. The door thunked again. Jason smiled over her shoulder, into the mirror.

'Jason!' She spun around, hitting him on the chest. 'What's going on?'

'It's your new job.' He smiled, his eyes like saucers. 'You've been promoted. Come on. Don't get fired on your first night.'

'What? How could you set me up like this?' Tears swelled in her eyes.

'You're a dancer, a fantastic dancer, so why not make us some money? You'll get way more than what you were getting as a basic glassy.'

Where could she go? Nowhere. He'd forced her into this. As she left the restroom, Gav stood in the doorway.

'This is for you.' He handed her a glass of bubbly. 'Congratulations, Steph. You're as good a dancer as your boyfriend told us. The job is yours. You could dance the pants off all these girls.'

She glared at him, digging her fingernails into her legs, numb in her mouth.

'Drink up,' Gav said. 'You're next on stage. Here, I've written down the job details. You're welcome to have a few more drinks on the house to calm your nerves.' He pushed the note into her jeans pocket.

The first glass of bubbly clung to her throat, the second made her swallow hard, and she drank the third like water. In a vague trance, she climbed the stairs and danced on the stage, listening to the beat and ignoring the audience, until Jason led her off.

'That's it for tonight, babe.'

'Huh.' Her voice sounded android-like.

They fell into bed together hours later.

'You're the hottest chick,' Jason said.

The next day, she found the note in her pocket.

Steph – new position/promotion
Waitress/dancer.
8 pm to Midnight,
Pick your nights in advance.
Minimum 3 nights a week must include Friday or Saturday night.
Endless tips each night.

'Jason.' Her teeth clenched. 'Fill me in on what happened last night. What exactly does this mean? Please tell me it was all a dream and you don't really want me to work in a men's club.'

'Babe, you're a great dancer. You looked great up there on that stage. Plus, we're behind on our rent.'

'Why don't you go and get a job?' She raised her voice and hand, wanting to hit something.

'I've got to finish uni. My parents are expecting me to finish.'

'So, I left school to pay for you to go to uni?'

'You hated school.' He brushed her hair away from her eyes. 'You said yourself that you didn't want to go anymore. I thought you'd be happy to get some more cash.'

'You think I should be grateful for you making me work in a strip club?' She pushed his hand away.

'Hey, hey, hey, it's a classy hotel. It's not a strip club.'

'But the first time you dragged me there, the girls didn't have tops on!'

'That's only after midnight.' He took the note from her. 'Look, Gav has asked you to work until twelve. You can leave your top on and stop getting your knickers in a knot.'

'I need to get out of here for a while.' Steph left, slamming the door behind her. As she wandered through the streets, clouds hung low and rain disguised her tears. She continued her walk. The cold wind and misty rain felt like sleet on her cheeks. She couldn't focus. She didn't understand who her boyfriend had become.

Why would he want me to do this? Her bare arms were shivering, covered with goosebumps. Her mind swayed towards Tabbie, and how uncomplicated her life must be. All Tabbie had to worry about was school. Life was so simple before Toowoomba, before Jason.

Her aimless wandering brought on an overwhelming need to tell Tabbie how much of a good friend she was. The thought gave her footsteps direction and she found herself on Tabbie's doorstep. She needed to let Tabbie know how much she appreciated her.

'Hi, stranger.' Tabbie opened the door.

'Hey.' Steph now had wet channels streaming down her cheeks.

'You're saturated. You must be freezing. Come in. I'll get you a towel.'

'I really miss you.'

'Is everything okay?' Tabbie rushed back with a bath sheet.

No, my life sucks. I've thrown in school for a psycho boyfriend. 'Yeah, after I rang you, I realised I haven't seen you in… forever.'

'It has been weeks. How's work?'

'I just got promoted.' Steph forced half a smile.

'That sounds great. More money?'

'Yeah, money is great.'

'How's Jason?' Tabbie looked Steph in the eye.

Steph glanced away. 'Great.'

'Really?'

'Yeah, we just had a bit of a disagreement today.' Steph dried her face.

'You're welcome here any time, day or night. You know Mum and Dad—'

'I know, I know. You've told me a million times. I'm okay, really. We'll be fine. Tell me about you. What's happening in your life?' Steph forced the corners of her mouth into a smile.

'I think I'm falling in love. Come upstairs. I want to tell you all about him.'

Tabbie had met a boy at her youth group, who was new to Sydney.

'Does he have a name?'

'Aiden,' Tabbie said, 'and he's got olive skin and blond hair and dreamy brown eyes. And he's really, really good-looking. He plays AFL, you know that funny game of football, and he's really sporty. He's—'

'Amazing, I'm sure.' He sounded too good to be true. 'You'll have to introduce your amazing man to me soon then.'

'Steph, what's it like?'

'What?'

'You know, *it*,' she said quietly. 'Sex.'

'Oh, Tabbie, is he pressuring you?' Steph wanted to protect her innocent friend.

'No, but when we kissed.' Tabbie closed her eyes. 'It's like, I don't know how to explain it, but something happens in my body and I just want to well… you know.'

It was obvious Tabbie had already fallen head over heels.

'But Tabbie.' Steph put on her most sincere voice. 'You said you wanted to wait. Isn't that what they teach you at that youth group?'

'But you wanted to wait and didn't.'

'I know, but you should. Just for a while.'

'What's with telling me not to? You went ahead and did it with Jason.' Tabbie leaned on her elbow.

'I know it sounds crazy, but—'

'But why should I wait?'

    Spiralling Out of Control

'Because if he really loves you, he'll wait. Don't be tempted.' Steph shook her head.

'What if I don't want to wait any longer?'

'Because this is important to you.' Steph knew she was the wrong person to have this conversation with Tabbie. 'I know if you wait for a couple more months, you'll be glad you did.'

'I don't get you.'

'You need to talk to one of those church people about this.'

'None of them would get it.' Tabbie picked at a piece of fluff.

'It's really serious. You can never go back.' Tears blurred Steph's vision. Everything in her wanted to protect Tabbie. 'It will change who you are. I wish I could have your life again. Tabbie, don't. Just don't.'

'You really don't think I should, do you?'

'No,' Steph said, her voice stable and strong.

Chapter Thirty-Three

STEPH FOUND IT HARD to keep track of the days. When she woke from her intoxicated sleep, she'd look at her phone or turn on the TV to check what day it was. Jason made her work four nights a week, to cover rent and partying expenses. Weeks blended into each other. Her inner tenderness had turned to dust and her outer demeanour hardened to save herself from pain.

The nights of Jason arriving to pick her up from work sober became rare. When he arrived intoxicated, he would drag her out on the town. When he didn't turn up, she'd catch a taxi home alone, entering their apartment with apprehension. Axel had started bringing his rum-drinking, pot-smoking yobbo mates home, and Jason often invited friends over who'd sponge off them and leave a mess in their wake. When she found Jason passed out, she was thankful she wouldn't have to gauge his mood. She drank champagne, beer, or whatever she could find to put herself to sleep.

'Why do you work after midnight?' Steph asked Cassie, another dancer.

'Don't you get it?' Cassie shook her head. 'You're the only one who doesn't work after midnight. It's why the other girls treat you the way they do.'

Steph walked away feeling stupid for asking. She'd heard them call her a prude and stuck-up, and welcomed the bubbly each night to dull her intimidation.

One night, Gav pulled her into a side room. 'You're doing really well.'

'Thanks.'

'Everyone seems to like you. There is something special about you.'

Steph raised an eyebrow. It sure wasn't the girls who liked her. *What does he want?*

'A couple of the girls have left, and the big boss has put the heavy on us to only employ girls that can work thirty-two-hour weeks to streamline the paperwork. What I'm hoping is that you'll be available to work four eight-hour shifts. You'll get far more money than you're earning now.'

'Yeah.' She scoffed. 'Working double the hours.'

'You'll get a lot of tips to make it worth it.'

'So you want me to start at four?'

'No. Six or eight,' he said, with a smile. 'Through to two or four. See, we're pretty flexible.'

'I'd rather keep the hours I'm working.'

'Steph, you aren't hearing me. Your current job has been made redundant.'

'Can I go back to clearing tables in the beer garden?' She chewed on the inside of her mouth.

'We've filled that position.'

'Can I think about it?'

'Yes,' he said. 'Finish your shift and let me know before you leave tonight.'

Steph left the room. She swayed as she walked with alcohol rushing through her veins. *I'll just get another job.*

Cassie was at the bar when she walked out. 'Was that the talk?' She punched the air with quotation fingers.

Steph searched the girl's eyes.

'We've all had it.' Cassie shook her head. 'It's the way it goes here. You work a couple of months, get used to the money then you basically get told to get your top off or leave.'

'Really?' Steph's jaw dropped.

'Come on, Steph. Look at where you're working.' Cassie scanned the room. 'It's no big deal. You'll get used to it.'

'So you like working here?'

'Conditions here are way better than anywhere else.'

'What do you mean?' Steph knew her innocence had surfaced.

'Gav treats us well. That's all I'm saying.' Cassie turned. 'You're next on stage.'

Steph walked up the stairs in a daze, grooving her body to the beat. Tonight she wanted to lose herself in the music and deal with it all later. But the new job proposal stayed in the front of her mind. That night she looked out to a sea of middle-aged men, most of them older than her father.

Her father had been leaving more messages than her mother lately. Something urgent he needed to talk to her about. But she couldn't talk to him. Not while she danced at The Groove at night. She'd sent a text asking him to reply in a text because she didn't have credit to return his calls.

The men sipped their imported beer as they undressed her with their eyes. Repulsed, she stared at a light in the back of the room. After a couple of songs, she was glad to tag another girl to dance and clear tables again. She walked towards the bar for another glass of bubbly when a pair of hands curled around her waist from behind.

'Ah!' she shrieked.

'Hey, babe.' Jason spoke into her ear. 'What's up? Who'd you think it was?'

'I'm working.'

'I know. I just need some cash. Have you got some on you?'

'Not until the shift finishes.' She squinted at him.

'What? Have we run out already?'

She nodded. 'You spent it all last night.'

'Wow. Don't remember that. Can you ask for your pay now?'

'Jason.' She walked away, shaking her head. 'I don't want to ask.'

'Why not?' He followed.

'I'm leaving tonight.'

'Why? It's a great job.'

'It's all changed. I have to work more hours and after midnight.'

'Whoa.' He laughed. 'Take it off, baby.'

'Jason!' Her eyes widened. *How could he?* Was this her boyfriend or some other idiot?

'Is it better pay?'

'Yes, but that's not the point.'

'Babe.' Suddenly, his face straightened. 'We need the money. I need you to do this.'

His begging eyes crushed her. She didn't know how to stand firm against him. *If I start at six, I suppose it'd only be two hours.* She shook her head, perplexed that she was even contemplating it. Steph continued to clear tables while Jason waited at the bar. On her next round, he was gone.

'Hey, that's great, Steph.' Gav nudged her shoulder as she passed him. 'I really didn't want to lose you. You really are a great dancer.'

'Huh?'

'Jason just said that you're happy to start tonight and work through until two. He said you were okay with me giving him your pay for the night.'

Steph bit her lip.

'It was okay, wasn't it? I haven't done the wrong thing by you, have I?'

'No, it's all fine.' That night, Steph drank as many free glasses of bubbly as Gav offered, and then bought some. In all her years of dancing, she never thought she'd be dancing topless.

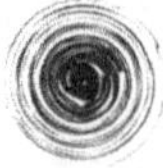

The next Saturday, Stephanie woke to a thunderous knock on the door.

'Did I wake you?' Tabbie looked at her watch.

'Yes, we got home late.'

'Work?'

In Steph's sleepy daze, she spoke without thinking, 'Yeah, and we went out after work.'

'Where?'

'Doesn't matter. What are you doing here? Why didn't you just ring?' Steph yawned.

'You want me to leave?'

'No. You're my best friend.'

'It's horrible.' Tabbie leaned forward, sobbing.

'Come in.' Steph pushed the door open.

'He was horrible.'

'Oh, no. What did he do to you?'

'He got really pushy and when I said no, he slapped me.' Tabbie touched cheek. 'He said I was leading him on.'

'Oh, Tabbie.' Steph held her friend in an extended hug until her tears stopped.

'You were right. I'm so glad you gave me that advice. He wasn't that nice after all,' she said through sobs. 'I wish I could find someone as wonderful as Jason.'

Steph swallowed, dropping the corner of her mouth. 'You deserve better than what I have.'

'I thought you were happy.'

'Well, I am. But it could be better,' she whispered.

'Why, what's up?'

'Not the right time or place… shh.' Steph pointed to the bedroom.

'Sorry,' Tabbie whispered. 'Why don't you come and stay a couple of nights back home?'

'Can't.' Steph looked towards the bedroom. 'Work.'

The outer hardness she had found in the previous months had been reduced to numb submission. Steph could no longer face her job sober. After a month in her new position, an over-exercised-bulging-muscled man stopped her. 'We're hiring. I think you'd be perfect.'

Steph squeezed her lips together. Her brain whirled in a fuzz.

'You can call me BJ,' he said. 'Here's my card. Call me tomorrow. If you don't call me, I'll be back to remind you.'

BJ's card fell out of Steph's handbag when she reached for her purse the following day. Vague memories of meeting him spiked her thoughts.

'What's that?' Jason said.

'BJ.' She read the card, 'Producer, dance video clips.'

'Why have you got his card? Is he trying to poach you?'

'Um, he said something about… I can't really remember.'

'It could be great. I wonder what he pays?'

'Why do you only care about the money!?' She snapped, now wide awake and alert.

'You're a dancer. Don't you want a career in dancing?'

Steph shook her head, heading towards the fridge in search of a quick swig of bubbly.

'Here, I'll call him and see what he wants.' Jason snatched the card from her and rang the number.

'BJ?'

She listened in to the conversation from the next room.

'You gave my girlfriend your card last night.'

She went to walk away but swayed, wanting to know what Jason would say next. He was silent for a couple of minutes, then said, 'She'd love the job. When can she start?'

Steph turned on the shower and allowed herself to relax, relieved. She didn't have to dance at the men's club anymore. A smidgeon of excitement grew in her core. Could this be her big break? Could she actually have a career in dancing? A smile found her lips.

'Hey, babe,' Jason called, when she stepped out of the shower. 'You've got a job dancing for music videos. You can start on Monday morning.'

'That's great. I'll ring the hotel and tell them I can't come in.'

'No, babe, don't quit yet. We need the money.' He walked towards her. 'Three more nights will pay for rent and the party.'

What party?

Each night for the next three nights, Steph repeated in her mind, *not long now, nearly finished.*

When she woke up unusually early after her last shift, the only person she wanted to see was Tabbie. Jason was still sleeping, so she slipped out without him knowing.

Steph let herself in to the Morays' place and found Tabbie sitting on the couch. 'You aren't going to believe what's happened.'

'You're coming back to school?'

'No way, better than that.'

'You've got an ordinary day job?' Tabbie clapped her hands together as if in prayer.

'Well, kind of.' Steph sat beside her. 'It's not ordinary, but I'm pretty sure it'll be day work.'

'What is it?'

'A music video producer asked me to go and work for him.'

'Have you been dancing?'

She paused. *How can I tell her? No, I can't. Not the whole story.* 'Yeah, a little.'

'When do you start?'

'Monday.' Steph jumped up, kicked one leg high and spun around.

'That's wonderful! I can't believe you've been dancing and haven't told me.'

'Enough about me.' Steph sunk back into the couch as her stomach churned. 'What happened with that boy?'

'Well and truly over him.' Tabbie laughed. 'I got a bit intense, didn't I?'

'No, you were just being normal.' Steph could only dream about having more normal in her life.

'School is going well. Too many assessments and exams and all the other stuff that bores you.'

'It doesn't bore me.' Steph yearned for the simplicity of Tabbie's way of life. She missed school. 'Tell me everything I've missed. I've been so preoccupied lately.'

Steph listened to Tabbie with more interest than she'd had in months. But soon she was haunted by the thought that Jason would be annoyed because she was visiting Tabbie. She'd have to deal with him when she got home.

Tabbie spoke without stopping until Steph was completely caught up on everything the girls at school were doing, what her brother was up to, and how loving and wonderful her parents were. Steph hadn't spoken to her sister, mother, or father in months. Their faces flashed in her mind.

'You haven't said anything about that church thing you go to.'

'The last couple of times I brought it up, you didn't seem interested.' Tabbie tucked a stray hair behind her ear. 'I'm actually about to head down to the beach with my church friends. Would you like to join us?'

'Do you mind if I don't? I'd love to catch up on a little sleep. This house is so peaceful.'

'Make yourself comfortable. I'll be back this afternoon. I think Mum and Dad are out all day, so the house will be quiet.'

Steph jumped up when she heard Tabbie at her bedroom door. She blinked away the sleepiness.

'Hey, hi. It'll be getting dark soon. Do you want to stay for dinner?'

'I'd love to.' Steph flashed a bright cheery smile. 'I'll just text Jason.' Her insides burned at the thought. *How will he react?*

'Mum can drop you back,' Tabbie said. 'Unless… you've changed your mind and you'd like to sleep over.'

'Thanks, but I'd rather go back.' *To what?* 'Jason will be expecting me.' If she didn't return soon, he would likely bite her head off.

'It's lovely to have you with us tonight,' Francine said as she served dinner.

'How is everything?' Tom asked.

'Good, thanks.' Steph gave a slight smile.

'You know you're welcome here any time,' Francine said.

'I know.' Steph looked up. 'Thanks.'

'I've spoken with your parents several times now. We can't keep accepting board payments when you live with Jason.'

'But—'

'They say they can't get in touch with you. Have you returned any of their calls?'

'I've just been in touch with them today. Everything is sorted.'

'Steph?' Tom deepened his voice.

'Look, I still live here. I just stay at Jason's.' Steph lifted a hand to her forehead. 'What's the difference really? Please just leave it. They don't care. They've got their own issues to deal with at the moment.'

'I think they care more than you give them credit for,' Francine said. 'You really need to talk to them more often, no matter what they're going through.'

'As Francine said, you are always welcome here. We'd much rather you stay here and visit Jason. Honesty is the best policy, and I suggest you tell the truth next time you speak with your parents.'

'But—'

   Spiralling Out of Control

'We will be letting them know how often we see you.' Tom placed his knife down. 'Peter is thinking of moving home, so we'll need to move your things into Tabbie's room.'

'So when you come and stay, you can bunk in with Tabbie,' Francine added.

'We'd all love you to stay. Please say you will. It'll be fun.' Tabbie nodded.

'Thanks.' Steph lifted her hand. It jittered, so she hid it in her pocket. She couldn't pinpoint what had hit her nerves. 'But I'd better get back now.'

Francine drove and Tabbie jumped in as well. Steph tried to control her shaking hands and trembling muscles.

'It's dark. Do you want us to walk you to the front door?' Francine asked.

'No, thanks. I can see a light on in the back,' Steph lied. 'I'll use my phone torch. I'll be fine.'

She waved goodbye and looked up again, hoping no one was home. Axel was often out. Jason might be asleep. When she let herself in, empty bottles filled the coffee table, ashtrays overflowed, bongs sat on the bench and half-eaten pizzas sat limp in their cardboard boxes. She wandered around to check that no one was crashed out in one of the rooms.

Annoyed with the mess, she poured herself a glass of champagne and flicked the TV on. The bottle was soon empty, and she found another. At some stage in the darkness, she put herself to bed.

Chapter Thirty-Four

'WHERE WERE YOU LAST NIGHT?' Jason asked as they stirred in the midday warmth. 'I threw a party and you didn't show.'

'Wow, what time is it?'

'Just after one. You didn't tell me where you were going.' Jason threw the cover off.

'I sent you a text.'

'When?' He looked at his phone. 'Oh.'

'I was at Tabbie's.'

He punched the sheets, inches from her face. 'What on earth were you doing there? I thought we agreed you wouldn't go back there.'

We didn't agree. You told me not to go back there.

'We'll have to celebrate again tonight then. Have you got some cash?'

'Celebrate again? What are we celebrating?'

'You.'

'My birthday has come and gone.'

'Not for your birthday, stupid. For getting into the music industry.'

'I'll be dancing. Not exactly getting into the music industry.'

'Still worth celebrating. Have you got some cash?' Jason left the bedroom.

'I think there's something left in my purse.' She reached down to only find ten dollars.

'Bingo!' Jason returned, shaking twenty and ten dollar notes in his hand. 'He always leaves cash beside his bed.'

'Jason!' Spending time with Tabbie had given her a burst of courage. 'You can't take Axel's money.'

'I'll pay it back.'

'Call him and ask.'

'He'll be fine. Don't worry about it, babe.'

Steph rolled out of bed in search of paracetamol. She looked up when she heard Jason's keys rattle. 'Back soon, babe.'

'Lock the door on the way out.' She needed a shower and was already undressing.

She watched the water fall until the glass screen fogged over. She stepped under the burning shower, letting her skin singe and turn pink, standing in a trance until the water flowed cold.

She shivered and turned the taps off. As the water stopped flowing, someone bashed on the front door. She wrapped a towel around her dripping body and checked the front door peephole. 'Oh, man. You don't have to bust the door.'

As she unlocked the door, Jason pushed it, bumping her.

'How long does it take you to open up?' he roared.

'I was in the shower.' Steph caught her footing and tightened her towel.

'I said I'd be back soon.' He forced the words through clenched teeth.

'Forget your keys, did you?'

'Why would I need keys when you're here?'

Steph bit the inside of her mouth. *Breathe.* Why were they arguing about stupid keys? 'This is ridiculous. I'm going to get something to eat.'

She pulled her clothes on, snatched her keys off the table and left, slamming the door. Jason must have lost Mr-Kind-And-Considerate somewhere while he was out.

She meandered along the concrete path to McDonalds, avoiding cracks and zigzagging to touch the grass on each side. Her stomach cramped in hunger when she ordered. As she turned away from the counter, her attention was caught by a perfect-looking family. She felt compelled to sit down and watch them as she ate. Hot fries burnt her mouth as she stared at the two girls, laughing and jabbing each other. Her heart raced. It had been months since she'd had a real conversation with April. She drank her juice to cool her burned mouth, keeping her eyes on the family. Her hand shook as she reached for her phone.

'Mum?'

'Well, what a surprise.' Her mother spoke in a sarcastic tone.

'Just wanted to say hi.' Steph rolled her eyes.

'Look, I spoke with Francine last week. She said you have something to tell me.'

'Yeah.'

'Well, what is it?'

Urgh. What was the point in keeping it from her any longer? 'I'm not staying at the Morays' much. I'm kind of living at Jason's.'

'Stephanie! Why?'

'It's too hard to get to work from their house.'

'Perhaps you should come home.'

'No way.' Steph stuffed another hot chip into her mouth.

'You shouldn't be living together.'

'I know. But it's just easier this way.'

'Why can't you get another job and move back to the Morays?'

'I've already got a new job.' Steph smiled, blinking away tears.

'Where?'

'I'm dancing.'

'A job dancing?'

'Yeah.' Steph swallowed the lump in her throat. Her mother never did understand her dream of becoming a professional dancer.

'Then you'll be able to stay with the Morays.' She could hear her mother shuffling something.

'No, Mum. Still too hard to get to work.'

'Humph. How is school?'

The new job clashes with school. She couldn't say that. Her mother would never understand. 'Is April home?'

'I'll put her on.'

'Hi, April.' Steph's voice quivered as tears swelled over her lashes. She reached for her juice again.

'What makes you call now? You haven't been bothered to talk to me for ages.'

'Sorry. How's gym?'

'It sucks.'

'Why? What happened?' Steph swallowed the thickness in her throat, again.

'Don't worry about it.'

'How's school?' Steph resisted the urge to race back to Toowoomba and hug her sister.

'Fine if I was someone else.'

'April, what's going on?' Steph continued to stare at the family sitting in front of her.

'Nothing. Here's Mum.'

Muffled scratching echoed as the phone was passed between hands. 'Mum, what's up with April?'

'She's just had a few difficulties. She stopped eating for a while there.'

'What? Like anorexia?' Steph fingered a nutrition label of the McDonalds wrapper lying in front of her.

'That's what the doctor said. She wasn't able to compete for several weeks and lost her place in the gym team.'

'She must be devastated.'

Steph heard April in the background, yelling, 'Shut up. You don't have to tell her!'

'She hasn't been dealing with it very well.'

'Oh.' Steph was distracted by the family in front of her, putting their leftovers in the rubbish.

'Stephanie, I'm not happy with your living arrangement.'

'Well, it's the way it is. I'm growing up, Mum. You can't make all the decisions.'

'Have you spoken to your father?'

'No. I'd better go.' The family she was watching walked past her and out onto the street.

'We do care, Stephanie.'

'Yeah, same. Bye.'

Stephanie. Her mum had called her Stephanie. It'd been forever since anyone called her Stephanie.

Steph threw her burger wrapper in the bin and drank her juice as she walked home and made a mental note to check in on April again soon. A couple of weeks at this new job and she'd have enough money to book a flight to Toowoomba. Maybe a weekend at home would be okay.

'Hey, babe, you happier now you've eaten?'

'Are you happier now you have a drink in your hand?' *Why am I reacting like this?* She didn't want to show any attitude that might trigger Jason's anger.

'Hey, if you'd just done what you usually do, you wouldn't have made me so angry. Anyway, here's some bubbly. Got some friends coming around soon.'

She sighed with relief. Copping the brunt of his aggression was something she didn't want to get used to. 'But I should get a good night's sleep before starting tomorrow.'

'Nah, babe.' He passed her a drink. 'You'll be fine. You don't have to be there until half past ten. Drink up. I was just about to go and get us a little extra to celebrate with.'

What does it matter anyway? It was only mid-afternoon. She'd have time to sleep it off.

     Spiralling Out of Control

Steph squeezed her eyes and shuddered when her alarm woke her the next day. She swung her arm onto the other side of the bed—bare sheets. *Jason?* The details of her night were hazy, mostly jumbled. Jason had invited people she didn't know. His new friends were rough and rowdy.

She remembered getting kicked out of a nightclub, and a vague sense that she'd walked along train tracks and seen bright lights coming towards her. A car with its siren blaring had scared her into hiding behind a tree. She remembered wrestling one of Jason's friends on the ground, pushing him off before he had his way with her. She had found a football oval where she lay flat on her back, watching the stars for what seemed like an eternity. At some stage during the night, Jason decided she should go home and put her into a taxi.

Still feeling foggy, she pulled herself from bed and walked around the apartment. Maybe Jason was still out. She rang his mobile phone, only to hear it ring in the lounge room. Without Jason to drive her, and only enough cash for a bus ticket, it would take three times as long to get to BJ's studio.

She shoved the dresser drawers open and closed, rattling everything on top. Jason had set this job up. He should be home to take her! She pulled on tights and a singlet, then threw an oversized T-shirt over the top. Knowing she had only minutes to catch the bus, she slammed kitchen doors in search of something to eat. The cupboards were bare. She slung open the fridge to find half a bottle of flat champagne. She drank straight from the bottle to calm her nerves before leaving to catch the bus.

Despite her frustration with Jason, a happy joy buzzed inside her. Today she was starting her new career. A career in dance. Something she thought would never happen. Today the sun was shining brightly, just for her.

She walked towards a large warehouse studio. With champagne courage and forced composure, she entered. 'Hello, is BJ here?'

'No, not right now.' A well-dressed man looked up. 'Can I help you?'

'He, um, I'm…' Her words jumbled together. 'He told me to start today, I'm a dancer.' *Yes, I am a dancer.* She pushed her chest out and shoulders back.

'Excellent. We need new blood around here.' He swung an arm and gave her a cheesy grin. 'Go and warm up, and we'll go through the routine in about fifteen.'

A group of girls stood chatting. Steph walked up to them glowing with enthusiasm.

'Hi. How long have you been dancing here for?' she asked.

'Long enough,' one girl said over her shoulder as she walked away.

'New girl, look out!' the girl beside her said, then wolf-whistled.

Another girl walked out of the group and spoke directly to Steph's face. 'Don't you go thinking you're getting the lead, because that's already been sorted.'

'Hey, I'm just here to dance.'

'You might be just here to dance, but there's a whole lot more you'll get, little Miss Happy,' another girl said as she stretched into the splits.

Steph found a spot behind everyone and warmed up by herself.

The man she'd met at the front door swished in with a tray full of champagne. 'Drinks.'

'Are you old enough to be drinking?' A girl snarled.

'Yeah.' Steph brought a hand to her cheek, realising she'd rushed out without make-up.

'Okay, girls. Cut the nasties. Are we ready?' He clicked his fingers, looking at Steph. 'Just watch for the first run through, then join in.'

Music blared from the speakers. The girls drank the bubbly like water and Steph joined them, taking the last glass from the tray, thankful to feed her body another dose of alcohol. She moved to the back as the girls all fell into step. Steph grabbed her jaw to stop it from dropping as she watched them dance provocatively. She'd never danced such skanky moves. She processed the routine in her mind, nervous as to whether she could pull it off.

'Okay, girls, really grind it this time.' The man from the front door danced in and around the girls. When he got to the back of the room he spun in front of Steph and stopped close, invading her personal space. His foul breath repelled her. 'Steph, is it?'

'Yep.'

'They call me Jam. Are you going to join in sometime today? Need another drink?'

'Is it okay if I have another?' Maybe the bubbles would help.

'Sure hu-ney. Make it a quickie.' He smiled, placing his hands on his hips. The other girls laughed.

After the next drink she fell into step with the other dancers, managing to deliver most of the moves. She knew her face was flushed as she worked her still-cool body. They worked on perfecting the dance, over and over, the same section, repeating the same moves. Stretching, twisting, grinding. Champagne continued to appear, but there was no water in sight. BJ arrived in the afternoon and all the girls ran to greet him. Again, Steph eased her awkwardness by finding refuge in another drink.

'Where's my new girl?' He pushed the others away. 'I see you need some training.' His voice boomed like he was the king of the world.

'I think she's getting another drink.' Jam laughed.

'Come here, my new little sweetie.' He linked his arm through hers and led her into an office.

She jumped when the door slammed closed, and spun around to face him.

'How are you finding everything?'

'Okay.' She didn't know what else to say.

'Good. Now, let's get a few things clear. When I arrive, you come and say hello. I'll let you off this time because you're new.' He poured vodka into two shot glasses. 'Have a drink with me.'

Steph's mind said no, but the alcohol had taken control and her body urged her to accept another drink.

'You'd better get back out there, and dance that little butt off.'

'What time will we be finished?' she asked.

'When you've got it right.'

'I just want to let my boyfriend know what time to pick me up.'

'Let him know when you're finished.'

She left the room with her head down, thankful for the fresh warm vodka buzz.

BJ stood in front of them while they practiced. Steph watched how the other dancers fussed over him. He was creepy. *Why on earth are they flirting?*

'Drinks!' Jam called halfway through the routine.

Again, all the girls ran to BJ and waited for Jam to bring another tray of drinks.

'Shoo,' he said. 'Steph, come with me. Paperwork to sort.'

She followed him into his office.

'Take a hit.'

'No, thanks.' Steph eyed the powdery line.

'You don't seem to understand. Now that you work for me, you do as I say. I own you.'

Her thoughts swelled in fuzzy confusion. There was so much in his words that scared her. She started for the door, but he stepped in front of her and locked it with the key. She tried to call for help but his hand clamped tight over her mouth before she could squeal. He was strong, stronger than Jason, stronger than anyone she'd known. His hand grabbed at her pants. With fear in her eyes, she shook her head as she fought against the hand silencing her voice.

'Yes.' He smirked. 'This is part of the deal.'

She didn't close her eyes. Instead, she focused on a nail on the wall.

          Spiralling Out of Control

'Stop kicking or you'll get bruises.' His mouth curled into a smile that churned her stomach. 'I can't have a dancer looking beaten up.'

Everything in her wanted to fight him off, but the alcohol had leeched her strength as he stole a piece of her that could never be retrieved.

'Right, are you ready to dance again?' He pulled his pants back up and fastened his belt.

She glanced at him with disgust, shaking her head.

'Before you go.' He unlocked a drawer. 'Just so we're clear, you go telling your boyfriend and… well, you won't have a boyfriend.' He pulled out a gun and fingered the trigger. 'Now, are you ready to dance?'

Steph trembled.

'See, sweetie, you do need a hit.' He pulled open a different drawer and picked up a syringe. In one smooth move, he stabbed her.

She was wilder and crazier and completely reckless. The rest of the day was a blur. She remembered to ring Jason to pick her up before they cooled down. When he arrived, she climbed into the car and Jason rushed inside. Steph's eyelids were already drooping when he returned. On the way home, she swayed between consciousness and dreamland. As soon as she'd made it up the stairs, she passed out on Jason's bed.

Steph woke during the night to filtered light, speared into the apartment by the street lights. Jason wasn't beside her. She walked out of the bedroom and found Axel watching TV. Not wanting to start a conversation, she retreated to the bathroom. She needed to wash BJ's filthy body odour and lingering aftershave off her skin. If she could get rid of the stench, she might have a better chance of forgetting what he'd done. She ran a shower and scrubbed from her head to her toes. Thank goodness he'd used a condom.

Pulling on her pyjamas, Steph found Axel had fallen asleep, so she silenced the apartment with the TV off button. Her stomach ached for food. In the fridge, she found some leftover pizza, and washed it down with a couple of glasses of bubbly. Jason must have stopped at the bottle shop on the way home. She was still thirsty, and drank some water to cleanse her body. Then she attempted to sleep again.

She woke a second time during the night, feeling alone with helpless betrayal etched into her bones. Jason snored beside her. She showered again, then tossed and turned sleeplessly. At dawn she looked through the window and found comfort in the sun. She wept, then slept.

The next day she wanted to tell Jason she'd been raped, but every time she opened her mouth the vision of the gun was clear in her mind.

'I don't like the job. I'll find —'

'No, babe, you're contracted. You have to —'

'Why can't I get an ordinary job?' She stood close to him, looking up with pleading eyes.

'Because we need the money.'

'You need the money for your stupid drugs!'

'You saying you don't need the drugs?' He laughed. 'You're kidding yourself. You need them just as much as me.'

'Do not! I could stop any time. I don't need them,' she shouted. 'Maybe I should move back to the Morays.'

His stare stabbed her. 'You wouldn't survive without me now.' He clenched his fists. 'Get ready. I'll take you.'

She shuddered at his anger. Still trembling, she pulled her dance clothes on and let him drop her off. Whenever drinks came, she took two. If she had to be there, she'd rather not remember it. BJ didn't turn up that day. Steph was relieved.

After work, she rang Jason to pick her up.

'Hey, babe, did you get paid?' he asked as he pulled up.

'Take it.' She threw the cash at him, and cowered into the seat. 'I don't want their money, I hate them.'

'What?'

'I just want to sleep.'

Steph dozed in the passenger seat, exhausted.

 Spiralling Out of Control

Chapter Thirty-Five

'WHAT ARE YOU DOING?' Jason woke her up, enraged.

She turned from him, recoiling at his booming voice.

'You're late,' he said. 'Don't go stuffing this job up.'

'I told you I hate them. Or was I dreaming?'

'Don't be so stupid. I ran into BJ yesterday and he said you're a great find.' Jason clenched his jaw. 'Now get ready and I'll take you in.'

'What are you on?' Steph curled her knees to her chest. His anger had to be fuelled by something. 'Have you been drinking all night, or are you stoned?'

'I said get ready!' He grabbed her by the arm to pull her out of bed.

She tried to get her feet onto the floor, but he gave her arm another tug and pushed her.

Tripping, she hit her head on the corner of the doorway. 'Stop it!'

Jason punched his fist into the wall, leaving a gaping hole. 'Now look what you've made me do!'

'Why do I have to go back?' Steph pulled herself off the floor, staring at the damaged wall.

'We need the money,' he said through clenched teeth.

'I'll get another job.'

'But I told BJ that you'd be there!' His breath whipped her face. Steph backed into the bathroom, away from him. She stood under a flow of cold water to numb herself. She yearned for a drink to warm her shivering body as she dressed.

'I'll make my own way there!' Steph left before he could argue.

'I'll be checking in during the day to make sure you're there!' he yelled as she was halfway down the stairs.

After catching the bus, her hands were shaking before she'd even walked into the studio. She was grateful for the drinks on arrival.

One girl, Gracie, spoke to her. 'You look too innocent to be hanging around here. Why don't you take off before they lock you in with threats?'

But it's too late. They've already threatened me.

'Oh, I see. They've already threatened you.'

Is my face that transparent?

'Look, do as you're told, follow us and life around here will be more pleasant. I know BJ's pretty sick, but he thinks of us like his harem.' Gracie walked a few steps away, turned to Steph and said quietly, 'Just stick close to me.'

Steph nodded, trying to look composed and strong as she followed her new friend.

'Decided you like it here?' one of the girls asked. 'Nice to have you stick around.'

Could this be a turning point? She'd made a friend in Gracie and the other girls were now at least speaking civilly to her.

At home, Jason was over-the-top edgy and explosive. Steph assumed he'd found another drug, but didn't want to ask for fear of him pushing her again. Leaving the apartment was a happy moment in her day. Being handed champagne on arrival at the studio made her feel like a star, if only for a second. There weren't many jobs that let you drink as much as you liked while working. She thought of stories she'd heard of where girls slept with the boss to get the job or promotion. Maybe it was just the way it went if you wanted to get somewhere in life. She justified it, pushing BJ's creepy repulsiveness to the back of her mind.

One afternoon, Steph was waiting outside for Jason to pick her up. She thought all the girls had gone home. After ten minutes or so, Gracie walked out.

'I thought you'd left,' Steph said.

'Nup.' Gracie pulled a tense smile. 'Guess it was just my lucky day to make BJ happy.' She oozed sarcasm.

'What do you mean?'

'Steph.' Gracie kept walking. 'Don't be so naive.'

The next day, she watched through blurry intoxication. Another girl was called into the office as they were finishing. The next day, a different girl was called back as everyone left. Each day, she'd rush to the door, hoping to escape BJ.

A couple of weeks into her job, BJ called her as she pushed the door open to leave. 'Steph, sweetie, can I see you?'

'Sorry, BJ, my boyfriend will be waiting.'

'Don't go against the grain, Steph,' Gracie whispered. 'It's not worth it.'

Clenching her teeth, she followed BJ.

'I take it you've kept our little secret?' he whispered after Gracie left. 'Now it's time for your reward.'

She'd tried to justify working for BJ, but the moment she was alone with him, her stomach churned. As he forced himself on her another piece of her soul shattered.

At home, a pile of overdue notices cluttered the bench. Steph didn't know where her money was going. It seemed to slip through Jason's fingers and his anger continued to intensify towards her. So many things bothered her while she was sober, so she drank.

Tabbie rang often, leaving voice mail and text messages, but Steph lost track of whether she'd replied or not. On Sundays, Steph would try to remember to text her parents and to fill them with lies that she was okay.

On the weekend, she attempted to leave the apartment to visit Tabbie, but Jason stood in the doorway in a rage. She sculled two bottles of champagne that night and woke with bruises and no memory of how she got them.

Days and nights became jumbled. Steph took in alcohol so she wouldn't feel the constant, silent tears that sat stagnant on the inside of her eyes. Over and over she dreamt of her sixteen-year-old self, and Tabbie knocking on the front door. At one stage she woke up, sure Tabbie was outside. Steph got up to check, but there wasn't anyone there.

During the second month of working for BJ, Steph woke up and rushed to the bathroom, vomiting. 'I'll have to ring in sick.'

'Isn't there something you can take for that?' Jason stood over her while she knelt on the tiles hugging the porcelain bowl.

'Must have been something I ate.'

'You'll be right by lunch.'

He was right. She'd stopped vomiting by midday and Jason drove her to work for the afternoon.

'You must be drinking too much. Go easy on it,' he told her when they arrived. 'You can't afford to take time off. Just don't go getting sick again.'

I can't afford? More like we can't afford it. Her hands shook and her legs didn't want to function in coordination. Just a couple. She just needed a couple of drinks to get through. When the next tray of drinks arrived, Steph drank to stop the shaking. It wasn't enough. So she drank more.

The following day, she woke up with the same symptoms.

'I said to stop drinking so much, you stupid cow. If you'd listen to me you'd be fine!'

'Okay, okay. I won't drink anything today.'

He pushed her and she shoved him back. He came at her with his arm raised, tensed to slap. Instead he cussed and pushed her with his elbow. She tripped, landing on the bed.

 Spiralling Out of Control

When she didn't accept the champagne on arrival, Jam asked. When she didn't accept a drink later in the day, BJ ordered her into his office. 'You look sick. What's up?'

'I think I may have a bit of a virus.' She swallowed. 'I've been vomiting the last couple of mornings. I feel a little queasy.'

'You stupid thing!' His hands clawed into her shoulders, shaking her. She lost focus as he threw her across the room. 'You've gone and got knocked up, haven't you?'

'What?' She felt like she'd had the wind dashed out of her. 'No, no, I couldn't be.'

'Fix it.' BJ threw money at her. 'Get yourself sorted out by the end of the week!'

He walked out of the room, slamming the door so hard against the outer wall it swung closed. Steph lost control and cried sinking to the floor. She hugged her legs, rocking back and forth. *How could this be happening?* Steph pulled herself together, fixed her eyes to the floor and rushed past the girls without saying goodbye. She was going to prove BJ wrong and took off down the street. At the first pharmacy she came to, she bought a pregnancy testing kit. She locked herself in a public toilet cubicle and read the instructions through tears. After peeing on the stick, she waited two minutes. Through squinted eyes she checked the result. It was clear. *Positive. Pregnant. Definite.*

Steph hailed a taxi from the street to take her home. Trudging upstairs she unlocked the door and fell onto the couch. Jason wasn't home. She rang his mobile, but he didn't answer.

Her whole body shook. She turned the TV on to distract her misery. Finally, as dusk darkened the room, he stormed in.

'Where have you been?' he roared. 'I waited at the studio but you didn't come out. I went in to find you and BJ told me to get out. What have you done?'

'Jason.' Tears trickled down her cheeks. 'I need you. I'm pregnant.'

'You slimy little…! Who've you been slipping under the sheets with behind my back?'

Steph pulled her hands to her face.

Jason looked from wall to wall, then back at Steph. 'BJ?'

Steph drew a sharp breath, then stood up, facing him. 'Jason, he made me. He said he'd kill you.'

Enraged, he grabbed her shoulders, shaking her slowly, then faster and faster, until he shoved her across the room towards the door. She hit the flimsy fly screen with a thwack. Her small body tore a gaping hole and she fell right through.

'But Jason, I'm sure it's yours.' Her voice was airy, winded. She stood and he dived towards her, pushing towards the stairs. *It has to be yours.*

'I thought you were on the pill,' he said.

I am. She lost her balance and tumbled, hitting the steps with her shoulder, knee, elbow, hip, head. When she stopped rolling, she opened her eyes to see Jason walking away from her.

Her body was limp, and pain shot through her limbs.

Unbearable.

She closed her eyes, and drifted into unconsciousness.

 Spiralling Out of Control

Chapter Thirty-Six

Steph was caught in a tangle of recurring dreams of Tabbie. In the dreams she was sixteen years old and happy. No dramas. The heaviness of the past year lifted from her shoulders. Freedom at last. She wanted to wake up and walk out of her dreams to live it as reality. But her eyelids continued to stick together.

'Steph.' She recognised the voice. 'Steph, can you hear me?'

Yes, I hear you.

But again, there was silence and dreams.

'I'm back.' Steph connected the voice to Tabbie. 'Just had to pop out for a few minutes.'

She managed to pull her eyes open slightly, her lashes fluttered, her head pounded, and her body hurt.

'Steph, it's me, Tabbie.'

She went to talk but no words came out.

'Don't try to talk if it hurts.'

Steph looked towards the stern voice. Her gaze darted around the room, questioning.

'You're in hospital. You're going to be okay,' the stern voice said.

'You should be thankful that your friend found you when she did. You've lost a lot of blood.'

'Tabbie.' Steph's voice rasped as she began to cry.

'You must have fallen down the stairs.' Tabbie smoothed the sheets. 'Do you know you're pregnant?'

Steph couldn't speak. How did Tabbie know? *Who else knows?*

'I found you at the bottom of the stairs at Jason's late yesterday afternoon.'

A nurse leaned over the top of her. 'Would you like us to call someone? Your parents, perhaps?'

'I don't want to see them,' Steph said with a scratchy voice. Tears rolled down her face.

'It's okay. Everything will be okay,' Tabbie reassured her, holding her hand.

She watched Tabbie close her eyes, murmuring quiet words she couldn't understand.

Steph fell asleep again. She dreamed of her parents yelling at her. Then she dreamed of blue skies and green fields. Her body began to shake uncontrollably.

'The next few weeks will be hard,' the nurse said. 'It'll take a while for her body to detox.'

She knew she was no longer dreaming. She was horrified when the nurse spoke about her like that to Tabbie. She wasn't an addict. Her body shuddered uncontrollably again.

'You'll get through this.' Tabbie held her hand. 'You are strong, just like your last name.'

'But I've really stuffed up.'

'It's not all your fault.'

'But I'm pregnant.' Steph could barely get the words out between the sobs.

'How long have you known?'

Blinking, she couldn't find the words to answer.

'There's a place I've heard about, somewhere you can go until you're feeling better.'

     Spiralling Out of Control

'What do you mean?'

'Like a home where you can get back on your feet.'

'Where?'

'Queensland.'

'April!' Steph gasped. 'I was going to go and visit her.'

'I'm sure you can see her soon.'

'No.' Steph tried to shake her head.

'What?'

'I don't want to go back to Queensland.'

'What if you visit your family, and maybe stay to get help until you're better?' Tabbie squeezed Steph's hand.

'Mum and Dad will want me to abort, or adopt the baby out. An unwed mother isn't part of their plan.'

'You are the only one who can make that decision.' Tabbie's brow furrowed.

Steph closed her eyes. *Where's Jason?*

'You get some more rest and I'll be here when you wake up.' Tabbie rested back in a chair beside the bed.

Steph nodded.

When she woke again, Tabbie was still there and a police officer stood at the end of the bed.

Steph looked at Tabbie, too fearful to speak.

'This is Sergeant Kearny.' Tabbie indicated the policewoman.

'Hello, Stephanie. When was the last time you saw Jason?'

'The day he … The day I fell down the stairs.'

'I'm afraid I have some bad news for you. Jason was found unconscious last night. He was shot. The paramedics arrived quickly. He's stable but still unconscious.'

Steph dry-retched, thrashing from side to side on the narrow bed. Tabbie grabbed the buzzer from under Steph's arm and pressed the button. The nurses insisted Tabbie and the officer leave until Steph had calmed down. An hour later, Steph demanded to see Tabbie.

'I really love him, Tabbie.'

'I know.' Tabbie pulled the chair close to the bed.

'I just wanted him to stop the drugs.' Steph looked away then back to her friend. 'How did it all go so wrong?'

Tabbie pushed Steph's hair away from her eyes.

'What if he dies?'

Tabbie shook her head.

'It's all my fault. How am I going to live without him?'

'Of course it's not your fault. Let's not worry about anything right now.'

'And the baby?'

'I'm sure Jason will wake up soon.'

Steph cried underneath her scratched, bruised hands.

When no nurses or doctors were within earshot, Tabbie spoke. 'Steph, what happened the day you fell?'

'We had another stupid fight.'

'Did you really fall?'

Steph shook her head.

'Did he push you?'

She nodded.

'Oh, Steph. I know you love him. But that's serious.'

'It was an accident. I made him angry. Just another stupid fight.'

'Let's concentrate on you getting better.'

'Which hospital is he in?' Steph didn't want to face the future without him.

'They haven't said. The police officer said something about a huge drug bust. Jason was involved. He might be charged when he wakes up.'

'Oh,' Steph sighed. Maybe she did need to go somewhere to work things out in her mind.

The nurse returned. 'Before we organise your transfer to rehab, we need to make sure everything is okay with baby and you. So you'll be here for another day or so.'

Steph blinked and waited for her to leave before she asked Tabbie, 'What's the place like? The one up north that you told me about?'

'I don't know a whole lot other than it's run by a church and the decision to go has to be yours—nobody can make you go.'

'Church? I don't think so. Would they make me go to church?'

'They'll help you make decisions, like where to go next. Basically, they'll help you sort your life out...'

More tears swelled in Steph's eyes. 'Thanks, Tabbie, but no. I don't want any religious people trying to fix me.'

'Okay. The doctor said something about having to detox before thinking about anything like that anyway.'

Steph nodded. Detoxing sounded ugly. 'Would you come and visit me in the rehab centre?'

'Sure. I'll never be too far away.'

'Thank you. You really are the best friend I could ever hope for.'

The Emails

Spiralling Out of Control

15th December

Dear Tabbie,

This place gives me the creeps. I'm stuck with a bunch of druggos. I don't know why they told me to come here. I'm not addicted to drugs. I'm not an alcoholic. I just want to get out of here. I need to talk to Jason, but I don't know where he is. Can you help me find him?

From Steph

16th December

Dear Tabbie,

Today I had to sit through stupid lectures on all sorts of junk. A therapist wanted to talk to me about my family and childhood. She made some analogy about being abandoned by my father. Abandoned—ha! Whatever. She told me my family might be disconnected. I'm the only one disconnected. Disconnected from the world! I hate this place. Did you find Jason? Oh, also, could you find my mobile for me? It must be in one of the boxes from the apartment.

Bye, Steph

17th December

Dear Tabbie,

I feel like I want to die. I didn't think I had an addiction problem, but they tell me I wouldn't feel this bad if I didn't. Can't believe Jason made me take all those drugs. Crap! Just want to feel normal again. This place is horrendous. It's like everyone is watching me all the time. If your God is real, can you pray to him—for me?

Love, Steph

18th December

Dear Tabbie,

Jason rang me. He's still in hospital, but can't tell me which one. I think he's going through detox too. He said he can't call me again. He's done some deal with the cops. He dobbed in BJ and some other drug dealers. Apparently the cops had been trying to shut them down for a while. But now he'll have to move to another city and said he won't contact me again.

I'm a mess. I can't stop crying. There's so many thoughts racing around my mind that I think it'll explode. So much I want to say. I'm telling everyone everything. I wish I could just shut up.

Love, Steph

19th December

Dear Tabbie,

There's a counsellor here. She seems to think it's best for me not to talk to Jason again, but to forgive him and move on. I've been trying to work out when things changed. I think it was way back in September last year, in Toowoomba, when he went away with his mates. He came back different. But everything was still kind of okay. But, we didn't have the best relationship in the end. I wish we could go back to what it was like when we met. Before the drugs. Before the drinking. But I have to look forward now. I have a baby growing inside me.

Your friend, Steph

20th December

Dear Tabbie,

Thanks for looking into that home for me, but I've decided not to go. I don't like the sound of it being attached to a church. I hope you understand.

I'm starting to wonder if this baby is a boy or a girl. I'll have to think of names. Can you come shopping with me to get a cot and clothes and all the things I'll need? I hope you can. There are loads of support groups I can join when I get out of here. But I don't think I'll need them. I just have to get past feeling so awful, then I'll be right.

Hope to see you soon,

Steph

21st December

Dear Tabbie,

They tell me I'm doing really well. Apparently, my state of mind is satisfactory. I have been wondering why Mum and Dad didn't ever come to visit when I left Toowoomba to live with you. I knew they didn't have much money. But I'm guessing they've been on the verge of separation for who knows how long. Maybe I wouldn't have made so many dumb decisions if they had visited and knew how I was living. But I know I can't blame them. Did I hide it all from you? Or did you know? I was a terrible friend this year. I'm sorry. I hope I can make it up to you.

I thought I felt the baby move, but the doctor assured me I wouldn't feel movement for another couple of weeks. I'm so excited at the thought of a little bub squirming around inside me. I hope I haven't damaged him or her with all the drugs and stuff.

How's your family? Your parents were so kind when I was living there. I never really thanked them. Could you please thank them for me?

I realised I've written to you every day. Guess I'll write again tomorrow. LOL

Love you my friend,

Steph

22nd December

Dear Tabbie,

Christmas is so close. I haven't done any shopping or anything. But, I'm hoping to leave here before Christmas Day. What are you doing for Christmas?

I don't want to go back to Toowoomba. Can I hang out with your family? If not, I'll stay here. Don't really have anywhere else to go.

They tell me I'll get some benefits from the government. I think I'll use it to rent something small and nice. It'll be fun setting it up for bub and me. It's scary to think I'll be a single mum, but they tell me there are special groups just for young mums. I love singing all the Christmas carols. I've just realised they are all about Jesus! Well, except Rudolph the Red-Nosed Reindeer.

Love, Stephanie

23rd December

Dear Tabbie,

I'm really looking forward to leaving. I know I'm not completely well, but I'm getting there. It's so noisy here. People are yelling all the time. It reminds me of how Jason used to yell at me. I never want to be in that kind of relationship again. I truly did love him. But he changed. Drugs change a person, hey? Most of this year has been such a blur. I'd be happy to wipe it from my memory altogether. Feeling sad again today. A guy twice my age hit on me just before. Hiding in my room now.

Chat soon,

Stephanie

24th December

Dear Tabbie,

I don't know why I'm emailing you again today when I'll see you in the morning. I can't help but think about the turns that life takes. I just made a couple of decisions that really screwed things up. I'm so glad to be out of that scene. I'll never go back there again.

I hope Jason is doing okay, but I've realised I never want to see him again. I'm glad he's being hidden in another city. Don't know how I'll explain the whole crazy story to this baby. But the baby will be better off without a violent dad. I don't think I could trust him now.

Oh, how could I have forgotten? How did you go at camp and exams? I'm such a bad friend. Sorry I haven't asked before now. I've got a bump. I really look pregnant. I'm sure you'll notice when you see me. I know it's only been ten days, but I'm sure my tummy has popped out! How is your youth group? I can't wait to hear about everything you've been up to.

I need to ring April. I have been worried about her. I think she needed a big sister around and I abandoned her.

Mum rang. She doesn't understand what's happened. She wants me to have an abortion or give the baby away. There's no way I can do that. She just doesn't understand me. Another reason to stay in Sydney. I know she's angry with me, but she'll have to deal with that herself. I know I'm only sixteen, but I feel older.

They showed me where the AA meetings are. They're all over the place. I know I've kicked the drugs, but I still crave a drink. I'm ready to take control. Ready to live a great life. I know it won't be easy, but I hope I can stop making a fool of myself and start being responsible.

Can't wait to see you and your family.

Love and hope,

Stephanie

25th December

Dear Tabbie,

Merry Christmas!

Thank you so much for visiting me today. I feel like I blabbered on and on about me and still don't know what's been happening in your world. I can't wait 'til my head is clear again. I know I'm not ready to leave yet. But I will be, soon. Maybe you could help me find a place to live. Just a small place that I can set up for me and the baby. I'll probably have to find a job to cover the rent, but I'm sure I'll be able to find a regular daytime job. No more late night or crazy jobs for me. You're right though—I could teach young girls a thing or two about dancing, and the dangers of the industry.

Hey, I spoke with April today. She's not coping well. I hope she'll be okay.

Perhaps we can hang out more next year. I know you'll be busy with study and I'll have a lot on too, but I honestly want to make more time for you next year. You really are the best friend in the world. Thank you for not judging me. Thank you for sticking by me.

Love you loads,

Stephanie xox

25th December

Dear Stephanie,

Merry Christmas.

My news isn't very merry and I'm sorry to be sending you this email today.

I'm also very sorry I have failed our family. Your mother and I cannot work things out and we will be going our separate ways permanently. I've moved in with Liv and her boys. She is lovely and looks forward to meeting you.

Your mother and I were so caught up in our own issues, we didn't keep up to date with what was happening with you in Sydney. I am sorry. We

　　　　　　　Spiralling Out of Control

should have listened. We should have checked in more often and taken more notice.

I do hope you will visit us.

With love,

Dad

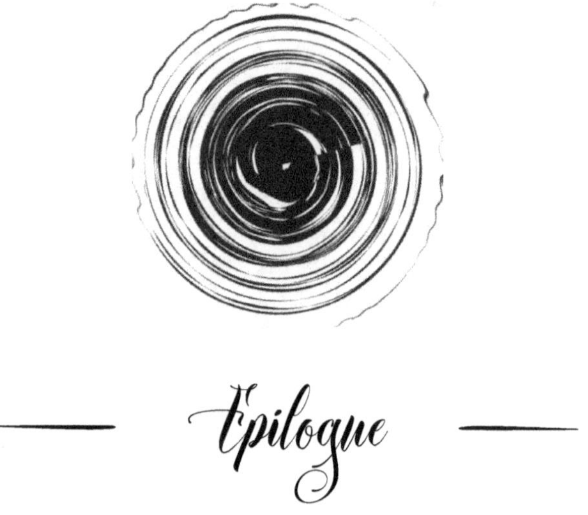

— Epilogue —

FRANCINE PULLED UP AT THE KERB.

'Are you kidding me?' Steph pushed the car door open.

'We know you don't want to move back in with us.' Francine cut the engine.

'And that transition house you'd agreed to was hours away.' Tabbie beamed a huge grin. 'So, this is ours.'

'Ours?' Stephanie walked towards the small block of units.

'Yep, yours and mine.'

After her parents had declared marital World War Three, Steph couldn't go back to Toowoomba. And living with Francine and Tom wasn't going to happen after what she'd been through, and what she'd put them through, even though she knew they would welcome her.

'You're willing to live with me after everything—' Stephanie eyeballed Tabbie.

'Yes.' Tabbie walked down the driveway. 'But there will be rules.'

Stephanie raised her eyebrows and followed. She could do with some boundaries. 'Which unit?'

'The end one.' Tabbie smiled and skipped ahead. 'Are you ready for the rules?'

'Can I make some rules of my own?' There should be equality in this new home.

'After you agree to my rules.'

'I promise I won't drink.'

Tabbie stopped and turned to face her, with policewoman seriousness. 'If you so much as touch a drop of alcohol or any drugs, that's it. I'm out of here, and you'll be on your own.'

'I'm clean now. I know I can stay that way. Now for my rules. Keep your religious mumbo-jumbo away from me.' Stephanie suppressed a giggle from rolling out of her mouth.

'You know I don't do religious mumbo-jumbo.' Tabbie laughed and continued to the front door. 'I'm a Christian. My lifestyle may be different to what yours has been, but look where yours got you.'

Steph shrugged, then nodded.

'So is it a deal?'

'Yep. I still can't believe you organised this without telling me. And I was joking about your religious mumbo-jumbo. I'm starting to think your prayers kept me alive.'

Stephanie followed Tabbie through the front door of their ground-floor unit. Tomorrow, the calendar would turn over to a new year, and Stephanie would start a new season of her life.

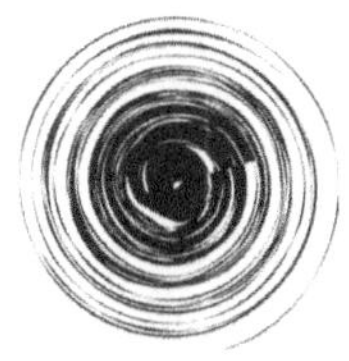

You were never designed to slip into depression
or have days of darkness.
Feeling down or depressed is not a weakness,
but a reality in our world.
Beyond Blue and Black Dog Institute
both have an abundance of
information and guidance
on their websites.
I urge you to seek help.
There is a way out of the darkness,
tomorrow is a new day and may just be the day
you turn a corner.

Beyond Blue **beyondblue.org.au**
Black Dog Institute **blackdoginstitute.org.au**

Aussie Terms...

Blu-tack	a sticky material used to attach paper to walls.
Bong	a device used to smoke marijuana.
Chuck a sickie	take a day off work or school with an excuse of being sick when you aren't sick.
Doona	duvet or quilt.
Esky	portable cooler box or bag used to carry drinks or food.
Exi	Expensive.
Glassy	person who collects glasses from tables in a nightclub or bar.
Maccas	McDonalds.
Pash	a passionate kiss – snog or French kiss.
Schoolies	the week after high school (year 12) finishes.
Scull	finish a drink quickly.
Take an early mark	leave before the shift is finished.
Wag school	take time off school without notification.
Yobbo	similar to a bogan or white trash.

Visit **MichelleDennisEvans.com**
to connect with Michelle on social media

I am passionate about seeing girls and women
pick up the pieces and move forward in life
after major upheaval.

I have two charities I love to support.
Destiny Rescue and A21 Campaign.

destinyrescue.org   a21.org

A portion of sales from all of my books
goes towards these organisations.

Thank You...

To my daughters, my son and my husband—
you bring joy and laughter into every day, and I am so
thankful we are family. I am also thankful to my parents
who first recognised my gift for writing back in my early
primary years when I chose to write dialogue for my
spelling sentences. Thank you to Roald Dahl who ignited
my passion for reading.

I have to give a shout out to my first reader Michelle. She
accepted the challenge when no one else would—I'm so blessed
to call you friend. Every author needs a cheer squad and I'll
be forever thankful to the girls who cradled me with their
encouragement when I thought I couldn't keep going—Birgit,
Denise, Jo, Karen, Linda and Michelle—I'm so very grateful
for those who've run the marathon with me to see this novel
published. Also, a huge thank you to all of my critique partners
and beta readers, some who stayed with me right through the
novel and some who just helped with a few pages. You are all
appreciated and I'm scared if I started naming you I'd miss
someone. I mustn't forget my online friends. Your support is
welcomed and appreciated and I hope to meet all of you
in real life one day!

And above all I am thankful to my Creator, the giver of life,
the one who showers me with crazy favour and ridiculous grace.

Spiralling Out Of The Shadow

Book 2 in the Spiralling Trilogy

Print book available at online bookstores, and MichelleDennisEvans.com

Spiralling Solo

Book 3 in the Spiralling Trilogy

Print book available at online bookstores, and MichelleDennisEvans.com

Sink, Drift, or Swim

A young adult novel in free verse

Print book available at online bookstores, and MichelleDennisEvans.com

Life Inspired

A beautiufl collection of poems

eBook available at Amazon